A Howl for Mayflower

Also by Dan Gilmore

Season Tickets: Poems and Stories

A Howl for Mayflower

Dan Gilmore

IMAGO PRESS
TUCSON ARIZONA

Published in the United States of America by:

Imago Press
3710 East Edison
Tucson AZ 85716

Names, characters, places, and incidents, unless otherwise specifically noted,
are either the product of the author's imagination or are used fictitiously.

Library of Congress Cataloging-in-Publication Data

Gilmore, Dan.
  A howl for Mayflower / Dan Gilmore.
    p. cm.
  ISBN-13: 978-0-9725303-8-5 (alk. paper)
  ISBN-10: 0-9725303-8-X (alk. paper)
  1. Widowers—Fiction. 2. Bigamy—Fiction. 3. Homeless teenagers—Fiction. 4.
Alzheimer's disease—Patients—Fiction. I. Title.
  PS3607.I4522H69 2006
  813'.6--dc22
  2006033836

Cover Photograph © 2006 by Barbara Stewart Thomas
Author Photograph © 2006 by Jennifer Gilmore
Book Design by Leila Joiner

ISBN 978-0-9725303-8-5
ISBN 0-9725303-8-X

Printed in the United States of America on Acid-Free Paper

To JoAn, Jennifer, Jeff, Quin, and Graeson,

that band of souls which awakens my sleeping heart.

ACKNOWLEDGMENTS

Thanks to my friends, all of whom helped me open the door of imagination and creativity a little wider—Mayflower Brandt, Fifi and Willard Day, Peggy and Dave Tyler, Linda Hook, Joe Hofmaister, Roy Phillips and Patricia Harmon, Bernadette Steele, Emily McKenty, Virginia Hall, Duncan Littlefair, Bruce Loessin, and the students and faculty of Thomas Jefferson College. And to my musical support group—Mike DeBellis, Dan Wolff, Jeff Lewis, Bill Martin, Alan and Madelon Rubens, and Sheryl Holland. Also to my friends, teachers and readers—Meg Files, Masha Hamilton, Nancy Wall, and Tom Speer. And a deep bow to Leila Joiner, my compassionate and tireless editor.

september

ONE

My custom that summer, when the heat made it impossible to sleep, was to go to the basement to cool off and read while doing my laundry. The last time I retreated to the basement was over a year ago, a night early in September. Past midnight. Silent. The other residents had settled in for the night. Before starting my washer, I took off my shirt and trousers and put them in the machine with the other dirty clothes.

Forty minutes or so later I was sitting there in my skivvies, reading a book on Gettysburg and waiting for my laundry to dry. Then I heard a door open and footsteps on the staircase. I have never been one to act without a plan, but the possibility of being caught in my underwear made me respond without thinking. I hid in one of the tiny storage closets that lined the wall opposite the washers and dryers. This was a mistake. The brick back wall was hot to the touch, the air too hot to breathe. Within seconds sweat was trickling down the backs of my knees. I felt light-headed.

I heard a woman's voice, but couldn't tell if she was talking to herself or another person. I thought she said "parquet floors and long corridors." I definitely heard "My dear Charles."

So I opened the door an inch or so and peeked out. It was my neighbor, Mayflower Bryant. I recognized her from behind because of her hair, a single gray braid that reached her waist. She wore black tights, a man's white shirt, and a black vest. In one hand she held a black cane with a silver ball on top—the kind magicians and show biz dancers use. She continued talking to herself as she inserted four quarters into the slot and started her washer. Clearly, she was going to be here longer than I could stay in the storage closet.

Mayflower plugged in a tape player, took aim with one long finger and punched a button. Nothing happened for a few seconds, then…*Boom.*

Out came this brassy version of "Me and My Shadow." Mayflower tucked her cane under her arm and started dancing.

She moved her hips right and left and around in a circle. She humped the air with pelvic thrusts and passed the cane slowly between her legs. She spun, swayed and shook her breasts with her shoulders. As the music got louder, she twirled her cane, flung her braid around her head, strutted a few steps forward and back and sang at the top of her voice: *No one else to tell my troubles to.* Near the end, the tempo cut to half time, and a screaming trumpet built to a grand finale.

One more time!

Mayflower stood tall, feet spread, one arm extended, hips rotating, pelvis thrusting. She belted out, *Strolling down, I said, strolling down. Come on down the av-vah-nue.* Then she shimmied all over. I'd never seen anyone do that. She reminded me of a wet dog. She braced herself on the washer, rocked back, kicked out a long leg, twirled her cane and wedged it under her arm. The music stopped. She took a slow, deep bow.

I almost clapped. Then it occurred to me there could be ethical and legal ramifications to my situation. To stay hidden and say nothing would be taking unfair advantage, pure voyeurism. To let her know I'd been watching could get me arrested as a peeping Tom. Worse, I had a problem with hiccupping. Even as a child, a loud noise or thinking someone might be hiding under my bed would cause me to hiccup. Once I started, I couldn't stop for hours. You see where I'm going here. If I had a siege of hiccupping in the storage closet and she heard me, she might call the police. Not being on the best of terms with the other residents, I imagined them smugly nodding their heads as the police put me in shackles, their suspicions confirmed that the loner in 201 was a sick old man.

It must have been over 120 in that closet. I felt dizzy. I had to get out of there. I slowly opened the door a few inches, sucked in some cool air and whispered through the crack, "Excuse me. I don't want to startle you, but that dancing of yours was top rate."

Mayflower jumped back. Her cane bounced on the floor and clanked across the concrete. She held the back of her hand to her mouth. "Oh, dear," she said. She collected herself, looked inside the empty washers, the sink, in the air vent, under the bench. Finally she stopped, put her fists on her hips and said, "Is someone here?"

I swallowed back a hiccup. "No need to be frightened," I said in my most reassuring voice.

"I'm not frightened," she said. "I just don't know if you're real or if I'm imagining you."

I opened the door another eight inches or so and stuck out my head. Sweat was pouring off my brow. I did my best to smile. "Hello, Mayflower."

She leaned forward and narrowed her eyes as if judging the quality of a brisket of beef.

"It's me, Tobias Seltzer, your neighbor in 201. Nothing to be alarmed about."

She rubbed her chin. "You're in the storage closet."

"Technically, that is correct, but—"

"Why?"

"I was doing my laundry. When I heard you coming, I hid in here."

"But why?"

"I was waiting for my clothes to dry—my shirts and trousers. Truth is, I'm wearing nothing except my shorts and shoes."

She moved her head to the left as if trying to see around the door.

"You make dancing look effortless," I said, wanting to switch the focus off me, "like you've been at it all your life."

She folded her arms under her breasts and settled into herself. "Why, thank you, dear. My mother insisted I take lessons as a young girl. I told her I was too tall and too clumsy, and she said that is precisely why she wanted me to take lessons."

"One doesn't expect to see dancing like that, I mean from—"

"An old woman?"

"No. I mean one does not expect to see dancing like that in the lint-filled basement of a broken-down apartment building. Sure, maybe at some fancy hotel in Miami, but not in Tucson, not in the middle of the night."

She smiled. "You're very kind."

There was an awkward silence, then I said, "I wonder if you'd mind turning around while—"

"Do you dance?" she said.

"Last time I danced was at my wedding almost fifty years ago. Even then I had the agility of a sack of cement."

She extended her arms. "Dance with me now."

"Thank you, but—"

"Nonsense. You'll enjoy it."

She selected another tune. It turned out to be something I recognized from a movie I'd seen years ago—*Picnic*. I remembered a dance pavilion on the lake draped with strings of colored lights. Kim Novak and William Holden swaying to the throaty sound of a woody clarinet, the swish of brushes on a snare drum. But, most of all, I remembered that primal, lust-filled pause when Kim's and William's eyes locked.

"Moonglow," I said.

"You certainly know your music." She held her arms out again and wiggled her fingers in my direction. "Come."

"I'm not dressed."

"Dear, I've seen men in their underwear before."

"Not me. I'm not doing this. Now, if you'll just turn your head, per-haps—"

"I'm not leaving until you come out."

"Fine," I said. "I'll stay in." A minute passed. I was definitely going to faint. So, having no choice, I stepped out and stood in my skivvies before Mayflower Bryant. "I hope you're happy."

She looked me up and down.

I gave my shorts a tug and ran my thumbs around inside the elastic band.

Suddenly, she moved toward me. "Come." She positioned my right hand on her left hip and placed her left hand on my shoulder. I wanted to pull away, but her hands felt sure and strong. We stood in place a mo-ment—me rigid as a Republican, aware of her hip moving ever so slightly under my hand. I confess I was slightly aroused. Truth was, it had been a long time since I'd experienced the soft angle of a woman's waist, the sub-tle rise and fall of a hip.

"Slow-slow, quick-quick," she said. "Left foot first. Ready?"

"Wait," I said. I took a deep breath. My knees were trembling. "For-ward or back?"

She gave a little nod. "Forward on your left foot. Now, your right."

After a minute or so, I started to get the feel of how the step related to the music. We were definitely dancing, circling, barely touching.

Self-confidence could be a delusion of old age. More likely, people probably lower their personal standards as they grow old. But, for what-ever reason, my impression was that I was a pretty good dancer.

She moved closer and placed her head on my shoulder. It was a bit awkward because she had to stretch down a bit to reach my shoulder. But she managed to snuggle in, and we danced for a while like that.

Then she whispered in my ear, "Oh, Charles, my sweet Charles."

At that moment it didn't matter what she called me. I would have answered to Nanook of the North if it meant holding on to that moment. I was enjoying the valleys and peaks of her. I liked how, when one part moved, other parts moved too.

We passed under the forty-watt bulb dangling from the center of the room. She gave it a push with her hand. The room expanded and contracted to the rhythm of the swinging bulb. My confidence grew. I added an extra little hop to the basic slow-slow, quick-quick thing and came down hard on Mayflower's foot. I grimaced and backed off.

"No, no. It didn't hurt. Try again."

"I just mashed your foot."

She straightened her back, lifted her chin and looked me directly in the eye. She had the largest eyes I had ever seen, wide-set, green as jade. "Slow-slow, quick-quick. That's it. Glide. Don't look at your feet. Look at me."

I couldn't look her directly in the eye, so I locked on a spot between her eyebrows. We settled in again, and I was dancing in a sea of lilac perfume, the clean scent of bath soap, hips, breasts. I was becoming aroused. I silently recited the Gettysburg address.

She stopped dancing, held her forearm to her brow and said something that sounded like, "Good God, I'm horny."

"Yes, it's very hot," I said.

"Start again," she said. "Come here." She pulled me against her. "You first this time," she said. "It's called leading."

I willed my left foot forward. She moved her right foot back. I stepped out on my right. It worked. Light played in the fuzzy halo of her hair. The tip of her braid brushed the back of my hand. A school of fish swam through my abdomen.

At the end of the tune, she arched her back and stuck out one leg. "Don't let me fall," she said, arching backwards. Her braid almost touched the floor. I held her there, ready to sign on for life, to give up books and my precious solitude and dance my remaining days away with this woman with the strange name. Cast us in bronze, I thought. Call it a life.

She came upright and fanned herself with her hand. "Whew, let's rest." We sat side by side on the wooden bench. Aware of my nakedness, I spread my fingers over my knees.

She held her braid off her neck and leaned forward. "That's the first time in years I've danced with a partner," she said. "There was a moment when we were really—engaged. Did you notice? No thoughts, no ideas, just us moving together."

"Uh huh," I said. I searched for something more to say, some tidbit to add to the conversation. "Jews in the camps often danced on the nights before they knew they were going to the ovens," I said.

"You were in a camp?"

I shook my head. "I read a lot."

"I suppose that, when you're certain your life is about to end, dancing is one thing that makes sense." She stared at the round window of her washer as if imagining a scene in Auschwitz. "Do you think they made love?"

"They were frightened, weak from starvation, confused."

There was a long silence, then she said, "I think I would try. Even if I could move only one toe, it would be a lovemaking toe. One should know when they are doing it for the last time, don't you think?"

I shrugged. I knew I was blushing. "Men and women together, anything is possible, yet…"

She picked up my book from the bench where I'd left it, looked at it and put it down without comment. She went back to staring at the window of her washer. "I used to dream of wearing a slinky red dress and spiked heels and dancing the tango with a man in tight black pants." She swayed back and forth as if moving to a tune in her head. She placed her hand on the one that was covering my bare knee. "Tango?"

Inwardly, my body recoiled, but I couldn't move my hand. Her touch had turned it to stone. "No."

"Me neither," she said. "But I love to watch it, don't you?"

I couldn't think of anything to say. We sat like that for a few minutes—me, catatonic, her, swaying and rubbing the back of my hand. My shoulder was starting to ache. I needed to move it but was afraid. Finally, her washer clicked off. She got up and placed her wet clothes in a dryer.

I rotated my shoulder to loosen it.

"What's wrong?"

"Who knows? Old age. Pleurisy maybe, arthritis, rheumatism. I seem to have just one ache. It burrows around inside me like a mole. Yesterday a leg, today a hip, tonight a shoulder."

"Here, let me rub it."

She touched me, and my shoulder tightened even more. "No need," I said. I faked a yawn. "A good night's sleep—"

"Nonsense." She moved behind me and placed her hands lightly on my shoulders. My upper lip twitched. I fought back another hiccup.

She rubbed my neck. "How does that feel?"

"Good," I lied. I had never been a touchy person. I didn't know what to do when someone hugged me. I felt repelled, almost painfully so, and at the same time wanted more of it.

"Close your eyes."

I closed my eyes.

"Breathe."

I took a breath.

She knuckled her way lightly down to the base of my spine, then up to my head and down again. By the third trip up and down, I was sinking into the center of a warm stone. She tapped her fingertips lightly on my skull. "Imagine rain drops," she said.

"Nice," I said.

She moved closer and pressed herself against my back. Her hand slid down over my chest and stomach. She pressed herself against me. Her lips brushed my ear. "Oh, Charles," she said. "Make love to me."

I stood involuntarily and faced her. My first inclination was to let her have her way, to pretend I was this person named Charles. In my imagination, she could be Kim Novak.

She loosened the knot in her shirt. At that moment, I lost my courage. I backed away, ashamed of my fear. "I'm not Charles," I said, "I'm Tobias Seltzer, your neighbor in 201."

The rest is a blur. I don't know how I got out of there. The next thing I knew I lay shivering on my bed, sweating and hiccupping. "Moonglow" still played in my head. My hand still rested on Mayflower's hip. I saw her face, wrinkled but filled with character. It was as if the outer layer of skin was a transparent sheath containing a beautiful young woman. I saw the way her lips parted just slightly before she spoke, as if she were tasting her words before saying them. I willed myself to get out of bed, knock on her door and beg her to let me in. I couldn't stop thinking that, at that moment, as we lay in our beds, our heads were separated only by the thickness of a single wall. I imagined knocking a hole in the wall, reaching through and touching her. But I didn't move.

It was a few minutes past one, and residents of the Coronado had started their middle-of-the-night rituals. Bennie the Hindu, in the apartment above mine, led off with coughing spasms. Down the hall a door slammed. Someone was playing Mexican music on a radio. Three toilets flushed in quick succession. The sounds were reassuring. In the past year three residents had died in their sleep. Two weren't found until someone noticed the stench of their rotting flesh. I'd come to think of these nightly rituals as the residents' way of letting others know they were still alive, a way of tending our collective flame of life and calming the fear of dying alone.

I stood at my window, watching the full moon glide smoothly toward the horizon. It was not reassuring to see this symbol of death and rebirth, the source of the spirit that turned Dr. Jekyll into Mr. Hyde. I recited the nursery rhyme about the cow that jumped over the moon, the little dog that laughed, the dish that ran away with the spoon.

I had never felt lonelier.

TWO

In the light of day, the night before seemed unreal. I made a pot of coffee and sat at the kitchen table eating toast with butter. I thought of Beatrice, her long illness, that huge lumpy body that contained such a shy little girl, how we were almost desperately attached to one another and at the same time suspicious, unable to believe anyone would consent to live with the likes of us.

We were still in our teens when we were married and, although our friendship had grown more secure through the years, physical intimacy of any kind became almost non-existent. We were like railroad tracks—traveling in the same direction but never touching. As the years passed, her obsession with food grew worse, and I escaped into my books.

Late in our marriage, one day shortly before her death, Beatrice asked me if I loved her. So help me, I couldn't tell her that I did. "Why do you ask such a question?" I said. "Who can say what love is?"

"But do you love me? I want to know."

"Of course," I said.

"You don't show it," she said.

"I take care of you. I give you your medicine. I cook your food. I wash your clothes and change your bed. What's that, if it's not love?"

Her eyes welled. "I don't know."

I sat down beside her bed, held her hand and said, "I love you, Beatrice." But it was too late. We both knew that, whatever it was she wanted, I wasn't able to give it. To my eternal shame, Beatrice died feeling unloved. And she was right. I'm not sure I was capable of feeling love. What I felt at first was duty and loyalty. As the years passed, I felt resentment. Then I felt nothing.

And although I was unable to love another human being, my love for books grew. I loved the smell of books, browsing the stacks and running my finger over the spines. I loved them because they didn't judge me or make demands on me. I loved them because they were intelligent and infinitely patient. I loved them because that's the closest I had come to feeling alive. After Beatrice died, I relished living alone, reading, thinking, writing an occasional letter to the editor, eating when and what I wanted, taking pleasure in leaving a pencil on the table and finding it exactly where I left it the next morning.

I washed my coffee pot and left it upside down on the counter. After taking a shower and dressing, I found my clothes folded in my basket outside my door. My Gettysburg book was there, too, along with a note: "Thought you might need these. Mayflower."

While putting my clothes away, I fantasized about having an occasional cup of coffee with Mayflower—perhaps, in time, developing a casual kind of friendship. Maybe all I needed was a shallow relationship, one similar to reading a trashy book, something I could pick up at my convenience and put down whenever I wished.

But not Mayflower. She was too excitable and unstable. Besides, she was a woman, and women expected things men didn't. Women showed almost no interest in facts, ideas, or reasoned opinions. Men were less intense, more drawn to logic, more accepting of the superficial. For my purposes, this was a good thing.

I came to believe I needed a male acquaintance, someone to talk politics or philosophy with, to have a drink at a bar while watching sports on TV, or The News Hour. It seemed to me that I could have a low-risk friend without having to change much about myself.

At the Coronado, I decided there were three male candidates—the Hindu upstairs, Bennie what-his-ananda, who triggered in me a mild case of xenophobia; Randall Pruitt from down the hall, who had tried to shoot himself through the head after returning from Vietnam and succeeded only in turning himself into a harmless moron; and a man named Howard Gardener, who had recently moved into the late Abigail Kaufman's apartment across the hall—Abigail, who died in her bathtub and soaked for a week before anyone smelled her. There was an advantage to having a friendship with a person who lived just across the hall. He could check on me occasionally, make sure I wasn't making a soup of myself in my bathtub.

I didn't know the first thing about how to make friends. To sharpen my social skills I searched my shelves for a copy of *How to Win Friends and Influence People.* Couldn't find it but ran across something similar called *Closing a Deal.* It covered such topics as "How to Control a Conversation," "Going for Yes," and "The Importance of Eye Contact, a Winning

Smile, and a Firm Handshake." It suggested practicing handshakes by squeezing a tennis ball. I didn't have a tennis ball, so I used a round of Gouda cheese.

Standing in front of my bathroom mirror, I extended my hand, smiled, and squeezed the Gouda. I managed to make dents in the cheese and took that as a good sign. But I didn't like my smile. My smile was the smile of a person who had eaten bad fish. I practiced a couple of different smiles. One looked like a grimace, the other a whine. I gave up. Then it came to me. So what if I had a lousy smile? At the Coronado, a smile was as rare as a jump rope. No one here had seen a decent smile in years. They wouldn't know a good one from a bad one.

I changed into my seersucker suit and bow tie and walked across the hall. I stood before Howard Gardener's door, trying to look relaxed and nonchalant, but I couldn't ignore the sweat running down my back. Finally I knocked. Nothing. I knocked again.

The door opened just wide enough for me to see a wrinkled shirt, baggy chinos, a crumpled jacket, a tie, and a very red nose.

I introduced myself and asked if he had a cold.

He shook his head. "My wife died." He scrunched up his face and blew his nose. "Jesus, that hurts." He dropped the tissue on the floor.

"Oh, I'm sorry," I said. I had made a mistake. I was about to get involved with a person who had just lost his wife. I had no interest in listening to this man's sad stories. I would leave as soon as I demonstrated some reason for knocking. "I wonder if you might lend me some canned soup?"

"What kind?"

"I like Campbell's Bean with Bacon, but any kind will do. I'm going to drive to Safeway tomorrow. I pay you back then."

"You own a car?"

"A car, a collapsed lung. Same thing," I said. "The passenger side window is missing, front bumper droops like a fat lip, both fenders are dented, blue smoke comes from the exhaust. But we go back a long time. I—"

"I don't drive," he said.

"Just as well," I said. "A car will put you in the poorhouse."

"I am in the poorhouse. We both are."

"Still," I said, talking to fill the awful potential of silence, "we have a history, my car and me. When it dies, I will grieve. I mean it. I love that car. Even for twisted steel, one grieves."

Howard opened the door wider. "You want to come in? I'll see what kind of soup I have."

"Sure," I lied. "For a minute. I have an important meeting."

His floor was covered with wadded-up Kleenex. No pictures, no tele-phone. The sink and counter overflowed with dirty dishes. Unpacked boxes lined the wall. A TV faced the window. Open books with "grief" in the title lay face down on the kitchen table. I paged through one, closed it and said, "Your wife is lucky she has someone to grieve for her."

"She's not lucky. She's dead." He let out a broken sigh.

There was a silence. I had to get out of there. Howard Gardener's suf-fering was a clogged drain about to back up into my living room. "I'm sorry," I said. "I've been insensitive. You must want to be alone." I turned to leave.

"Wait," he said. "Your soup."

I could feel the quicksand of him sucking me into his world. Yet, one can't just take a can of soup and run. I made the mistake of asking a stu-pid question. "Are you all right?"

In the old days, when you'd ask this question the other person would feel obligated to say, "Fine, and you?" Today, people aren't so courteous. You ask them how they are, and they bury you under an avalanche of true confession. People these days seem to assume that other people are actu-ally interested in their state of mind. You ask a person if he's all right and, instead of being polite and saying, "Great," he tells you about his colon cancer or liver spots or, worse, his houseplants or grandchildren.

"Fear," Howard said. "Comes in waves, as if something terrible is about to happen. I'm afraid to go out."

"Who isn't?" I said. "It's scary out there."

"A band of steel tightens around my chest."

"It's the steel band of sanity," I said, inching toward the door. "In this neighborhood, to go outside when you don't absolutely have to is a sign you are missing certain faculties."

"I can't read a newspaper, watch TV, or even look out the window without getting terrified."

I opened the door and stepped into the hallway. I stuck my head back in. "This has been…great. Perhaps we can talk again." I clicked the door closed behind me, grateful to escape Howard Gardener's black hole of despair.

Next evening I discovered that, once started, ending relationships was about as easy as kissing your elbow. Howard knocked on my door and asked me to come to his apartment with him. He said there were things he wanted to show me. I could see he'd been crying. I was overwhelmed by a sense of doom. "I'm on my way to my Optimist Club meeting," I lied.

"Just a minute of your time."

All humans suffer. I know that. No one has a monopoly on misery. Suffering is dealt out in equal shares. Even the most privileged must fret occasionally about their lamb being too rare or their yacht leaking. But Howard's was a kind of kamikaze suffering. It fell from the sky and exploded in your face. There should be a law about foisting this kind of suffering on another without first getting his permission.

That aside, Howard's will was too strong. "Please, just give me a minute," he said. "Come to my apartment."

I was out of practice at saying no. I followed him to his apartment.

He'd unpacked—pots and pans were scattered about the floor, books thrown about, a mountain of dirty clothes in the center of the room, a blue plastic box on the kitchen table. The box contained Howard's wife's ashes. I knew about ashes because Beatrice's ashes were in an identical box. I still had them under my bed, not sure what to do with them. To flush them down the toilet or toss them in the garbage seemed disrespectful. To keep them under the bed also seemed disrespectful. "I see you're unpacking," I said.

"I'm giving everything away," he said. "I don't want it anymore."

"This is probably a good thing," I said, "shedding your past, so to speak, like a snake."

He sat down in the middle of his dirty clothes. "Take whatever you want. It doesn't matter. I'll put what's left on the street."

"I ask for a can of soup, and you offer me the whole supermarket. You should have a garage sale."

"Do you have a Mr. Coffee?" Howard asked.

"I have an old percolator," I said.

"Take my Mr. Coffee," he said. "It's programmable. Helen was the coffee drinker. Caffeine makes me jittery."

I believed with absolute conviction that nothing in life is free, that I would pay in some way for what I was about to receive. Still, what choice did I have? If a man really wants to give me his Mr. Coffee, there's no polite way of stopping him. So I took his coffee maker.

"What else?" he asked.

My initial resistance turned into a kind of shopping frenzy. "That skillet might be nice," I said. "And that big pot there. A few of your books look interesting." I debated about asking him for the tie he was wearing and decided that would be a little too personal. This is the way it is with me. If I decide to do something, I hardly ever do it. If I decide not to do something, two minutes later I'm doing it. So I caved in to my lesser self and said, "If you want, I'll take that tie you're wearing."

"Not the tie," he said. "It was a gift from Helen. I'll need it." He stroked it with a hand that seemed too large for such delicate material.

How does one explain the nature of greed and desire? I'm not especially impressed by the "forbidden fruit" explanation, but in this case it seemed appropriate. As soon as Howard denied me the tie, I wanted it even more. I began to plot my strategy for getting it. I started by telling him how my father started one of the first cleaners in Tucson, how Beatrice and I ran the business for thirty-two years before we went bankrupt and lost what savings we had.

I felt his lapel. "Wrinkles like these we called red-tag wrinkles," I said. "I always told the customer to expect the worst with red-tag wrinkles. That tie, however, is nothing to be ashamed of. Oh, it's not a great tie, but it's a good one, the kind you see on college professors."

"You can't have it," he said.

His obstinacy was like gasoline poured on my fiery determination. I had to have his tie. I needed another tack. I looked around and pointed to the blue box. "That must be Helen," I said.

"Yes," he said.

It was a diversionary tactic. I asked him to tell me about her and listened attentively to his answer. He told me more. I kept listening.

Helen was fourteen years younger than Howard, a teacher of anthropology at the university. The two of them had spent their best years together remodeling an old Victorian on Second Street near the university. He told me about putting in sheet rock, bricks, the Japanese garden Helen had wanted. I was drowning in brain-numbing information. As soon as he took a breath, I said, "She gave you that tie, huh?"

He followed me back to my apartment, carrying his Mr. Coffee and a sack of groceries, including some Swiss cheese, a can of chili, even an unopened bottle of tequila. While I was going through the grocery bag, Howard made another trip across the hall and came back with his portable TV on his shoulder.

"Will you take it?" he said.

I had tossed ours out the day Beatrice died. "Do I look like a man who eats raw sewage?"

As Howard lowered his head, I had second thoughts about the TV. I hadn't watched TV in years. Maybe it had gotten better. There'd be another voice in my apartment, one I could switch off and on as my mood dictated. "Come in. We'll talk."

Howard slumped on my sofa, still cradling the TV.

I stood over him. "Don't take offense if I don't leap at your generous offer," I said. "You see, I live on social security. These books lining my walls are my world, yet I can't afford new ones. The truth is, I can't afford electricity to run a television. If you were to offer me something, say a few dollars, to take it off your hands, well—"

Howard looked up at me over the edge of the TV. "I'll give you twenty dollars to help pay for your electricity."

I had always thought of myself as a basically good man—not a great man, not a man of major *mitzvahs*, but at least one who doesn't take advantage of others. Now, suddenly, I was a weasel, caught up in coveting a tie that I didn't particularly like, unable to stop. I rubbed my chin as if considering his offer. "Tell you what," I said. "I'll take the television and the twenty if you toss in the tie."

"Not the tie."

"Fine," I said, giving up on the tie. "I'll take the TV and the twenty."

While Howard watched, I attached the cable wire to the TV, curious to test the quality of the picture. To let Howard know it was time for him to leave, I feigned a stretch and a yawn. "Getting late," I said.

"If you don't mind, I'd like to stay a few minutes," he said.

"May I ask why?"

"To watch TV with you."

What could I say? I was trapped. "Sure, stay as long as you want," I said.

I made popcorn and served it with tepid water from the tap. Howard ate like a hyena, kernels flying into the air, bouncing off his lap into creases of my sofa.

"More popcorn?" I asked.

He burped and shook his head. "Gives me gas."

"A bicarbonate, perhaps?"

"Nothing."

We watched two sitcoms. Howard was a sigher, but he seemed not to be aware of this annoying habit. Every time the automatic laughter came on, Howard sighed. He kept sighing while we watched the local news, the Leno show, the Late Show, the Late-Late Show, and a Japanese movie about a man and woman who lived in a hole in the sand that kept caving in on them. They spent their entire miserable lives shoveling sand out of their hole. Sighs and more sighs.

"I knew a man once who sighed all the time," I said. "Once he won a few thousand in the lottery, and all he could muster was a sigh."

Howard sighed.

During a commercial, he walked around my apartment, examining my books. Books everywhere—on the floor, sofa, refrigerator, air conditioner, windowsill. "I see you're a reader," he said.

"You're quite the detective."

Howard picked up a thick book I had bought for a quarter to use as a doorstop: *History of Modern Art.* He sighed and said, "I used this book teaching my art appreciation class."

I sat up. "You were a teacher? All my life I've wanted to be a teacher."

"Of what?"

"Anything. American History. Philosophy. Anything but gym. What's it like? To teach, I mean. Sometimes I imagine those eager young faces soaking it all in. I mean, it has to be the most meaningful, gratifying—"

"I was adjunct, part-time. Helen was full time, the real academic. After a while you give up your idealism." He opened the book and turned a few pages. "It's nice to know someone who's interested in art."

"Truth is, I'm interested in art insofar as it tells me something about an age, how people lived, how they saw the world. The trouble with art books is they have too many pictures."

Howard sat on the sofa and yawned a gaping yawn. His head fell back. "I should go," he said, but he didn't move. Within seconds he was snoring.

I covered him with Beatrice's old afghan, tucked it neatly under his chin and sat for a few minutes watching him. All my life I have liked watching people sleep. You watch a person sleep, you feel differently about him. It's hard to judge a sleeping person negatively. As a kid I used to sneak into my parents' bedroom and watch them sleep. For most of my life, whenever I wanted to stop being mad at someone, I imagined them sleeping. After watching Howard for a while, I felt my body soften, and I saw him for what he was—the saddest and loneliest man I'd ever known, a man who venerated his own sadness. Although I was not necessarily a happy person, next to this man I was Bozo the Clown.

The following morning he was gone. The afghan was folded and on top of it lay twenty dollars and the red tie. He'd left a note that read, "Tobias, thank you for putting up with me. Enjoy the tie."

 THREE

The morning sun was blaring full force as I walked to the Bread and Butter. No wind, no clouds, barely enough air. Pieces of newspapers, paper cups, hamburger wrappers lay on the sidewalks and in the gutters. To keep panhandlers at bay, I kept a book tucked under my arm and walked quickly with my head down, imagining myself a scholarly man, filled with clear distinctions, adept at pure reason and exacting logic, a man of letters on his way to prepare his next lecture.

If a beggar approached me, I had a standard routine, a kind of Saint Vitus Dance. I had discovered in my years on Fourth Avenue that psychosis is the best defense in a world populated by people who have nothing to lose. Even psychotics were afraid of psychotics.

Despite wandering off into an emotional dead end for a couple of days, despite close encounters with Mayflower and Howard Gardener, my life was intact. I also had a new TV, a nice skillet, some extra food, a bottle of tequila, an almost new Mr. Coffee, twenty dollars, and a red silk tie.

The Bread and Butter was crowded. The smells of fresh baked bread, melted butter, and Miss Choy's coffee lifted my spirits even more. I was once again aloof, smartly cynical, unmoved by the pervasive pain in the world. I sat at the counter on a stool toward the back and looked around. I liked it all—the silo coffee urns, the counter stools with red vinyl covering held together by duct tape, the old cash register that still worked with a manual crank. I'd turned that crank a few thousand times before Beatrice got sick.

Miss Choy placed a cup of coffee before me. "You come back. Work for Miss Choy."

"I can't," I said. "I have too many books to read before I die."

"Books, books, books. You always reading crappy books. Books a bunch of bullshits. Miss Choy's cash drawer never balance no more. I no punch right button. Miss Choy not know if she rich or poor. Government sons-of-bitches on Miss Choy's ass. Virgil say Miss Choy is intuitive type. Virgil full of crap." She looked at me, her neck bent like a bird about to peck at a worm. "What you want?"

Who could feel anything but happiness around such a woman? I ordered my usual boiled egg with rye toast and orange marmalade.

"Same-same everyday," she said. "Same egg, same toast, same marmalade. The day you tell me you want something different, the elastic in Miss Choy's drawers pop."

That cheered me even more.

Virgil Sears, the cook, called through the kitchen window. "Hey, Tobias."

I deepened my voice and tried to match his Native American monotone. "Hey, Virgil."

When I left, Virgil would say, *See you, Tobias*, and I would say, *See you, Virgil*. I enjoyed the comfortable sameness of my visits to the Bread and Butter—the well-defined boundaries, the ritual. I took a sip of coffee and let the metallic taste of it wash over my tongue.

Miss Choy stood on a stool and filled a coffee urn. I was admiring her flexed calf when the front door opened and Mayflower Bryant entered. I could almost hear a fanfare.

"Hello, dears," she called out to those assembled.

Forks hung suspended in midair. Everyone in the diner looked at her. She wore linen slacks and a blue silk blouse with the sleeves rolled up just past the elbows. She came straight towards me, addressing everyone as she passed. "I must have taken a wrong turn," she said, sitting next to me. "I'm afraid my sense of geography is deserting me. I've walked these streets for years. Now every direction I turn holds another surprise." She nudged me with an elbow. "Hello, Tobias. It is Tobias, isn't it, the man who dances in his underwear?"

"I'm sorry I—"

"Nonsense. I thoroughly enjoyed myself."

"Thank you for folding my laundry."

"Yesterday afternoon my social worker asked me to count backwards from a hundred by sevens, and I couldn't do it."

"Ninety-three, eighty-six, seventy-nine," I said. "Like that?"

"Sometimes I feel as if I'm watching a movie, knowing at some point the film will break and—poof!—there I'll be with nothing except the glare of a blank screen. I close my eyes and try to glimpse the exact instant in which time and space will cease to exist. I know if I look in a mirror at that moment, there'll be no one looking back." She folded her hands and rested her elbows on the counter.

I smelled alcohol on her breath. Her bracelets trickled down her arm and reflected the morning sunlight that poured through the windows. Her teeth and eyes sparkled. "You shouldn't be wandering around this neighborhood alone," I said.

"I find it charming, filled with life."

"It's filled with derelicts, drug addicts, and people who would cut your throat for a nickel. It's dangerous."

"But what isn't? I think it's sad what most people are willing to give up to feel safe."

"Fear. They give up fear."

"No, they are still afraid. They are afraid of being attacked by terrorists, or some new virus, or not being able to afford their next Botox treatment. What they give up is their souls, their capacity to experience passion and joy. Then they stop experiencing anything, even terror."

"Still, a nice gated community, a swimming pool, a new SUV, a bodyguard—"

"I see you like my bracelets," she said. "You're staring at them."

"Dazzling," I said.

"What a lovely word, dear. Say it again."

"Dazzling?"

She closed her eyes and said the word as if tasting it. "Daz-za-ling."

Miss Choy set out a linen napkin and silverware, apparently Mayflower's own special supply, and poured hot water into Mayflower's special teapot.

Mayflower ordered an English muffin toasted "devilishly dark with some of your delicious strawberry jam and three pieces of burnt bacon." She turned back to me. "Oh, you like marmalade. I prefer strawberry."

"Why burnt?" I asked.

"My nose has all but stopped working," she said. "Has yours? I hope I'm not wearing too much perfume. Sniff me."

I leaned closer. "You're not," I said.

"Oh, good. Since I can no longer enjoy olfaction, I find myself preferring crunchy things more. Textures. I used to like my toast lightly browned. Now I prefer it extra dark and crunchy. I'm learning to enjoy the feel of food." She stroked her braid, absently flicked the bushy end of it at me, then tossed it over her shoulder. "How do you feel about toast, Tobias?"

All I could manage was, "I saw some nice looking used toasters over at the Thrift and Gift."

"I've been intending to go there," she said. "I need a new toaster. Perhaps we can explore together."

I didn't say anything.

Mayflower leaned closer and whispered, "I'm going to read some Whitman later this morning. Would you like to fan the literary fires with me?"

"I've had some bad news," I lied.

"I have too, dear. I found Cordelia dead in her cage this morning. It never occurred to me that birds actually die of old age. I thought they went on forever."

"I'm sorry for your loss," I said.

"At least I was there to find her." She ate a piece of bacon in three bites. "And what is your bad news?"

I shrugged, unable to think of anything. "Nothing, really."

"Oh, dear. I've made you angry, haven't I? I abhor people who butt in with their misery when I've got my own. I won't let you leave here until you tell me."

I made up something. I told her a friend of mine seemed to be going mad.

"And what is wrong with that, dear? I've come to value certain aberrations. I think of them as the costume jewelry of character." She filled her cup with tea, took a sip and smiled. "Isn't this fun?"

"I suppose—"

"I so enjoy our little chats, don't you? Talking about this and that, not having to worry about a job or the stock market or the price of oil."

"As a matter of fact, I do worry about the price of oil."

"I think we'd all be better off if we ran out of it." She took another sip of tea and smiled. "A dog kept me awake half the night howling at the moon."

"I heard it," I said, feeling like a flying Garibaldi reaching for the next conversational trapeze.

"Maybe that was me you heard, dear. I called out the window and told it to hush. Then I looked up at the harvest moon and knew why it was howling."

"Why?"

"For love, of course. I took it as a kind of prayer. Are you religious?"

"My religion is the opposite of religious."

"How do you mean?"

"I'm anti fairy tale."

"I love fairy tales."

"I recently learned an interesting fact about the moon," I said. "Did you know if you bend over and look through your legs at the huge full moon on the horizon, it appears to be normal size?"

She furrowed her brow. "I think I'd prefer not knowing that, dear. I like my moon romantic, huge and orange. Only under the most unusual circumstances would I consider bending over and looking at it through my legs." She touched her napkin to her lips, then raised her fist in the air. "'Get on with it, you moonstruck beast,' I called. 'Howl to your heart's content.'"

Silence.

Mayflower laughed. "And he did. He howled for hours. So I had a few gins and howled with him. It was marvelous, the two of us howling like that." She looked directly at me. "Tell me, Tobias, when was the last time something pierced your heart so deeply you howled?"

I whispered, "I have never howled."

Mayflower leaned in my direction. "Then you must. Let's do something rash, dear, something alive and magnificent, even destructive."

"Like what?"

She thought for a moment. "Well, perhaps we could go to the zoo, climb into the lion's den, rip our stomachs open with a sharp knife, and wait to be consumed." She laughed.

I stared at a speck of pepper on my uneaten egg, waiting for my next thought. "I'm sorry," I said. "I—"

She shrugged. "I suppose I'd better do a little sorting. It's slow work, you know. I'm more a gatherer than a sorter and organizer. Order interferes with surprises. I'm re-reading my old love letters before I burn them. We collect stuff our entire life, then fret that someone will find it after we're dead. So we ship it off to the city dump. It's sad, isn't it, that others often view as degenerate smut what we value most? Some of my best letters are the smuttiest."

"I read that the average person writes only two letters a year," I said. "That's down from twenty, three decades ago. E-mail's the thing nowadays."

"Utterly tragic. Letter writing is good fun. Once I was having an affair with a shy prince from Kuwait. He'd rule for a while and then, when he'd had his fill of Islamic purity, he'd fly to Paris and play with me for a week or so. Poor dear never tired of writing dirty letters. He adored saying *fuck. Fuck* this, *fuck* that."

I looked around, but my embarrassment didn't faze Mayflower.

"I suppose religion often makes us want to talk dirty, doesn't it?" she said.

"Tell me, did you actually know a prince from Kuwait or did you make him up?"

"Both," she said. She folded her napkin. "Some fact, some fiction. I'm not interested in knowing the difference. My stories serve me well just as they are."

"How can something that's not true serve you in any reasonable way?"

"They connect me to you. Don't you feel that connection?" She checked the wall clock. "Well, I really must be wandering on. Last week I ended up in the rectory of Our Mother of Sorrows. The priest and I had a rather heated chat about universal birth control. My dearest hope is that, if we are destroyed by overpopulation and forced to stand on the edge of someone's compost pit and shoot ourselves, I'll be among the last to go." She leaned over and whispered in my ear. "You need some interesting stories of your own, dear. You must tire of reading other's stories." She waved a royal wave to everyone in general and left.

I finished my egg and headed back to the Coronado. Meeting up with Mayflower seemed to have changed my body chemistry. The more I tried to be bold and unafraid the more anxious I felt. A skateboarder almost ran over me. Across the street a religious zealot stood on an upside-down garbage can, arms flailing. I could see his mouth move but there was no sound. The new Fourth Avenue merchants' trolley on its way to the university seemed to be moving too fast.

Nothing seemed familiar, not the sidewalk, not even the Coronado sign in the distance. I needed something familiar. Then I saw Caravelo, the one-handed juggler.

A crowd had gathered. I pushed through it. I focused on the ball that rested on Caravelo's forehead. The ball leapt into the air, landed on the back of his neck, stayed there for a few seconds and disappeared down the back of his shirt. My panic began to subside. This man amazed me, the miracles he performed with his one hand.

Calm now, I paused at the Windsong Studio Gallery. A sign on the door read "BACK AT 6:30." Katherine Peterson, the owner and resident artist, sold her paintings mainly to men for three to six hundred each.

With every payment in full, the buyer could, if he wished, receive a "private showing" on her purple sheets in the back room of her gallery. I looked in her window and considered buying a small painting. A stupid idea. I needed discourse, not intercourse. I kept walking, thinking how lucky I was to have my books.

FOUR

Like Thoreau, fairly early in life I came to believe that the vast majority of humans, including most saints and great thinkers, live lives of quiet desperation, neither producing nor thinking anything of significance most of the time. The lives and thoughts written about in history books have been culled from the wasteland of ordinary numb and empty lives, the one-thing-after-another crap we fill our days with. Hence, the value of history is its efficiency. History distills life into one great moment after another. Writers of history sort the ordinary from the truly outstanding and offer up only the most delicious morsels of life. I, for example, am not interested in the fact that Pythagoras had an irrational fear of beans or that he refused to allow his followers to sit on a quart jar. I'm interested in his theory of harmonics and its relationship to Plato's idealism. The suggestion that Lincoln was gay or that Van Gogh was psychotic is of minuscule significance compared to Lincoln's political life and the beauty of Van Gogh's paintings. Long ago, I decided I wanted to associate with the best and brightest, but only when they were at their best and brightest. The same logic applied to my own life.

Most of the time I bored myself. No one was at home. Nothing I did or said made the slightest difference in slowing humanity's slide into the septic tank of the ordinary. I had excuses, of course—I blamed it on politicians, TV, advertising, Beatrice's long illness, her pain, her need for round-the-clock care and company. She was a talker, Beatrice was, right up to the end. Her last words were something about a sale of Vienna sausages at Safeway. She was addicted to Vienna sausages, scoured the paper for sales, sent me off to every supermarket to buy them by the case. I tried to work, to think, but who was I to deny a dying woman her Vienna sausages?

In the years since her death I tried to become more productive and creative, woke up each morning prepared to *carpe diem*, but by noon my good intentions had given way to fiddling with a dripping sink or staring out the window holding an open but unread book in my lap while watching ordinary people go about their stupid ordinary days, feeling, well, stupidly ordinary.

Ordinariness is a great social force. Its power to leach vitality from the human soul is at least equal to the black plague. But on that day, after running into Mayflower in the Bread and Butter and being energized by her passion and vitality, I vowed to change my life. I felt a kind of emergence of the greater Tobias, the productive Tobias, the Tobias with an inner will of coiled steel.

I would clean my apartment, align my environment with my inner purpose, then I would read and think—perhaps even think a grand thought, come up with an idea that would break open the mystery of evil or shed some light on the illusive nature of love.

By noon I had scrubbed the orange stain from my sink, swept and mopped my floors, cleaned my corroded toilet and bathtub, and polished my chrome and glass coffee table. I found a dozen cans of Vienna sausages at the back of the pantry and set them aside for the Salvation Army.

Housekeeping lifted my spirits. I found Beatrice's medicines, some of her lipsticks, her hairbrush. Her illness was long and painful. At times I grew weary of caring for her. Now, every cupboard, every drawer I opened contained something that reminded me of her. I tossed away her old medications and cosmetics, her old toothbrush and found two new ones at the back of a drawer. I tossed out three unmatched bobby socks. Beatrice's dresses went into a bag for the Salvation Army. I held her robe to my nose, inhaled the rancid perfume of it and hung it up in the closet. She had worn it throughout her sickness. I couldn't throw it out, not yet.

I reorganized my books according to the time in my life I'd read them. I opened a dog-eared copy of *Goodnight Moon*, the first book I'd read on my own at the age of three. My mother had inscribed it "To my darling Toby on his second birthday. May all your dreams come true." None of my dreams had come true. I'd dreamed of being a college professor, a man who published learned papers and gave brilliant lectures. Recently, I read that dreams had no meaning; they resulted from random firings of neurons in the brain, and to interpret them was tantamount to interpreting the sound of a jackhammer. This seemed to go along with my experience.

After cleaning the apartment, I sat on my sofa staring at the first page of Durant's *The Life of Greece*, waiting for the first line to sink in. I couldn't concentrate. The words were disconnected, as if some internal mechanism had broken down. Images of dancing with Mayflower flitted across my mind. I tried not to think about her and thought of Howard instead.

Was his bizarre display of generosity a gesture of misguided friendship, an effort to get my attention, or a sign of abject hopelessness? I resented even having to ask the question.

I tossed my book on the table and looked around. I needed a break. I made some popcorn, added liberal portions of melted butter and salt, slipped on Beatrice's robe and turned on my new TV. A soap opera had just started. Karen and Steve were about to separate, a good thing, too, because Laurie, Karen's good friend, was in a coma and pregnant with Steve's baby, and Steve was denying all responsibility. I cursed Steve. I lectured Laurie. I felt almost nothing for Karen.

Three days later I hadn't turned off the television. Mayflower had knocked several times, but I hadn't answered. I didn't want her to see me in such a pitiful condition. I hadn't taken a bath or brushed my teeth or washed my dirty dishes. My apartment smelled like butter and Vienna sausages. I had eaten all of them, dipping their little tubular, pale bodies in strawberry jelly and tonguing them against the roof of my mouth.

I lay on the sofa, feeling nothing except the electronic buzz of fear. When I did move even an inch, static electricity snapped at me. A sock clung to my bare chest like an argyle leech. My hair was standing straight up. Finally, in a last desperate effort to reclaim my life, I crawled to the television and switched it off.

The silence was like a knife in the stomach. I held back tears as I yanked the plug from the wall, hoisted the TV to my shoulder, staggered across the hall and entered Howard's apartment without knocking.

It was like walking into a tomb. The air was laced with the dead scent of the previous tenant, Abigail Kaufman. Howard sat at his kitchen table, hunched over a yellow pad. He turned the pad face down.

"I'm giving your TV back," I said.

Howard didn't look up.

"What are you writing?" I asked.

"Nothing."

I placed the TV on the end of the table and sat in the chair adjacent to his. "I'm not blind. I can see with my own eyes you're writing something."

"You're wearing a woman's housecoat."

"Don't try to change the subject," I said. "Tell me it's none of my business, but don't say 'Nothing.'"

"It's none of your business."

"Fine," I said, lifting the hem of my robe. "I'm going."

"I don't want the television back. A deal's a deal."

"It takes two to make a deal, but only one to cancel it," I said. I grabbed the yellow pad.

Howard folded his arms on the table and rested his head on them.

I read: *To whom it may concern, I can no longer tolerate the pain of living without Helen. She was my breath, my essence, my only meaning. Therefore I have decided to end my life—* I snickered involuntarily and tossed the pad onto the table. I picked it up again and finished. The letter was long and self-indulgent, filled with clichés and massive doses of self-pity. "And how do you intend to end your life?" I asked.

He stared at his hands. "Jump off the roof."

"Are three stories enough to kill or just maim? I mean, if you jump you want to be killed, don't you? What's the point of feeling excruciating pain and paralysis the rest of your life? You should definitely go off head first."

He shook his head and shuddered. "I couldn't do that."

Suddenly I disliked this man for imposing his elephant-sized problems on me. His suicide marginalized my TV addiction. I wanted to leave, but I wouldn't have been able to live with myself if I left and Howard actually committed suicide. I sat down and spelled it out, point by rational point. "You've lost your wife," I said. "You're depressed. Depression isn't such a bad thing. I've been depressed most of my life. Depression is a natural reaction to the world we live in. If we all killed ourselves when we were depressed, there'd be no one left. There'd be no bank tellers or secretaries or bus boys."

"Please, go away."

Then I got it: giving his stuff away was part of his suicide plan. I wanted to punch him for being so unspontaneous. All the while, he'd been planning his own death. "Look, you dump this suicide crap on me, then you tell me to leave you alone?" I stood straight up. "Fine, I'll leave you alone. Come to think of it, it's possible the world already has enough people who believe they are the center of the universe. Maybe your urge to kill yourself is nature's way of ridding herself of too much selfishness. Best not to interfere." I turned to leave.

Howard grabbed my elbow. "Stay. Look, I'm having a difficult time. Will you help me?" His lower lip jutted out.

"Tell me, Howard, have you noticed that your misery seems bigger and more important than other people's misery? I have misery, too, you know. I've been eating Vienna sausages by the case with strawberry jelly and watching TV for three days. I set out to do one thing, and I do the opposite. You think you've got problems. You see standing before you an uninteresting person living a meaningless and uninteresting life."

Howard drooped his head like a dog that was being punished. I was feeling better. My blood was starting to flow again. "Here's the truth, Howard. This grieving of yours is making me antsy. You're not only depressed, you're depressing. Your depression is like an oozing mass of toxic waste. Your depression makes lethargy seem like something to be celebrated. Here's what you don't get—there are civilized ways to behave. Even when you're depressed, courtesies must be extended. Manners, Howard. You ever heard of manners?" My upper lip tightened involuntarily.

Howard sat up and crossed his arms. His eyes followed me as I walked around the table, talking, gesturing wildly not only to make my point but because it felt good. I wasn't sure I was making sense, but I knew I needed to keep talking because Howard needed me to keep talking. I'd seen it on TV. You keep the suicide guy talking. "Life is difficult," I said. "Suffering is the price we pay for living. We live a little; we suffer a little. Tit for tat. There's some cosmic principle at work here."

This was very good. I was interested in what might come out of my mouth next. "Just about every good thing is balanced by an equal amount of crapola. You help an old lady across the street, next day your cat gets run over. That's the way it goes. Good-bad, happy-sad, up-down. That's life. Dying is an easy way to get rid of the pain, but it also interferes with living. Still, dying has its appeal. Nature even cooperates with our dying. It urges us on, tries to absorb us back into it. Living means resisting its call. When we are dying, our brains secrete a sedative that blocks the fear. Ask Holocaust survivors. The amazing thing is they weren't afraid. Ask scientists." I paused. "Ask me if I'm afraid to die."

"Are you?"

"Of course not," I lied. "Death is as easy as—falling off a horse, but it's harder to stay on this bucking bronco called life. There's no chemical that takes away the pain, and if there is it should be banned. Booze doesn't help, not for long anyway. Neither does sex or television, not even grief."

"I feel empty, afraid."

"So do I." I paused a second, thinking about what I had just said about feeling empty, surprised I had said it. Then I went on. "I'll bet Helen wasn't afraid. I'll bet she fought a lot harder to live than you." I paced around the table, gesturing, scowling, sweating, liking what I was saying. "It takes time to get over losing someone you love. But you fight. You don't whine for two years, and you don't kill yourself." I poked the air in front of Howard's face to emphasize each word.

Howard pulled back. "How long did it take you to stop grieving after Beatrice died?"

"To tell you the truth, I don't know if I ever grieved. I still have her ashes under my bed. I'm afraid to keep them and afraid to scatter them. A few days ago I tossed out her lipsticks and medicines. It sent me into a tailspin."

Howard remained upright, attentive.

I lowered my head and squinted into his eyes. "You don't kill yourself, Howard. You take a laxative. You read a book. You get laid. You get drunk. But you don't kill yourself."

"The pain won't stop."

"Depression is a like a stray dog. Don't feed it and eventually it leaves. In the meantime you pretend you're alive even when you'd rather be dead. You get a hobby. You do something. You clean your apartment. You bake a cake. You dig a hole."

"I don't want to dig a hole," he said. "I want to stop feeling like this. I want to feel excited about something. Once, I was enthusiastic about being alive. I miss my enthusiasm, my vitality."

"Maybe you need another woman. Maybe you need to get laid."

"I have no interest in sex."

"Maybe even another wife. With a wife, sex is optional. You're still young. What, sixty? Sixty-one? As a matter of fact, there's a woman named Katherine Peterson who runs the Windsong Gallery, a real looker, tits like giant burritos. She lives just east of the Coronado on the other side of the vacant lot. You two have an interest in art in common. Talk to her about buying one of her paintings."

Howard narrowed his eyes. "Do you believe in an afterlife?"

"I don't even believe in this life."

"Seriously."

"Look, I believe we have one shot. As for you and me, this is it. Our heaven or hell is here in the Coronado Apartments. Is this not depressing? Why are you asking me these childish questions? Are you religious?"

Howard stood and gazed out the window. "I was as a kid. Remember the heaven we believed in as kids? The golden streets, deer and lambs all around? I think of Helen in a place like that, all light and gold." He picked up his suicide note and looked directly at me with dead eyes that revealed no hope.

A chill crossed my shoulders, and for the first time it occurred to me he wasn't kidding about taking his life. "Look, you need to—think of something else." I remembered the tequila he'd given me. "We'll have a few tequilas and limes, then instead of you jumping off the roof—" I looked around. "We'll fling the television off. How's that for an idea? We'll kill the goddamn TV."

Howard rolled his eyes. "It seems so—contrived."

"So what isn't? You have to *do* something, break free of your mind, lift a leg on lethargy. Think about it while I get the limes and tequila."

An hour later I was drunk and seeing double. The bottle was almost empty.

"Wait here," Howard said. He kept one hand on the wall and made his way into the bedroom.

I was expecting him to return with a pistol, having decided to put us both out of our misery, me first, then him. I wasn't even afraid. If this was it—too bad. I was too drunk to care. Instead of a gun, he came out carrying three thick photograph albums filled with pictures of Helen. For the next hour we looked at photographs of Helen.

She was a good-looking sixties-type—two parts lynx, one part ocotillo, a little hemp. She wore natural fabrics, kept herself trim. Sophisticated in a hippie sort of way—dark eyes, narrow nose, high forehead. When sitting, she always revealed a knee. I found her attractive. "Nice knees," I said.

Howard nodded. "Incredible skin."

"Beatrice wasn't attractive," I said. "She gained a lot of weight. What probably killed her." Suddenly, I missed Beatrice, or at least a feeling I sometimes had about her, a feeling that could best be described as family. Beatrice was family. I had no idea I felt that way. I missed having a family. "When she was sick, I'd rub her legs with lotion. She liked that. As a matter of fact, I liked it too. Sex, for us, wasn't that important."

Howard held up a picture—Helen wearing a bikini.

I was horny and drunk and feeling a little sorry for myself. "Get a load of that," I said. "What'd she weigh, one twenty-five, one thirty?"

"We never talked about our weight."

"Now she's—" I pointed to her ashes.

Howard's eyes welled.

I drifted away, thinking of ashes, all the ashes of all the people in the world, how the ashes left by one of Bertrand Russell's books would probably outweigh the ashes of Russell himself. "Just imagine," I said. "Ninety-nine point nine percent of the most interesting people who have ever lived are now dead. If this is not a reason for reading history, I don't know what is."

Howard's face scrunched up, his lower lip extended. He was about to cry again. "Snap out of it," I said.

"I can't," he said.

"Yes, you can. Think on the bright side."

"There is no bright side."

"Of course there is." An idea came to me. "Let's play a game called—optimism. I'll name one thing worth living for, and then you name one. Back and forth. I'll go first. Let's see. Miss Choy's chicken noodle soup at the Bread and Butter. Your go."

Howard pointed to a picture. "The first time I walked Helen home from a concert in the rain. We didn't have an umbrella. I still remember the scent of her hair."

"Good one. Here's one—the way Mayflower's lips move before she talks, like she's tasting her words before she says them."

"Who's Mayflower?"

"Never mind. Go."

"The time we lived above a bakery. Helen smelled like fresh bread all the time."

"Hold it."

"Huh?"

"Let's concentrate on the present. Give me something not in the past, something happening now."

Howard looked at his feet, then at me. "The smell of an artist's studio."

"Good." I said. "Hey, you could be an artist. You know about art. You taught it, for Christ's sake. Who is more valued in our society than artists? You can paint pictures of Helen. You already have all these photographs. I've read about projectors that enlarge pictures and flash them on a canvas."

"Interesting you should say that. Just before she died, Helen told me I should start painting again. I told her art didn't need another mediocre artist, and she said it didn't matter what art needed. I needed art."

I studied the picture of Helen in the bikini, her thin waist, her great legs. "She has a certain—grace."

"An incredible presence."

"Grace was not Beatrice's strong point, except when she ate. I loved to watch Beatrice eat roast turkey," I said.

Howard stared at Helen in her bikini.

"It was beautiful in its way. She took very small bites. I liked watching her pick off tiny strips of meat. I loved the way her small mouth moved when she chewed. She possessed great powers of concentration when she ate, almost moved into an altered state."

Howard locked his hands behind his head and smiled. "It's good to talk like this, isn't it? I've not talked to anyone this way since Helen died." He turned a page and paused. "Look at this one."

Helen was heavier in this picture. She wore a loose dress. Her knees didn't show.

"She doesn't look—like the same person."

"I took this photograph the day she left for a visiting professorship at Drake University in Des Moines. She said she needed time away from me, that she wasn't sure she wanted to stay married. See the strain in her face, how she holds her body? That school year was the worst of my life. I thought I'd lost her."

"She came back."

"Yes, but it was never the same. At times I'd watch her sitting at her desk, sipping tea, staring at the wall with a smile on her lips. Then, from nowhere, she'd start crying. Or sometimes she'd laugh as if someone had sneaked up and breathed on her neck. I felt as if I were in the back row of a theater watching her perform, and she was looking off-stage, seeing things I could never see." Howard leaned closer. "I wished we'd had children."

"I know," I said. "Sometimes I wish I'd insisted that—"

"It was my fault. Something about the temperature of my scrotum."

Not eager to hear about Howard's scrotum, I slipped into a drunken silence. Finally, with what little coordination I had left, I reached for the bottle, finished the last few drops, and said, "Come on, Howard. Let's go kill the TV."

FIVE

For some reason I got stuck with carrying the TV. Howard hadn't asked me to carry it—he was too occupied with his own depression—but he acted as though I was the designated lackey. It made me angry. Yet I was unable to tell Howard that it was his turn to carry it. Apparently, somewhere along the line, I came to believe that being suicidal excused a person from heavy lifting.

As we made our way down the hall towards the elevator, it became clear to me that, after tonight, I had no interest in being this man's friend. His depression was too monumental, too demanding of my time and energy.

The TV pushed against my bladder. Sweat poured off my face. I needed to sit down, but Howard bounded on ahead, stopping occasionally to look back and motion me on. My idea of killing the TV suddenly struck me as stupid. I leaned against the wall, tongued the sweat from my upper lip and looked at Howard. He was waiting by the elevator, holding the door open. I came close to telling him to kiss my ass.

I paused in front of the elevator door. "Let's rethink this," I said. "We're drunk. Maybe we can kill the TV tomorrow."

"No, you're right," he said. "It's a kind of ritual, a symbolic way of fighting back at all the stupidity in the world. The more I think about it, the better I like it. It's original, to the point, fresh."

"Shut up," I said.

The elevator stopped on the third floor. We walked the rest of the way. My stomach felt like it'd been occupied by a whirling dervish. I was about to drop the TV.

Howard stepped on to the roof and held his arms out as if he were embracing the sky. He turned in a slow circle, exhibiting himself to the universe, inviting the cosmos to admire the simple fact of his existence.

"What a night," he said. "I feel better already. Can you smell the creosote? Just look at those stars. I'd forgotten how beautiful desert nights are."

Overcome by vertigo, I collapsed like a folding chair, crossed my legs, and remained perfectly still.

"Ready?" Howard said.

"Ready," I muttered.

Howard picked up the television and held it over his head. He loomed above me like a prehistoric bird. "Shouldn't we say something?"

"Just fling the bastard over, Howard."

He staggered back, turned a complete circle and ran toward the ledge.

The world slowed as if someone had shut off the power. A lazy blur of movement fluttered past me, several Howards accordioned together, many televisions, washes of black on black. I had an awful premonition that Howard was going to die.

I tried to call out, but couldn't make a sound. Howard extended his arms and heaved. The television rose and disappeared into the darkness. Howard disappeared, too. First his head, then his chest, hips, and knees. His wingtips seemed to cling to the parapet for an instant before he vanished.

A sickening silence. Suicide had had its way. It had drafted me into its service and used me as its instrument to kill Howard.

I prepared myself for the *whump* of his body hitting the alley. A second passed, then another. No sound. Nothing. I crawled twenty feet to the ledge and peeked over. A security light cast a greenish-amber glow on the dumpster below. I didn't see Howard anywhere. He'd vanished in thin air, been absorbed into the night. Then I spotted his body lying face up in the dumpster, cushioned by a pile of black trash bags. At his feet the television's one eye glared up at me accusingly.

I tried to call out, but my tongue stuck to the roof of my mouth. The stillness and utter silence was awful. Howard lay twisted and motionless. I didn't know if he was dead or completely paralyzed. I remembered seeing men who had to suck on straws to control their wheelchair, a paraplegic who painted with a brush held between his teeth. My awful destiny became clear. I would spend the rest of my life pushing Howard around, cooking his meals, feeding him, brushing his teeth, wiping his ass, cleaning his brushes.

Then he moved. He turned over, sat up, and slowly looked around. His eyes glowed green in the light. He called up to me. His voice had a breathy quality, something I associated with people who meditate a lot.

"My body's vibrating with this incredible energy," he said, "yet I'm inwardly calm."

"Stay put. I'll call 911."

"Don't. I feel fine—better than fine, I feel alive for the first time in years. This is how I want to feel. Life is surging through me." He brushed himself off, flapped his arms a couple of times and climbed down from the dumpster. He looked up. "I have an idea. Meet me in my apartment."

"I can't move," I said. "Legs won't work."

"I'll come get you."

Two minutes passed, then the door flew open. I watched in horror as Howard swept me up and carried me fireman-style across the roof. "You're light as air," he said. "I feel like I could fly."

"No flying." For a moment I thought he might go over the edge again, test the fates, so to speak—a tandem jump with me draped over his shoulder. "It's the adrenalin," I said. "You're experiencing something akin to religious conversion. Don't do anything impulsive."

Howard carried me toward the door and sang in a deep baritone, "To dream the unbearable dream—"

"Impossible dream," I said. "It's a song about hope, not nightmares. Get a grip. Look at yourself. First you're committing suicide. Now you're singing Broadway songs. You're suffering from the delusion of feeling chosen."

"I'm happy," Howard said. He took the stairs to the second floor.

"Put me down," I said.

Howard lowered me and tried to hug me.

"No hugging. You need rest. We both do."

Howard's eyes widened. "You want to hear my idea?"

"No."

"We'll scatter Helen's and Beatrice's ashes around the neighborhood. Helen loved this part of town. She insisted we eat at least once a month in the patio at Caruso's. She shopped at the Food Conspiracy. She bought the red tie I gave you at one of the vintage clothing stores."

I leaned against the wall. "I get it. Fine, you win. I'll give back your tie and the twenty."

"Forget it. You were right. We must move on. Optimism. You said it yourself. Go get Beatrice's ashes. I'll get Helen's."

"It's not safe to be on the streets after dark," I said.

"I'll protect you. We'll give our wives a proper sendoff and finish our grieving once and for all." He looked me over. "You'll have to take off that robe."

His passion was too strong, his grandiosity too complete. I had no will left. I changed into a pair of trousers and t-shirt, and ten minutes later we were on Fourth Avenue.

I was scared and saw nothing that reassured me—the punk rockers' greasy clothes and spiked hair, the endless rumble of cars spewing out exhaust as they circled the block, the neighborhood wild dog walking down the middle of the sidewalk dragging something that resembled intestines.

I had transferred Beatrice's ashes into a quart-sized plastic baggie. Howard carried Helen's ashes in their original blue box. In the midst of my fear and anger, I had to fight back the feeling that somehow Howard's ashes were better than mine.

He paused at the Food Conspiracy. "Helen loved this place," he said, his eyes still glowing with an inner fire. "She bought all our vegetables here." He scattered a few ashes in the entranceway. I did the same.

Two purple-haired girls approached us. They were talking about nipple piercing. As we passed, one of the girls propositioned Howard. "Hey, mister. Wanna fuck me?" She was fourteen at most. Her eyes and lips were heavy with black eyeliner and brown lipstick.

"Not tonight, dear," Howard said.

"Keep moving," I said, pushing at his back.

Howard wanted to help a drunk who clung to a parking meter. I pulled him away. "There's only one way to survive here," I said. "You have to act crazier than the others. Even a psychotic is afraid of a person who's more psychotic. Watch me." A group of young people huddled together— primal slime inching its way down the sidewalk. I lunged ahead toward them, head down, arms swinging, shouting gibberish. They split like the Red Sea. We walked through, unharmed.

Howard maneuvered his way through the crowd as if he were getting off an elevator, arms up, tiptoeing at times. "Pardon me, Miss. Excuse me, sir."

In the next hour we spread Beatrice's and Helen's ashes in the entranceway of several stores, in the fountain of Caruso's restaurant, at the Dairy Queen, and at the feet of a man and woman who were playing "King of the Road" on saxophones.

Despite my fear, I felt a sense of release. Beatrice would sit for hours looking down on this street, yearning to be part of it, to be accepted by it. After the cancer spread, chemotherapy had caused her to lose her hair. During those last days, she'd sit at the window, breathing deeply to relieve the pain. The day before she died we spent the afternoon together, sitting side-by-side, looking out the window. It was one of our best days together. I imagined her at the window now, watching me and Howard.

A bully wearing a Levi jacket, boots, and torn pants almost knocked me off the sidewalk. He stopped and sneered.

I prayed that Howard wouldn't say anything.

The bully came closer and stopped inches from Howard. "You owe me an apology."

"For what?" Howard said.

"For blocking the sidewalk," the guy said.

"Excuse me?"

The human wart poked Howard's chest with a finger. "You sound queer. You queer? Huh? Huh?"

Howard stumbled back, holding Helen's ashes with both hands. "Sir, I—"

He kept poking Howard.

I considered running. Then, taking my own advice, I stepped between them, jumped up and down, flapped my arms and crowed like a rooster. The guy backed off just enough to be absorbed by the crowd.

"We have to get back to the Coronado," I said.

"You go," Howard said. "I'm staying."

"Listen to me. Contrary to what you may think, you are not immortal. The meek will not inherit Fourth Avenue. You're going to get us killed."

Howard wasn't listening. He'd become fascinated with Caravelo, the one-handed juggler, who was bouncing balls off the sidewalk and wall so fast they produced a continuous rope of light. Caravelo turned a complete circle and caught the balls in a bag attached to his waist. The last ball landed on the back of his hand and, like a small bird, leapt to the back of his neck. It circled his head, came to stop on his chest and sat there, pulsing like an external heart.

The crowd cheered. Howard gave Caravelo a dollar and dropped a few ashes at his feet. "Let's sit down," he said to me, pointing to a bench that circled a lemon tree. He put more ashes at the base of the tree. "Helen and I used to sit here," he said.

I put the last of Beatrice's ashes there. "That's it for me," I said. "Let's get out of here."

Howard held up his plastic box, still two-thirds full. "I'm staying," he said.

Two girls walked by talking on cell phones.

"Mae West said youth was wasted on the young," I said.

"They grow up," Howard said.

"They get bigger, but they don't grow up. Their little thimbles of knowledge are filled with clichés and pop culture. They think what they don't know isn't worth knowing."

"Don't be cynical. Relax. Enjoy the evening. Remember optimism?"

"Hey, asswipe." The same guy who'd wanted the apology stood ten feet away, hands on hips. "What's in the box? Leftovers?"

"Don't you ever get bored with yourself?" I asked him. As soon as the words left my mouth, I wanted to take them back.

He came toward Howard and snatched Helen's ashes.

"Give those back," Howard said.

"Come get 'em, pussy."

Howard grabbed for the box, but missed.

All my life I had kept my distance from violence, thinking of it as lowbrow and common, an activity reserved for the uneducated masses. I preferred to learn about the shadow side of humanity through books. I prided myself in cultivating a healthy fear of my own blood, in having enough sense to walk away from a dangerous situation. I held these beliefs with great conviction. So to observe myself leaping through the air and landing on the thug's back astonished me. I didn't know what to do.

He began to spin.

I wrapped my arms and legs around him and squeezed so hard my eyes went out of focus. Stuck to his back, I noticed every detail—the rancid heat radiating from his body, the sweet scent of cheap aftershave, the blackheads in the crease of his neck, the saxophonists playing, "I Don't Know Why I Love You Like I Do."

He was still spinning. I willed myself to let go and run, but something in me was enraged. I wanted to do harm to this wasted piece of humanity. My hands gripped his neck and hair. "Run, Howard," I yelled.

He whirled faster. My legs came loose and stuck straight out.

You never seem to want my romancing.

My anger grew more intense. My fingers climbed the washboard ridges of his windpipe. With all my strength I tightened my grip. I felt a crunch.

The only time you hold me is when we're dancing.

I brought my head forward and my teeth found his right ear. I bit down hard. He screeched and whirled even faster. My teeth tore and ripped. Half his ear came off. I spat out an oblong hunk of gristle and went back for seconds. It didn't matter what happened to me now. My whole existence had only one purpose—to take this bastard down—to bathe in the blood of my enemy. And there was something else. Somewhere from deep within this hatred came another emotion, one so strong it staggered me.

I wanted Mayflower.

The goon went to one knee. He still held Helen's ashes.

I let go and stood over the one-eared mutant who was kneeling before me, rocking, holding the side of his head and moaning. All was silent for a moment except for his moans. I looked around at the crowd, fully prepared to take on my next victim. They backed off. The neighborhood wild dog appeared, sniffed around the injured man, licked some of his blood from the sidewalk and ate his ear.

Sirens screamed in the distance. Howard loomed at my side. "We have to get out of here," he said.

"The dog ate my ear," the thug screamed. "Stop him."

"Give me that box," I said.

"Go fuck yourself." Blood streamed from his ear. He got to his feet and tried to kick me. I jumped back, and he missed. I heard a piercing screech, steel against steel. Ten feet away, a garbage truck strained, locked its metal pincers around a container, lifted it high into the air, and dumped the contents into itself.

The sirens were closer.

The one-eared bully stumbled toward the garbage truck. I saw what he was up to, but couldn't move fast enough to prevent it. He tossed the blue box into the truck. The truck wheezed, settled back and sped off.

"Helen," Howard cried, pointing. "Stop that truck."

The sirens were a few blocks away.

"Let's go," I said.

Howard was devastated. He couldn't stop talking about how incredibly cruel it was that Helen would spend eternity in the city dump.

"Only a part of her," I said. "A very small part."

Inside the Coronado, a few people sat in the game room staring blankly at the TV. Mayflower was asleep in an overstuffed chair. *Leaves of Grass* lay open in her lap. We tiptoed past her. A minute later, we stood at Howard's door.

Howard took a deep breath and rolled his head around. "Why do people do that?" he said. "Where does all that anger come from? Why'd he toss Helen's ashes into the garbage truck? It's all so stupid, so unfeeling, so hateful."

We stood for a moment in silence. "I've never been that angry," I said. "I could have killed him. It's stupid, but a part of me wants to go back out there, find him and finish him off."

"Get some sleep," Howard said, touching my shoulder and guiding me to my apartment. He waited in the hall until I closed my door.

I washed the blood from my face and hands. My heart was still pounding. I felt alive, vital, heroic, unconquerable. I put on a clean shirt and went back to the lobby. It was dark except for the reading lamp beside Mayflower's chair. This time I wouldn't run away. I wakened her. She looked up, her eyes blank.

"I was wondering," I said, "if you'd like to drink some gin and read some Whitman together."

She smiled and held out her hand. "Walk me home, Charles, dear."

I escorted her into the elevator. The doors closed. "I've been in a fight," I said. "I bit off a man's ear."

She looped her arm under mine and yawned. "Good, dear."

We made our way down the hall to her apartment. I waited, hoping she would invite me in, but she thanked me, said goodnight and disappeared behind her door.

I went back outside. It had started raining. The vacant lot between the Coronado and Katherine Peterson's place was already flooded. The mud reminded me of a recurring dream—thousands of mud-babies beneath the ground struggling to dig their way out, calling my name. That dream had always frightened me. If they got out, I would be attacked and killed by a brigade of angry babies. But now, as I stood on the front steps of Katherine Peterson's place, I felt confident, unafraid.

Her light was on. I approached the door, ready to inquire about terms for buying a painting. Then, through her window, I saw a man's silhouette. He had a drink in his hand. She reached out and placed a hand on his shoulder.

I walked down Fourth Avenue in the rain, half hoping someone would try to mug me. I broke into a jog and jabbed the air. "Boom, bam," I said. I kicked at a puddle and threw an uppercut. But, except for a few bums sleeping in an entranceway, the street was empty. Nothing to do, no foes to conquer. I headed back to the Coronado. On the way, I decided I would rescue the TV.

In the dumpster behind the Coronado, the caved-in trash bags still showed the imprint of Howard's body. I cradled the TV in my arms and carried it to my apartment, where I watched an old John Wayne movie until I fell asleep.

During the night, I woke with a terrible headache. My sheet and blanket were piled at the end of my bed. Toilets flushed, floors creaked, air conditioners hummed. A dog howled in the distance. Everything, even my own breathing, seemed too loud and disjointed.

I got out of bed, stood at my window and stared west at the silhouette of the empty downtown area—the squat, abandoned buildings, Tucson's version of big city skyscrapers. I thought of Mayflower—what might have been if we had met when we were young, what might have happened in the basement if I had not run away. I got in bed and turned off my light. A few minutes later, I heard a sound—three taps on the other side of the wall behind my head. I lay perfectly still. Three more taps. Everything in me wanted to answer, but I couldn't move, couldn't make a sound.

SIX

5:00 a.m. After a restless night, I lay awake, trying to remember how it felt to be Tobias the Fearless, the horny, throat-crushing, ear-biting warrior. No luck. That wasn't me, just a doppelganger created by booze and adrenalin. I shuddered.

I stood before my sink, filling my percolator. I didn't like myself. My life was falling apart. My experiment with relationships had been a bust. I wanted my old life back, the life of the contemplative scholar. I took two aspirin, drank two glasses of water and made a pot of strong coffee.

I wouldn't go to the Bread and Butter this morning. I wouldn't leave my apartment. I was still thinking of Mayflower, her tapping on my wall. That was all the hopeless fantasy of a part of me buried years ago. I refused to turn into a dirty old man out on the street ogling women, rubbing up against ash cans in the park. I thought of St. Augustine, Kazantzakis, Jesus, Luther, Gandhi, Thomas Merton, their lifelong struggles to climb the steep mountains of morality while battling their baser instincts. Their lives and thoughts had inspired me, served as models for how to live *in* but not *of* the world. I remembered something James Hillman had written—to become a truly authentic dirty old man, one had to give up sex and love and live totally in the imagination, for it was only in the imagination that the purely erotic existed. He was right. It was my imagination I needed to cultivate, not relationships. I would spend the day reading the words of wise men.

After a bath, I stood before the mirror, a naked old man seized with self-loathing. I didn't want the company of the bow-legged, cave-chested jerk I saw in the mirror. I'd go for a walk. I'd walk until my depression vanished, and I felt at home again with myself.

Puddles from last night's rain dotted the street. New weeds peeked out through cracks in the sidewalk. I passed a girl's bicycle that had been chained to the same lamppost for years—tires missing, paint faded from deep blue to pale green, its leather seat crumbled by time and the Arizona sun. This bike and I had a history. After complaining about the bike to the city and getting nowhere, I'd written a letter to the editor insisting on its removal. But nothing happened. Then, over the years, the bike became one of the few stable things in the neighborhood. I wrote another letter, explaining how this wrecked bicycle had become an aesthetic object, one that had a kind of stabilizing influence on the neighborhood, how this abandoned artifact had become a piece of art. I touched its seat and ran a finger over a rusted fender.

At the place where I'd bitten off the man's ear, I paused to examine the rusty stains of blood on the pavement. My stomach churned as I heard and felt the gristly crunch of his ear between my teeth. I was lucky to be alive. I'd done a stupid and dangerous thing. I vowed to be more careful, stay home more, become less conspicuous, keep my mouth shut, be as invisible as possible. I would look up the poor bastard with one ear and ask his forgiveness. Maybe not. That would be asking for trouble. Best stay as far away from him as possible. But what if he came looking for me?

I turned into the Bread and Butter and positioned myself on a stool in the rear with a good view of the door and easy access to the back door.

Miss Choy brought my coffee. "Same?"

I nodded.

She shrugged and left. Virgil waved a knife instead of saying his usual greeting. I took a sip of water. It tasted metallic. I waited for the one-eared guy to come through the door, machine gun in hand. Twenty minutes passed. Ten people with twenty ears came through the door.

I bolted down my breakfast and hurried back to the Coronado, intending to take a nap. As soon as I closed the door behind me, I opened it again and went out. I knocked on Howard's door. No answer. I knocked on Mayflower's door. I could hear her inside, a muffled, "Oh, dear. Oh, dear." A minute later she poked her head out, sleepy and disoriented. "Yes?"

Suddenly, I was overcome with exhaustion and embarrassment. "Just wanted to make sure you were all right," I said.

"I'm fine, dear." She smiled a crooked smile. "Anything else?"

"Not really," I heard myself say.

She closed the door.

Finally, I went to sleep. I must have slept close to an hour before I was awakened by someone pounding on Howard's door. I glanced at my watch—eleven o'clock. I looked through the peephole and saw a skinny girl with long, unkempt blond hair. At her feet sat a rope-bound suitcase and a shopping bag.

"Hey," she called. She knocked harder.

The banging hurt my head.

When she turned, I saw she was pregnant. She was holding a piece of paper with something written on it. She looked like a thousand other girls I'd seen over the years who had drifted in and out of the Fourth Avenue district. They were all looking for something—the father of their child, drugs, a place to stay, money, maybe even love or at least their version of what they imagined love to be. They were too old and too beat up to be children and too young to be adults. They were trapped in their own prisons of ignorance and emotional turmoil, poverty and drugs. But this one was knocking on Howard's door. She must know him.

I opened my door. "I don't think he's at home."

"You got a bathroom?" she said.

"Well, I'm not sure—"

"Sorry, mister. I don't have time to have this discussion." She pushed past me, paused and looked around.

"Through the bedroom," I said.

The bathroom door slammed.

"Are you okay?" I asked.

"Stay out."

I heard water running. She opened the door. Her hair was soaking wet. She dripped her way across the floor and plopped down on the sofa. "What's your name?"

"Tobias."

"Mine's Naomi." She moved a strand of hair stuck to her cheek. "Morning sickness, my ass. It's almost noon. A woman on the bus said it would go away. I've been puking my lungs out for six months."

"Look," I said. "I also have an upset stomach. You may rest here for a minute, dripping on my sofa, then—"

"So get me a towel."

I brought her a towel from the bathroom and waited while she dried her hair. She wore a dark skirt with dusty, black tights underneath. I couldn't guess her age but she was young. She looked vaguely familiar.

"Better?" she said.

"Are you a friend of Howard's?"

"Who?"

"The person who lives in the apartment across the hall."

"Not really."

"Then why were you knocking?" I stood for a moment looking down at her, waiting for her answer.

"That's my business," Naomi said. She held out a hand. "Help me up." Her hand was softer than I expected. She lunged forward and stood up, then went to my kitchen and opened a cupboard door. "You got any food?"

"No," I said.

She looked in the refrigerator. "How about you fixing me a fried egg sandwich? I'd like it with a thin slice of onion and dill pickles."

I hiccupped. "Excuse me. I don't have either."

Naomi came closer and raised one eyebrow. "Are those hiccups?"

I hiccupped again.

She stood a foot away. "Look at me."

I settled for a spot between her eyes.

She was whispering now. She leaned in. Our faces were inches apart. "Focus on my eyes."

"I'm not good at this eye business."

"Look into my eyes," she said, louder this time.

I forced myself to look, first one then the other.

Her voice softened. "That's it."

Tendrils of red streaked the whites of her eyes, a few freckles dotted her cheekbones, a strand of wet hair stuck to the side of her face.

I hiccupped again.

"Relax," she said.

I tried to breathe normally. My heart raced.

"That's it." She waited until I hiccupped again and, before it was fully out, she screamed, "Stop it!" No, it was more than a scream. It was a shriek, an ax to the temporal lobes, a spike in my ear. My heart leapt into my throat. My knees turned to water. I held on to her, trying to stay upright.

"There," she said. She returned to my sofa.

I could barely talk. "There what? There you have given me a stroke? There you have my neighbors calling the cops?" My voice cracked. "Is this any way to treat a person who helps you, who allows a perfect stranger to puke in his toilet, who brings you a towel?"

"First, I'm not sure what you're up to, but I am sure you're not trying to help me. Second, you're cured. You're over your hiccups."

I waited for my next hiccup. It didn't come. I tried to force it. Nothing happened. "Incredible," I said. "All my life I've—"

"You got an extra toothbrush?" she asked.

"Do the words *personal property* and *tact* mean anything to you?"

"Someone stole mine in the bathroom at the bus station. Bitch. Who would steal a used toothbrush?"

My better judgment told me to ask her to leave. But there was something raw and direct about her, maybe a little dangerous. Worse, she had nothing to lose. Then it occurred to me that I didn't have that much to lose either. Brushing my teeth alongside an indigent teenager would not destroy my life. I went to the bathroom and came back with my two new brushes. I handed her the red one.

She raised an arm and sniffed her armpit. "You can smell me, can't you? I haven't had a real bath in a week, just those bus johns. I'll bathe in your tub. Is there a washer and dryer?"

"In the basement. I think before we go too far with this, you may want to get my permission."

"You can do my laundry while I bathe."

"Aren't you capable of doing your own laundry?"

She pulled her hair back, held it over her head, and jutted out a hip. "You're attracted to me, aren't you?"

"No."

"I know when men are attracted to me. Sometimes I know before they do." She moved closer. Her breath was in my ear. "Wouldn't you like to try some of this young stuff just once? How long has it been?"

I pulled away. "You're mistaken."

"Am I? I'll bet you lie about practically everything, especially when it comes to your pecker."

"You don't know anything about me," I said. "I'm not a liar. The thing I value most is honesty."

She went to the window and pulled the shade closed. She looked at the kitchen table with the four chairs, opened my cupboard and looked at my mix and match dinnerware for two, opened a drawer and held up my can opener, my new soup pot. She touched the TV screen with a finger, inspected my Mr. Coffee, the card table in the corner with my typewriter on it, my floor lamp with the green lampshade, my books. It was as if she were probing my body.

She saw Beatrice's dressing gown. "You married?"

"I was."

"And?"

"She died."

"When?"

"Five years ago."

"How?"

"Cancer."

"Yuck."

I straightened the shade on my reading lamp, put a couple of books back on the bookshelf. "Howard should be back anytime," I said.

"Are you going to fix me something to eat or what?"

"One fried egg sandwich. That's it. Then you must leave."

She sat at the table while I made two fried egg and mayonnaise sandwiches—one for her, one for me. She ate hers in three bites and followed it with an entire glass of milk. Without asking, she took the other half of my sandwich.

I wanted her to leave but, as soon as I thought this, I wanted her to stay. Then I wanted her to leave again. Truth is, it wasn't my choice. She was going to do exactly what she wanted to do.

She wiped her mouth with the back of her hand, looked up and burped. "What are you looking at?"

"Nothing," I said.

"You were staring at me, thinking about asking me to leave. You were wondering what the hell you've gotten yourself into."

"Not really, I—"

She made a swipe at her nose, then tucked a strand of hair behind her ear. "I'd like to brush my teeth now."

"Fine. Help yourself."

"We'll brush together."

My shoulders tightened. She was testing me, seeing how far she could go. "Why would anyone want to brush their teeth in front of another person?"

"Too intimate for you?"

"What's intimate about foaming at the mouth and spitting in the sink?"

"Follow me." She led me to the bathroom and loaded our brushes with toothpaste. "That's more than I'd use in a week," I said.

She gave me the blue brush. "Stand next to me and brush," she said.

"No," I said. But I stood next to her and brushed.

"Harder."

Foam ran down my chin and forearm. I nudged her to move over and spat into the sink.

"Get your gums," she said.

I brushed my gums.

"And tongue."

I brushed my tongue.

"Spit."

I spat.

"Rinse."

I rinsed.

We stood side by side looking at our toothbrushes.

She nudged me. "Do you want to give me a bath?"

"No."

"No charge."

"What then? What's in it for you?"

"Who knows? Sometimes nice things happen. Clean bodies, fresh mouths, you know, that kind of thing."

"I'm not interested in bathing you or having sex with you."

"Then what do you want? Why haven't you kicked me out?"

"I don't know. Maybe I think I can help you."

"Bull."

"Why were you knocking on Howard's door? There are social service agencies, you know—shelters for pregnant girls." I followed her back to the living room. "You can't stay here."

"I'm not staying here," she said. "I'm going to Alaska to look up my friend Brendan. He said if I was ever in trouble—"

"So how did you end up in Tucson?"

She looked at me for a few seconds, then rifled through her shopping bag and found a letter. She handed it to me and sat on the sofa.

The letter was dated May 7, eight years earlier.

My Dearest Daughter,

Today is your tenth birthday. I have hired a lawyer to locate and deliver this to your adopted father and mother. You were snatched away so quickly. I saw you, then you were gone. I remember your cute nose, your tiny toes and fingers. I don't even know your name. I hope you have a wonderful name and someone in your life who makes you feel special.

Forgive me for intruding on your life. I have no right, nor am I certain your parents will show you this letter. There are things, though, I want to tell you…

I glanced down at the signature—Helen Gardener. My mind flashed to all the pictures I'd seen of Howard's wife. I scanned the last paragraph and saw a reference to Howard. "Your mother's name was Helen Gardener?"

Naomi hugged a sofa pillow. "She lived here in Tucson. The address is on the letter. When my adopted father kicked me out for being pregnant, he gave me that letter and enough money for a bus ticket to Tucson. So I came here. I planned to ask her for money. But guess what? Sweet little Helen is dead. The couple who bought their house told me she had a husband named Howard, and they thought he lived in town. So I found him—across the hall. That's why I was knocking."

Someone knocked on my door. "Hey, anyone home?" It was Howard.

"Just a minute," I called. I held my hand on top of my head, closed my eyes and forced myself to take a long, slow breath. I turned to Naomi. "Do you know who your biological father was?"

"Not this Howard guy. In the letter she says he was named Alan Shade, a student of hers who was killed in Vietnam. Who knows? People's mouths are just the front end of their assholes. I was hoping this Howard Gardener might give me enough money to get to Alaska. Brendan said he was going to move to Juneau."

"Tobias, you in there?"

"You gonna get that or what?" Naomi asked.

"Just a minute," I called. I tried to remember exactly what Howard had told me about Helen—her trip to Iowa, her indecision about their marriage, the dreary photo of her before she left. "There's something I need to tell you," I said. "I'll explain later but for now you have to trust me." I tried to make eye contact, but her gaze was too threatening. "The person that's knocking on my door—that person is Howard Gardener."

Her eyes narrowed. "Ah, he's home."

"Yes, but you can't show him that letter. I'm not even sure he should see you. You resemble Helen."

"How do you know?"

"I've seen pictures. You can't tell him about Helen—not yet, anyway."

"Why not?"

"He just tried to commit suicide because he couldn't get over Helen's death. She was his entire life. He has no idea Helen was unfaithful to him, much less that she had a child by another man. A man lives his life believing he knows what has gone on. Then he suddenly discovers his life is fiction. That can send a man like Howard over the edge."

"Tobias," Howard called.

"Coming."

"You think I care? Maybe he'll give me money just to get rid of me."

"That's not the point. In his mind, there's a life he created with Helen. It's all he has. You can't just tell him his entire life was a lie. Think about it."

Naomi was standing now. "It's not my fault he lies to himself. We all make ourselves up."

"You aren't old enough to get philosophical."

"You don't get it, do you? I couldn't care less about Howard Gardener's little life. I need money. He owes me."

She headed for the door. I blocked her. "You have to trust me on this." I touched her arm.

She pulled back. "Get your hands off me."

"We have to move slowly here. To destroy a life is—"

"Whose life? *You* go live on the streets then, and *I'll* stay in your cozy apartment."

Then I heard my own voice saying, "You *can* stay here. I'll give you my bed, food, even money to get to Juneau if that's what you want. I don't have much, but enough to get you there. Just don't tell him, at least not until we've had time to think it through, come up with a plan. Say you agree."

"How much money?"

By working at the Bread and Butter, I had managed to accumulate five thousand dollars in a secret savings account over the last ten years, and I wasn't about to give it all away. "Five hundred."

She looked at the door, then me. "A thousand."

"You must be kidding," I said. "Seven fifty."

"Twelve hundred. Want to try again?"

"Fine. A thousand."

"Put it in writing."

"Later. There's no time."

"Now."

"I'm waiting," Howard called.

"Just a minute, Howard." I scribbled out an IOU for one thousand dollars on a yellow pad and gave it to Naomi. "Promise."

She studied the note. "Okay, I agree," she said, "at least for now."

I seriously considered going through the window and down the fire escape and never coming back. But that was not my nature. I opened the door.

Howard was wearing a blue work shirt with rolled up sleeves and baggy trousers. He was holding a rake.

He glanced at Naomi, then back at me. "I need a ride to the dump," he said.

 SEVEN

I managed a smile and tried to act carefree. "Howard. How are ya?"

Howard peered over my shoulder, did a double take and ducked behind me as if he didn't want Naomi to see him—either that or he didn't want to see her. "What's going on?" he whispered.

I stood aside and gestured toward Naomi. "Howard, I'd like you to meet my friend, Naomi. She's visiting from the Midwest."

Howard studied her as if he'd found a shard of pottery and was trying to imagine what the whole bowl looked like. "Hello," he said.

Naomi, almost in a gesture of contempt, pulled her shoulders back slightly. "What's with the rake?"

Howard cocked his head from one side to the other, dog-like, then turned to me. "You have a car, right?"

"Such as it is."

"I can't leave Helen's ashes in the dump. She doesn't deserve that. We have to try to find them."

"Howard, my God, the dump is half the size of Rhode Island."

"It's a long shot, but I've got to try. I couldn't live with myself otherwise. I've called the waste disposal people. The attendant should be able to show us yesterday's garbage if we get there before noon. After that, it will get covered up. Will you take me?"

"Helen's ashes?" Naomi asked. "How did they end up at the dump?"

I gave her an abbreviated answer about last night's adventure on Fourth Avenue, omitting the part about me biting the man's ear off, and ended with, "The guy tossed Helen's ashes in a garbage truck before we could stop him."

Howard was still staring at Naomi. "What's your name again?"

"Naomi."

"And you're visiting from where?"

"I'm on my way to Alaska as soon as I get some money." She glanced at me and said, "I figure I'll need about two thousand."

Howard turned back to me. "We have a chance to find Helen's ashes if we leave now."

"Dumps are dangerous places," I said. "Birds thick as locusts, packs of mad dogs."

"I'll go with you," Naomi said.

"No. Absolutely not," I said.

"We could use an extra pair of eyes," Howard said.

I was determined to stand my ground on this one. I was on the verge of saying a loud and emphatic *No,* when I heard myself say, "Fine. If that's what you want, let's go to the dump. Maybe we can pick up a few psychopaths on the way to help."

I followed Howard and Naomi downstairs. A dry yellow leaf clung to Naomi's sweater. I picked it off and put it in my pocket.

"Where are you staying?" Howard asked Naomi.

She glanced back at me. "With Tobias—at least for now."

Mayflower stood in the lobby wearing a red silk evening gown and white pearls. I thought of an exotic plumed bird.

Naomi stared, her mouth open.

"We have to get going," Howard said.

Naomi walked over to Mayflower, held out her hand and introduced herself. "That dress you're wearing is beautiful," she said.

"Thank you, dear. Will you be in Manhattan long?"

"I need to learn how to drive," Howard said.

"Not long," Naomi said.

"We were just leaving," Howard said.

"I'm to meet Charles," Mayflower said. "He's late. We're going to the opera, then to dinner and dancing at a small out-of-the-way place he's found. Charles likes to have at least three martinis before an opera. He says he can survive a musical with one drink and a serious drama with two, but he needs three for the opera. We're seeing *Madame Butterfly.* Such a sad and passionate story of love. We've seen it three times. Charles actually cried last time. You know, when she kills herself in the end?" She glanced around. "He should be here by now."

I approached her. "I don't think Charles will be coming tonight."

She held her watch to her ear, looked at me, then back to her watch. She stood perfectly still for a few seconds. "I've done it again, haven't I?"

"A minor lapse," I said. "It's nothing to worry about. Chalk it up to an active imagination."

"I'm not worried, dear. I'm *disappointed*. I'm damn disappointed. I was so looking forward to seeing Charles." She straightened her dress, held up her head and brushed something from Naomi's shoulder. "You must join me for tea, dear. Have you seen a doctor?"

"No."

"You should, for the baby's sake and yours. Are you married?"

Naomi shook her head. She'd lost her edge.

"Good for you. I've done many foolish things in my life, dear, but marriage hasn't been one of them. Early on, I learned an important lesson—that having sex with someone doesn't necessarily mean I love him. Although, for me at least, loving them almost always made me want to have sex with them. Have you had a lot of different men?"

Naomi practically whispered, "I'm from Pella, Iowa."

"When I was your age I had a constant erotic buzz at the base of my spine. I think of it as a kind of divine madness that so often disappears in the marriage bed. Now poetry and the arts give me that feeling. Do you like poetry, dear?"

"Once I read a book by Sylvia Plath. It was depressing."

"Yes, Plath's depression is awe-inspiring."

"We'd better be going," Howard said.

I touched Mayflower's elbow. "I'll take you back to your apartment."

"Thank you, dear. The last time I wore this dress was to the Met. I thought I was the most desirable woman alive. Charles spent the whole evening cracking his knuckles. Afterwards, I insisted we go somewhere to dance. He had absolutely no sense of rhythm. I dated several state department men and none of them had a sense of rhythm. Obsessively organized men almost never have a sense of rhythm."

"We really have to go," Howard said.

"Come with us to the dump," Naomi said.

"She should rest," I said.

"Nonsense, dear. I'm tired of resting."

"The dump is filled with rats the size of pigs. I don't think—"

"Sounds like Manhattan," Mayflower said. "How delightfully dangerous. I've never been to a dump. Frankly, I've never considered it a place one actually went to."

I eyed Naomi and shook my head.

She ignored me. "Some guy chucked Helen's—I mean, Howard's wife's ashes in a garbage truck. Howard wants to find them."

"How gallant of you—what's your name again?"

"Howard Gardener."

"She's coming with us," Naomi said. The implication was clear. If Mayflower didn't join us, Naomi would tell Howard about Helen.

"We'll wait while you change," I said.

"Please hurry," Howard said.

"I'll wear this, dear."

"Isn't it a little too dressy?" I said.

"Tobias, my days of having my wits about me are limited. What you see before you is the best I'll ever be. If I wait for an appropriate occasion, I'll never wear it. In the few moments of clarity I have left, I'd like to continue to do exactly what I want. And I would advise you not to be so prissy."

"You're…a hedonist," I said.

She smiled broadly. "If you insist on labeling me, I'd prefer freedomist. No, even better, I'm a polytheistic freedomist."

"Many gods just compound the problem."

"Or solve it altogether."

Howard herded us out the front door.

"What's a hedonist?" Naomi asked.

"Someone who seeks out and values pleasure, dear." She pushed Naomi's hair back and let her hand linger on the side of her face. "What pleasure do you want, dear?"

"Right now?"

"At this very moment."

"A deep, long, warm bath."

"Then you'll have a bath as soon as we get back from the dump. I will personally prepare it for you."

"Jesus," Howard said.

Mayflower held Naomi's hand. "Come, let's enjoy ourselves."

Howard, rake in hand, led us to the parking lot. Mayflower and Naomi followed. I brought up the rear. As I walked, a bouncy old Beatles song kept running through my head, the one about everyone living in a yellow submarine…

 EIGHT

Heading east on Speedway I felt as if I'd been abducted by three aliens and forced to drive them to the dump. Only days ago I was certain I would spend the rest of my life reading, thinking, and learning from the masters. Now I, Tobias Seltzer, a small, timid man with no history of deviance, had bitten a man's ear off and was on my way to the dump accompanied by a bereaved widower, a disturbed woman in an evening dress, and a pregnant teenager who just happened to be the daughter of the woman whose ashes we were going to look for. In my lifetime I had never been in such close proximity to so many seriously disturbed people.

I wasn't prepared to go to the dump. I was a man who, before doing something new, educated myself on relevant facts, anticipating every possible disaster and how I would deal with it. I didn't know the first thing about scavenging. I glanced in the rearview mirror. Mayflower and Naomi were looking out at the scenery, oblivious to my impending anxiety attack.

The gate attendant at the dump had a forehead that extended out over his eyes like a porch roof. "Two dollars," he wheezed from behind the shadow of his face. He held a book, but I couldn't see the title.

Ahead of us were mountains of smoldering garbage. It was worse than I'd imagined. Thousands of birds pecked and tore at moldy casseroles and rat-infested mattresses. The stench was shocking, an immense flatulence from the backside of consumerism.

"So this is the way the world ends," Mayflower said. "This could be the most sobering moment of my life."

"No erotic buzz," Naomi said.

"No buzz whatsoever, dear."

"Two dollars," the man said.

I waited, but Howard made no move to pay. I gave the man two dollars.

"Excuse me," Howard said to the attendant. "Could you tell us where we might find yesterday evening's garbage?"

The man pointed "Over there, where those people are."

A few hundred yards away, on a flat spot, a dozen or so people were digging through the waste. "What are they looking for?" I asked.

He shrugged. "Most people come here looking for something they've thrown away."

"Do they find it?" Howard asked.

"Sometimes, I guess. Mainly they find other stuff. Stuff they don't really want, but it sort of justifies their making the trip."

"Maybe we'll get lucky," I said and drove away.

My tires bounced and shimmied so violently I had trouble holding the steering wheel. The muffler and front bumper were close to falling off. The glove compartment popped open and a screw fell from somewhere into Howard's lap. He handed it to me.

"Toss it," I said. "I saved them for years, but I could never find where they came from."

I wasn't prepared for the enormity of this place, the palpable sense of being on another planet. I had a hundred questions. Did one stake out a territory or was it survival of the fittest? How deep did one dig? Was there a right and wrong technique? What did one do if he found something illegal? Drugs perhaps, or an aborted fetus?

As we approached, the scavengers paused, shielded their eyes, and looked at us. A man in a long overcoat dragged a folding bed frame past us and gave us a suspicious look. A mangy dog lapped something from a yellow puddle.

I turned off the engine and opened the window. I could hear the sound of the composting garbage digesting itself. At first no one moved, then Naomi said, "What are we waiting for? Let's get at it."

I chose a spot at the base of one of the piles and toed things around. Something moved. I jumped back. It was a rat the size of a football. It lumbered through a pool of brown muck, paused, looked up at me, and wiggled its nose. It sat on its haunches and began cleaning its genitals. It was the fattest, most contented rat I'd ever seen. It finished cleaning, scratched behind its ears a couple of times and ambled back into the gunk.

"Dear me," Mayflower said from ten feet away. She pushed aside a soiled diaper with her toe and picked up a bottle of Black and White Scotch. "It's never been opened," she said.

Howard held a limp celery stalk between his thumb and forefinger.

"Rake, Howard," Naomi said. "Push stuff around."

I talked to the other scavengers and told them we were looking for a blue plastic box half-filled with ashes, and that we'd be grateful if they kept an eye out.

A black man carried a box filled with books and magazines and dumped them into the back of his truck. He held out his hand and a seagull landed on his arm. "Ain't that something?" he said.

"Is it safe?" I said.

"Ain't nothing to be afraid of out here, mister. This is bird and rat heaven. They're all too happy to be worrying about you."

I asked the man what he intended to do with the books.

"Take some to a swap meet. Leave the rest."

I sorted through the books and found a 1940 edition of *Handbook of Obstetrics,* written for nurses, and a paperback by Dr. Spock called *Baby and Child Care.* Maybe Naomi could use them. I gave the man a quarter for both books.

"Hey, you gonna help or what?" Naomi yelled. She was standing atop a mound of garbage, feet apart, hands on her hips.

I moved aside some garbage bags pecked open by birds and lifted some old drywall. As I dug, the garbage began to speak to me. Torn up photographs told of loss and broken hearts. A pair of bloody panties hinted at shame. A bag filled with frozen dinner containers said something about loneliness. I found a wristwatch that didn't work, the hands stuck at 11:59. A doll with a small crack in the head. It struck me that this place was devoid of beginnings and middles. Like old age, it was a museum of endings. I found a three-pound coffee can with the top on. I tried to muster enough nerve to open it but couldn't force myself.

Within half an hour Naomi held up Helen's ashes. I half expected her to clutch the box to her chest and cry, "Mama," but all she said was, "Let's get out of here."

In the car Mayflower opened the Scotch, sniffed it and took a sip. "Wonderful outing," she said, "exhilarating." She offered the bottle to Howard. He took a sip and passed it to me. I passed it back to Mayflower, and she had another sip.

Howard was more relaxed, but subdued. His fingers drummed on the top of the box containing what was left of Helen ashes.

"Does anyone mind if I stop at Safeway on the way?" I asked.

ᐸᐳ

Safeway felt like a well-organized dump in which fancy packaging hid the fragile and temporary nature of the truckloads of stuff lining the shelves. Today, everything was new and exciting—tomorrow, on its way to sewage processors.

Howard headed for the produce section. Naomi stuck with him.

Mayflower, a little wobbly after her Scotch, stayed with me. We walked down a lane of nothing but snacks. "My goodness," she said. "I had no idea there were so many different kinds of potato chips." She selected a bag of vinegar and salt flavored.

When we caught up with Howard and Naomi in vegetables, Howard was holding a tomato up to the light and inspecting it.

Mayflower walked around touching vegetables.

Howard put the tomato down and studied Naomi's face with the same attention he'd given the tomato. He stepped to the side and studied her profile. "For a moment there, I thought you looked like Helen," he said. He turned to me. "You saw Helen's pictures. Does Naomi look anything like Helen?"

"Nothing like her," I said.

Howard moved in front of Naomi, used two fingers to lift a strand of hair from her face, and cocked his head. "Nope, not even close." He turned his attention back to the tomatoes.

"I'd like to see for myself," Naomi said. "Will you show me Helen's pictures?"

Mayflower joined us. She was holding an eggplant. "Isn't it lovely?" she said.

"It's best if we all stay together," I said. I took the eggplant from her and put it in my basket.

Mayflower and I made our way past bins of carrots, turnips, and baby zucchini. She had a story about everything. "Once in Southern Italy I lived a summer with a painter named Giovanni something," she said. "He claimed the eggplant, not the circle, was the most perfect of all shapes. The man was fanatical about food. He'd spend an hour selecting a dozen oysters. Do you like oysters, dear?"

I was exhausted. Caravelo juggling balls was nothing compared to juggling people. "Never had an oyster," I said. "Here, try to keep a hand on the cart."

She looped her arm through mine. "I'd pose for Giovanni while he cooked and painted and drank wine—a splash of blue, some fresh basil added to the marinara sauce, some violet for shading, the smell of chopped garlic, a sweaty glance at me, a wash of yellow. It all blended into one thing. I can't remember ever feeling quite so consumable."

"I still can't believe we found Helen's ashes," I said.

"And a bottle of Scotch," she said.

"Do you notice any similarities between the dump and Safeway?" I asked.

She tightened her grip. Her breast pressed against my arm. "Personally, I'd prefer a long conversation at a quiet little bar with a good piano player to either Safeway or the dump."

An electric current was traveling down the back of my neck and across my shoulders.

"Pomegranates," she said. She held one in both hands. "Rilke wrote about how princely they look. See their crown on top here, their leathery texture? He said when they're ripe they burst of their own fullness, that they had slits with purple linings, like noblemen in grand apparel." She put the pomegranate back, grasped my arm and said, "I think of you as a ripe pomegranate, dear. How do you think of me?"

I glanced around. "Honeydews," I said.

At the oranges, Mayflower told me that Henry Cabot Lodge, the famous statesman, drank a mixture of orange and prune juice every morning when he woke up. At a bin of limes she had a story about a woman friend who, at the age fifty-three, ran away to Mexico to marry a man who kept bees and grew limes. "She said she fell in love with his honey and lime scent."

"Is it true you've lost your sense of smell?" I asked.

"Yes, dear, for the most part, but I have an excellent memory for scents. It's almost as good." As if reading my mind, she added, "I imagine your scent to resemble—let's see—ripe apples."

"You smell like lilac and bath soap," I said.

Mayflower picked out peanut butter and jelly, an assortment of soups and cheeses, eggs, milk, tuna, breakfast cereal, some chilled dill pickles from the deli, and a cheese ball for no other reason than she thought the word "cheese ball" had a festive sound to it.

When we caught up with Howard and Naomi again, Naomi said there were a few things she'd like me to buy for her—ice cream, canned chili without beans, soda crackers, Coke, Spam. I bought one of each.

Mayflower was starving. She opened the bag of vinegar-and-salt chips and tried one. Her eyes watered. She smacked her lips. "I haven't had a potato chip in years," she said. "I don't remember them being—so aggres-sive."

Naomi chose a pound cake, some strawberries, a bag of double-filled Oreos, and two packages of Fig Newtons. I put back one package of Fig Newtons. Naomi gave me a defiant look and added a package of Chips Ahoy.

At the baby food section Mayflower and I examined the little jars of food. "How sweet," Mayflower said, holding a jar of pudding called Hawai-ian Delight.

There were baby jars filled with broccoli, carrots, squash, green beans, banana cream pie, liver, chicken pie. Mayflower pointed out Zwieback toast, disposable diapers, and infant formula. I made a mental note about location and prices, but I was certain that Naomi would be out of my life long before her baby was born, maybe even before the sun rose tomorrow. I held up a jar of puréed liver for Naomi to see. "Look at this," I said, "creamed everything."

Naomi turned away.

I whispered to Mayflower, "I've read about women like her—Mary Baker Eddy, for instance. She started Christian Science but abandoned her children shortly after they were born."

"Give Naomi time, dear."

At the checkout stand Naomi thumbed through a tabloid newspaper with the headline *Diva Gives Birth at Intermission, Completes Concert.* "Dumb bitch," she muttered.

Mayflower pointed to the cheese ball. "What do you think?"

"Help yourself," I said.

Howard appeared with a dozen roses—six for Mayflower, six for Naomi.

Mayflower pinched off a small bite of cheese ball, closed her eyes, sa-vored it and offered some to Naomi. Naomi scooped out a glob the size of a ping-pong ball and ate it off her finger as we left the store.

In the car, Naomi held Helen's ashes in her lap and sniffed her roses.

Mayflower drank more Scotch. "My earlobes are still growing," she said. "Look at the poor floppy things." She held one between her thumb and forefinger and moved it. "I've always thought of myself as having perky little ears."

"I'm getting hair in mine," Howard said. "But it's disappearing from my legs."

"My ears ring all the time," I said.

"This is really interesting," Naomi said.

On the corner of Speedway and Sixth Avenue, a car had broadsided a pickup filled with kids. We were two blocks away from the Coronado. Paramedics were covering the body of a child that lay sprawled and motionless in the street. A man slumped beside his smashed vehicle. A small girl sat on the curb, her arms wrapped tightly around her knees, rocking. Ambulance and police lights swirled, two policemen directed traffic. Another policeman stood on the curb writing something on a clipboard. Men in white uniforms swept shattered glass into neat shimmering piles. Firemen in glowing yellow coats diluted spilled gasoline with a spray of water. Medics laughed and conversed while they inserted small bodies into ambulances and whisked them away.

There was a disgustingly professional efficiency about all this death, an efficiency that covered up the horror and prevented me from feeling it. But tears still came to my eyes. I didn't know if something in me was dying or if something was coming alive. All I wanted was to get back to my apartment and lock the door. That's when I felt Mayflower's hand on my shoulder.

"I have to go to the bathroom," Naomi said. "Are we almost there?"

I touched the accelerator and pulled into the long line of traffic that inched forward like a wounded snake.

NINE

I parked in the shade in the vacant lot on the east side of the Coronado. Howard and Naomi walked ahead. Howard carried groceries. Naomi carried her roses and Helen's ashes.

"Howard has a bounce in his step," Mayflower said.

"He is a man who apparently knows no middle ground," I said, "a man who could easily end up in a religious cult or become a convert to Amway."

Naomi walked beside Howard, asking questions. "Did Helen like anchovies? What was her favorite color?"

Mayflower carried her roses, her cheese ball, and her Scotch. She was wobbly on her high heels, so she held onto my elbow. I carried the two baby books and my groceries. I intended to see her to the door and leave. I was exhausted.

I heard a buzzing drone and thought it was coming from above until I spotted a rosemary bush in full bloom, swarming with bees. "Careful," I said. I directed Mayflower around the bush.

"Those bees are like the rats and birds at the dump, dear. They have no idea we exist. Rosemary blossoms have driven them mad with ecstasy. They're too in love with their queen to be capable of anger." She lost her balance and tightened her grip. "Have you ever imagined what it must be like to be a bee?"

"A bee stings once, it's dead. I'd have been a goner years ago."

"The drone has no stinger. Its only reason for existence is to serve the queen and help her produce more gatherers. Would you prefer being a drone?"

"I'd prefer being Alexander the Great."

She stopped at the rosemary and bent over to get a closer look. "Imagine what it must be like," she said.

"In the Torah, Samson tears apart a lion and finds a swarm of honey bees inside," I said, because I happened to know it.

Mayflower laughed and looped her arm through mine. We walked on. "I like you worrying about me," she said.

"Poets need worriers to look out for them," I said.

"Why, thank you, dear."

On the near corner a man bent long balloons into a giraffe. Across the street another man with white hair played guitar and sang a blues song. Mayflower insisted we slow our pace to match the beat of the music. Our walk took on a ceremonial air.

"I feel like I'm about to be initiated into the Knights of Columbus," I said.

She laughed again. I liked making her laugh.

We made our way across the lobby, and Mayflower pushed the elevator call button. Once inside, she pulled my shoulder snug against her. The ride to the second floor seemed much too short. In the hallway she told me to nod to the poor people. I didn't know if she was delusional or playing a game, so I nodded to the nearest wall lamp and asked, "Who invented the middle class, anyway? They're such pests."

"We walk well together, don't we, dear?"

"Indeed," I said.

When we passed Howard's door, I heard his laughter and took it as a good sign.

Mayflower's apartment was crowded with objects—an overstuffed sofa and chair, dozens of scented candles, a cuckoo clock that didn't work, fancy cups and saucers, commemorative plates of the Eisenhower, Truman, and Kennedy presidencies, dancing figurines, ribbons sorted by color in small wicker baskets, a drinking glass filled with sharpened pencils, orange and red scarves draped over the backs of chairs, glass animals, poetry books stacked high on the side table, old letters tied with ribbons, fine wine glasses, a leather-bound journal, a Chagall reproduction, another by Cezanne, and a Henry Miller watercolor of a nude signed by the artist.

"Not many people know he turned to painting in his later life," I said. I asked her if she knew his book, *To Paint is to Love Again.*

"One of my favorites," she said. "I have a signed copy."

"You knew him personally?"

"I met Henry in Paris at a party my parents had insisted I attend. What I liked most was how Henry loved surprises—to start out for the museum and end up at a brothel, as he put it."

"I've never known anyone famous," I said. I placed her roses in a vase and asked if she had an aspirin. She went into the bathroom and came back with a bottle. I put one in the water and took two myself.

She sat on the sofa, folded her hands over her crossed legs and smiled up at me, looking perfectly placed in her surroundings. "I just love all my stuff," she said.

When I placed the roses on the coffee table, she leaned forward and touched my hand. Neither of us moved. My entire body felt like a phantom limb, completely there but unavailable for use. I pulled away and said, "I'll get your groceries. They're at Howard's."

Howard's door was ajar, so I went in. Naomi stood at the kitchen table flipping through Helen's photo albums. She paused, picked one up and preened, using the photo as if it were a mirror. Enough of this charade, I thought. I will tell Howard who she is, get it over with.

"Howard," I said, "there's something I have to tell you."

Naomi's eyes flashed.

"What?" Howard asked.

"You should know—" I stopped. I couldn't do it. Four simple words could have changed Howard's life—*Naomi is Helen's daughter*—but I couldn't say them. The lies I'd told Beatrice just to get out of the apartment, the fictions I'd created by pretending to be a college professor seemed to coalesce and prevent me uttering those words of truth. "Are these Mayflower's groceries?" I asked.

They ignored me.

Naomi took the top off Helen's ashes and looked in. "Was she ever unfaithful?" she asked.

"Excuse me," I said. "Mayflower's groceries?"

Without looking at me, Howard pointed to two bags on the counter. "Never," he said. "She liked people, though, liked being with them. Sometimes, at the end of a semester, she would cry." He told Naomi about the Japanese garden he and Helen had built just after they moved into the Victorian. "One of her favorite students designed it," he said. "Nice boy. Needed work. Helen felt sorry for him, took him under her wing. Poor guy got killed in Vietnam, as I remember. Helen cried when she heard about his death."

I couldn't take this any longer. As I was leaving the apartment, I heard Naomi ask, "Do you think I'm as pretty as Helen?"

I had to put Mayflower's groceries away. She was in no condition to do it. Her refrigerator contained a quarter-loaf of stale bread, some wilted carrots, and a tiny piece of yellowed Brie. There was nothing in her cupboards except lemon-scented furniture polish and a dead spider, its legs wrapped around the empty shell of itself.

I insisted she eat something. I made toast with peanut butter, but it seemed too plain. In Mayflower's presence, one tended to set a higher standard. I sliced the toast diagonally and served it to her on a gold-rimmed plate with a linen napkin.

She broke off a corner of toast. "Do you like to cook?"

"I liked cooking for Beatrice."

"You must miss her," Mayflower said.

I paused before answering. "I've missed her more lately. Little things I never paid much attention to seem important now."

Mayflower took a bite. "It's always the smallest things that are the most important," she said. "Give me an example."

"I liked watching her eat."

She smiled.

"I like watching you eat."

Mayflower returned the toast to her plate and dabbed her lips with her napkin. "I'm afraid I'm more tired than hungry, dear."

"Finish half your toast. I'll eat the other half. You want a dill pickle with your peanut butter?"

"I haven't had a peanut butter and dill pickle sandwich since I was a child. I'd forgotten all about them."

I opened the pickles, snapped one in half and held the broken end up to Mayflower's nose. "Nothing smells as good as a dill pickle."

She took a small bite and patted the sofa cushion beside her. "Sit beside me," she said.

I sat at the far end of the sofa, my knees together, back stiff, and did what I usually do under pressure. I talked. "Some people hate dills. I love them," I said. "I like prunes, too. I don't love them, but I like them. Four a day keeps the plumbing clear."

There was a long silence. I no longer wanted to go back to my apartment. I wanted to keep talking. I wanted to be admired by this woman. If I could have tap danced, I would have. I remembered reading about women liking men who were honest with their feelings. It was time to give it a try. "May I say something I've never told anyone?"

"Of course, dear."

"I really am a worrier. I worry about everything. When I'm not worrying about something, I worry about having missed something that I should be worrying about. Like Safeway, like all the food that's bought, digested, and put back out on the planet every day. I mean, mathematically, it won't be long before we're suffocating in our own waste. I worry about Naomi—no, not her so much, but her unborn child. I worry about the enormous number of children born every day and raised by really stupid people—people who are addicted to drugs or have no homes or money, who have never experienced an insight and have no self-knowledge. I worry about dying alone in my apartment and not being found till I stink up the place. I worry about not having anyone come to my memorial. I worry about having a stroke and becoming totally dependent on others. I worry about the possibility that there's an afterlife, and I'd have to spend eternity with people who have bad taste. I worry about others becoming totally dependent on me. For this reason I avoid people who might make my life more pleasant."

"Yes, there's plenty to worry about, dear."

"I'm a self-perpetuating worry machine. I even worry about the way they feed last meals to people on death row. It doesn't take a genius to know all that voltage has to loosen their bowels. Last meals are not a good idea, you know. There are so many bad ideas floating around."

"I see your point."

She seemed pretty impressed. "*Baruch Hashem*," I said, raising my pickle. "Thank God for all goodness."

We took a bite and looked at each other. Her eyes sparkled in the light that reflected from the cut-glass vase. It cast small rainbows across her dress. "You don't look like most women," I said.

She cocked her head.

"I mean you have a quality about you, a quality that is the opposite of anything I have ever known, an acceptance, a willingness to participate in life. You seem to be at ease with yourself. I spend a great amount of my time criticizing and judging. I mean, if I didn't have criticizing and judging, I would have almost nothing. I'm not judging you for not being judgmental, you understand. The opposite. I mean you seem to live better than I do."

"Do I?"

"Look at us. We're both living in this rundown hotel in a rundown and dangerous neighborhood on this rundown and violent planet. What's to be happy about? Yet you seem happy."

"Sitting here with you, talking, eating toast with peanut butter and pickle. That makes me happy. Aren't you happy? I mean, right now?"

"I don't think so. I don't think I've ever been happy. I'm genetically prone to malaise. I've never worried about happiness much. At least there's one thing I don't worry about. I mean happiness is something kids feel on their birthdays. I hated my birthdays. At the parties my mother insisted on giving me, I worried about who was getting more than their share of cake, who was peeking when we were trying to pin the tail on the donkey. My world seems dangerous, untrustworthy, filled with evil and conniving people. Yours doesn't. You mentioned your ears on the way home, how they're becoming larger. I've worried about my ears from the time I was five. Other children teased me, said I looked like Bugs Bunny." I grasped the tops of my ears between my index fingers and thumbs and pulled them up. "See?"

She leaned over and placed a hand on my shoulder. "Please don't do that, dear. Don't make fun of yourself. You're a handsome man, certainly better looking than Bugs Bunny."

"I can't stop thinking about those children killed in that accident. I mean what's the point, if death is so random and meaningless?"

"Tell me about the last time you were happy," she said.

I didn't want to lie to this woman. I wanted to tell her the exact truth. "Dancing in the basement with you the other night. I was happy then."

"Just dancing?"

"Talking, too."

"I liked the touching. Did you?"

"Yes, of course, that sort of thing."

"Until I frightened you away. Oh, dear."

"I panicked. I'm not good at—whatever you call it."

She moved over and placed her hand on the back of my neck.

I cleared my throat. "A few years back, maybe a month after Beatrice died, I was restless one night and drove around. I stopped at the bowling alley up on Speedway and spent the evening watching men and women bowl and drink beer. They struck me as happy. Whenever someone made a strike or a spare, they'd pump their fists and jump around. So I rented a pair of shoes and bowled a game. I got a spare in the first frame and a strike on the second, and I didn't feel anything. Bowling depressed me. What a stupid game. I don't understand why people bowl, or play golf, or watch racecars go around a track in a circle. I don't know why people go to Disneyland or watch so much TV or buy so much crap. It seems pointless."

"You don't have to do those things to be happy."

"The truth is I want something more than happiness. I want—substance, depth. But I don't know how to get it, and the years are passing me by. I'm ordinary, maybe less than ordinary. I'm getting forgetful. I don't think as well as I used to. My need to improve myself is in a life or death struggle with my deteriorating brain. I thought books would give me answers. I've found answers but not *the* answer. You know what I mean? Sometimes, I fake it. I pretend I'm more substantive and deeper than I am. I pretend I believe something when I don't, that I know more than I actually know. In that sense, I lie a lot."

"You do?"

"For example, that accident, those injured children. Their deaths didn't seem real to me. It never got in. It's like there's a layer of thick ice below the tundra. I wanted the paramedics and firemen to hurry and clean up the mess. I wanted them to wash the blood off the street, sweep up the broken glass, get rid of the bodies. The fact is—I wanted all the horror sanitized."

She squeezed my hand and closed her eyes. "It got into you. I saw it."

My throat ached. "You want the whole truth? Here's another one. I wear my suit and tie when I go out so people will think I'm a professor at the university or somebody important. I always wanted to be a college professor. Now it's too late, and I go around pretending to be someone who knows the answers."

"We need people who have answers even if they're pretenders. Otherwise, we'd all go mad."

"Yes, but nothing gets in. Nothing penetrates. You want a real feeling? Here's a real feeling. My life feels small. Itsy-bitsy. I'm sixty-eight and my life has amounted to nothing. I've spent my entire life trying to follow the rules, trying not to draw attention to myself, and all the time I'm plotting about how to get more attention, how to be admired and adored by more people. Yet I don't want to be adored close up. I want to be adored from a distance. I don't want to feel obligated. I don't want to owe anything to anyone. And I feel guilty for—well, for telling you all this. It's like I'm flunking or something."

Mayflower turned to face me. She rested her arm on the back of the sofa, and her hand squeezed my shoulder. "I knew a woman, Jenny Krebs—the wife of the sculptor, Martin Krebs. After he died, she lived alone until she was ninety-six. She painted, entertained friends and wrote her memoirs for hours each day. She also drank a fifth of gin a day. She was happy. Then her recently born-again son came and tried to get her to stop drinking. When Jenny refused, he committed her to a residential alcohol treatment program. Well, she quit drinking, then she quit writing, then she quit talking, and she died six months later, cured."

I shook my head. I didn't get her point.

"It's about happiness, dear, doing what inspires and vitalizes you, paying attention to the small gifts the world offers you every day, to your own gifts. Not always following the rules."

"My gift is I'm a compulsive rule follower. I even measure things exactly when I cook Hamburger Helper."

Mayflower laughed and yawned at the same time. "Excuse me, dear. I'm so tired. It must be the Scotch." She moved to the end of the sofa, lifted her legs, rested her head on my lap and closed her eyes.

I sat there for a full minute, one hand on the sofa arm, the other against my chest, afraid to move. I looked down at her face. Even a little drunk, she had a quality about her, a perfect correspondence between who she was and who she appeared to be. "I want you to stop having Alzheimer's," I whispered.

Her eyes opened. "What?"

I sat back, cleared my throat. "I like your dress," I said.

"Charles thought it too revealing. He insisted I wear a bra."

I moved a hand to the back of my head. "How long did you know him?"

"Off and on for twenty years. The State Department kept him on the go. He was Catholic and strongly against divorce. Proper to the point of prudishness. I thought I could save him, make him happy. Childbearing isn't the worst curse of women, dear; it's the belief we can save men. Charles and I would steal an occasional weekend. I don't think we saw each other more than two or three times a year." She closed her eyes. "I've had other loves, of course, but with Charles there was a special feeling, a meeting at some deep level. We were never together long enough for the intensity to wear off. Then he became ill and moved west. We lost contact. Maybe that's why I decided to settle in Tucson, to find Charles and say a proper goodbye. I don't know. I haven't thought of him for years, but recently I can't stop thinking of him. Maybe I'm regressing, trying to recapture my past. Sometimes I wonder if I'm making him up, if he is anything like the way I remember him. I think we tend to create people in our own image. Maybe that's what I've done to Charles."

"What's his last name?"

"Robins, Charles Thomas Robins. He'd be in his mid-seventies now, if he's still alive. His children are in their fifties. His coworkers called him C.T. Sounds stuffy, doesn't it?"

"There are computers at the library, reference librarians, search services. I'll try to find out what happened to him. If he's close by, maybe we can go see him."

She looked at me for a long time. Her eyes welled. "Thank you, Tobias. I don't know if I could bear seeing him. Things have changed so much. I have changed so much. I know you can't believe this, but I used to be beautiful. I don't think of that now but, when I think of Charles, I want to be beautiful for him. I want to be that person he knew. At least, I think I do. Sometimes I don't know what I think."

There was a long silence. Pale yellow light had filled the room. The faint scents of dill and roses lingered.

"See that vase," she said, "the one the roses are in?" She smoothed her dress. "It's cut crystal. Someone important, a president or a statesman, gave it to my mother, but I can't remember who. I used to be able to quote from all the Democratic presidents' inauguration speeches. I could name everyone who had been a senator from New York. I could recite dozens of poems by heart, even remember what my mother was wearing on my third birthday. Now I can't remember who gave her that vase. I have to try so hard to remember anything. We laugh at our fading memories, but mine are fading in a different way. They are disappearing in a vat of black tar. Like the new man, Howard, who went to the dump with us. I can't remember his last name. It's completely gone, dissolved."

"Gardener. Howard Gardener. Look, I can't remember names either."

"Howard Gardener, Howard Gardener." She moved her head forward with each repetition as if to force the name into a fold of her brain. "He seems like a nice man. And the girl?"

"Naomi. Naomi Kuiper," I said, determined to teach her these two names, to prove to her that she was okay.

She looked across the room, lost in thought. "Yes, Naomi. I see something of myself in her. I was pregnant once, but decided on an abortion."

"Charles?"

"Yes. He never knew."

"Naomi has waited too long. Abortion isn't an option."

"I know."

"I may invite her to stay with me until she has her baby." I was surprised to hear this come out of my mouth. How strange. This conversation felt different from any I could remember. Normally, I chose my words carefully, stayed on the lookout for sudden moves and hidden agendas. I baited others, tried to get the upper hand, maintained a healthy level of skepticism. But at that moment there was nothing I feared revealing, nothing I was trying to get, nothing I had to prove. I'd told Mayflower things about myself I'd never told anyone. This was a remarkable thing.

She reached over to the coffee table and turned on her radio to an "all oldies, all music" station, then touched a rose petal with the tips of her fingers. "Will you dance with me?"

"Of course."

We danced without moving, close, her fingers touching the hair at the back of my neck.

A passing trolley shook the floor. A dog barked. Far away, another radio played Mexican music. We stood swaying together for a long time. She sighed deeply.

"Are you sure you're okay?" I asked.

"I'm not, dear. I'm approaching the point where I'm no longer capable of caring for myself. I feel the fog creeping in. My social worker says it's time I move to a care facility. She's found a place for me. 'A place has been reserved,' she said. I hate passive voice, don't you? Its implied blamelessness? 'War has been declared.' 'A murder has been committed.'" A new song started on the radio. She turned it off and stood facing me.

"You're leaving the Coronado?" I said.

"Yes."

"When? They're not just going to tote you off tomorrow."

"I'm moving to a place called Elderhaven right after the first of the year."

"I don't want you to go."

"Thank you, dear. I must."

"What about all your things?"

"I'm allowed two suitcases. I have to decide what to take and what to leave behind. So much of my life is wrapped up in my things." She held my hands. Her eyes welled. "I am so afraid."

My throat ached. I couldn't speak.

She held out both arms and stepped toward me. Our lips touched. Her lips were soft, softer than I'd imagined, welcoming, open. A stinging sensation darted across my forehead. My temples throbbed. I pulled back, and we looked at one another. I saw the wrinkles at the corners of her mouth and eyes, the small scar on her cheek, the pores in her nose. We kissed again, deeper this time, a kiss tasting of Scotch, peanut butter, dill, and vinegar. I'd had kisses before, but I knew what those kisses meant. I had no idea what this kiss meant.

She pulled back a few inches and held my head between her palms. "You're a good and kind man," she said.

"You don't know me," I said.

"I feel it here." She held my hand to her breast.

Good and kind man echoed in my ears. I could have jumped up and down like those bowlers, given high-fives. "Already I'm planning my next act of goodness." I led her by the hand to the bedroom. "Lie down. I will remove your shoes." I took off her pumps, pulled her bedspread up to her waist, and sat on the end of her bed.

In a few minutes her breathing slowed, and I left her apartment, amazed at my own buoyancy. So what if the compliment of one's life comes from someone with Alzheimer's? It had been a long time since I'd been kissed, and I don't think I'd ever been called kind and good. People go entire lifetimes without being told they are either good or kind. Now this woman, this intelligent and worldly woman, this talented and beautiful woman who seemed capable of sucking the marrow from life's bones had kissed me, placed my hand on her breast, and told me I was both good and kind.

I couldn't go back to my apartment. A good and kind person should be in the company of others. I hurried down the stairs to the lobby, hoping someone would be there to see me, to receive my goodness and kindness, but the lobby was empty.

The TV room sported a new exercise bicycle someone had donated and a new large-screen TV. I rode the bicycle for a while, pretending I was riding down a street lined with people cheering for me. How good and kind my imaginary admirers seemed. How good and kind the whole world seemed. After five minutes or so, I found an old newspaper, folded it under my arm and wandered around, checking the plants, dusting here and there with my handkerchief. I stood for a long time alone, looking out of the window in the manner of a good and kind man, thinking of Mayflower, thinking she was surely the fountain of any goodness and kindness I might have. I was terrified at the thought of losing her.

TEN

Naomi spent the entire evening at Howard's. I sat on the sofa in my apartment waiting for her, a good and kind man, a man at peace, still feeling the soft touch of Mayflower's lips, still hearing the reassuring sound of Mayflower's voice, still trying to grasp the reality that she was leaving her own life, leaving the Coronado, leaving me. I would not allow it. I was smart. I could think of something. On the other hand, a time would come when she would have no recollection of me, when she would not remember our dancing in the basement or our talk after returning from the grocery store. I couldn't handle this. I had to protect myself. I couldn't allow myself to stay close to her.

On the off chance that Naomi would actually come back, I made my bed on the sofa, lay down and paged through the Spock book I'd bought at the dump, casually at first, more curious than concerned. Warnings, danger signs, and cautions filled every page. Ears and noses bleed. They have to be cleaned. Rectal temperatures have to be taken, bowel movements examined and classified. Some babies hardly sleep. Others sleep too much. Some never stop crying. Others never start. On their stomachs, they die in their sleep. On their backs, they choke on their own vomit. They have to be washed and changed, watched constantly, fed certain foods regularly and often. Almost as an aside, Spock had written that babies often show *blue mottling* on their bodies. Blue mottling? I looked for more information on mottling in the index and found nothing. You wake up one morning with a blue mottled baby, and there's no explanation, no reassurance, just instructions to consult your doctor immediately. And what did immediately mean? Within the next sixty seconds or tomorrow?

I turned to the index: Abscesses, Animal Bites, Artificial Respiration, Bleeding, Choking, Contusions, Glandular Disturbances, Objects in the Nose and Ears. All these could happen *after* the baby was born. What about before? What about those first few weeks? How does an arm know it's supposed to be connected to the shoulder and not the forehead? How does the right foot know it's a right foot and not a left one? What small chemical shift makes the difference between the baby having one head or two heads? I felt as though the prevention of major catastrophes depended upon me learning all this information.

I'd had no idea how complex raising a baby was. Even if you were Beethoven writing the last movement of the Ninth Symphony, and the baby had a movement of its own, you stopped composing your masterpiece and changed your baby's diaper. If you were Moses receiving the Ten Commandments, and the baby needed feeding, you excused yourself and fed it.

After an hour I concluded I'd rather sort entrails in hell than raise a baby. Naomi had to read this book. She had to know about the horrors. But even if she read all the books on raising babies, would she become a better mother? Did books change anything? People had been reading the Koran and the Bible for centuries, and they were still buggering one another. I'd read almost an entire library, and I was pretty much the same person I was before I got my library card.

Still, based on my limited knowledge of babies, I could not resist trying to get Naomi organized. I made a list of supplies she needed to have on hand: COTTON SWABS, THERMOMETER, BABY ASPIRIN.

I read for another hour and, as I read, my restlessness turned to anger. What was Naomi doing at Howard's all this time? Was she seducing him as she'd tried to seduce me? Was she worming money from him? I opened my door intending to knock on Howard's door and give them both a piece of my mind about courtesy, responsibility, and the importance of a full night's rest. Instead, I returned to my apartment, placed the Spock book in the middle of the kitchen table, and wrote a note—NAOMI, READ THIS! I drew a thick black arrow pointing to the part about blue mottling.

I must have fallen asleep. I was awakened by a loud bang. My body sprang up like a jack-in-the-box, but my mind lagged behind. A tall female person with stringy blond hair stared down at me, so pale she looked like a ghost. I knew who she was, but couldn't remember her name.

She wiped her nose with the back of her wrist and smelled it. "What you looking at?" She turned on the television, stood before it and sniffed her armpits. "I stink. I'm going to have that bath you promised me."

Naomi, that was her name. My mouth was dry. My tongue stuck to my lips when I tried to lick them. I worked up some saliva and said, "You must not turn on the TV when you don't intend to watch it. Or slam the door like that. You must find some purpose in life other than giving me a stroke."

She looked at me as if I were spoiled meat.

"Rather than a curled lip, a simple 'I'm sorry' would be appropriate." I waited. "You aren't sorry, are you?"

"Kiss my ass."

"You take pleasure in obscenities? You like to shock people? Are you aware that you have allowed your life to become an obscenity?"

From her pocket she produced my IOU. She held it up at arm's length. "Give me my thousand, and I'm out of here."

"I'll give you nothing, not until you tell me what you were doing at Howard's all this time."

She sneered. "I didn't tell him about his slut wife, if that's what you're worried about." She went into the bathroom and slammed the door.

I followed her and shook my finger at the door. "You can't stay here if you don't show some respect. You have responsibilities."

"Not to you, I don't. And I don't respect you."

"Did you have sex with Howard?"

"None of your business." Water rushed into the bathtub, making further conversation impossible.

I walked back to the living room and switched off the television, fully awake now, determined to find some order in this chaos or, if not find it, manufacture it. I heard the sound of toilet paper rolling on and on, and imagined Naomi's hand wrapped in a giant mitten of tissue. One roll lasted me six weeks. If by any chance she stayed, I'd limit her to two or three tissues per wipe. She flushed the toilet, waited for the reservoir to fill and flushed it again.

The bath was still running. Two inches of water was more than enough to get clean. Why was she using a full tub? Soaking is for the rich. On a yellow pad I wrote: RULES: NO SLAMMING DOORS. NO LOUDNESS OF ANY KIND. NO PLAYING THE TV AND NOT WATCHING IT. NO WASTING TOILET PAPER. LIMIT BATHS TO TWO INCHES OF WATER. NO TELLING ME YOU DON'T RESPECT ME. I felt better. This was my apartment, my domain.

If she stayed here, she'd stay on my terms. NO BITING FINGERNAILS AND SPITTING THEM ON THE FLOOR. FOLD ALL

CLOTHES AND PUT AWAY. READ BABY BOOK EVERY DAY FOR
AN HOUR. The bath water was still running. Inexcusable. She was one of
the bottom feeders. To invite a person like this into my life would be inviting misery and suffering also. I'd ask her to go tonight, tomorrow at the
latest. NO LEAVING FAUCETS DRIPPING. I imagined her dirty bath
water, the greasy ring it would leave around the tub. CLEAN TUB AFTER
YOU USE IT. I added COMET and BLEACH to the list of things to buy.
She had put her toothbrush in my hole, insensitive and provocative. KEEP
YOUR TOOTHBRUSH IN THE BACK HOLE. She'd probably use my
towel. No telling what germs she might be carrying around. KEEP YOUR
HANDS OFF MY TOWEL.

What had I gotten myself into? Mayflower was dead wrong about me
being good and kind. Mother Teresa was good and kind. Albert
Schweitzer was good and kind. Gandhi was good and kind. I wasn't even
close to good and kind. My strengths were more analytical, more supervi-
sory in nature. I was no drone. I had to be strong, assertive, willing to
draw the line. What did it mean to kiss a woman with Alzheimer's? It
meant I had been seduced by lust. There'd be no more kisses and dances
with Mayflower. And who was Howard to think I was his chauffeur? No
more trips to the dump to look for ashes. And no more pregnant teenagers slamming doors and bathing in my tub. NO SPEAKING UNLESS
SPOKEN TO. Let her live with Howard, become Helen's surrogate. I was
too old to put up with such nonsense. NO TALKING TO HOWARD
UNLESS TOBIAS IS PRESENT.

I heard Naomi's wet flesh scooting across the porcelain tub. NO
MAKING FLESHY SQUEAKING SOUNDS IN THE BATHTUB. I sat on
the bed, yellow pad in hand, and stared at the bathroom door, ready to
show her my list. I'd not let this streetwalker pull me into her game. I
stopped, read my rules over again, then ripped them into tiny pieces and
buried the shredded pieces in the trash. To have rules meant I was assum-
ing she'd stay. I wasn't ready to make that assumption. Besides, I didn't
need rules. I needed gumption. I needed resolve. My future had never
been this indefinite. I sat on the sofa and filled a whole page of my yellow
pad with one big question mark. I stared at the question mark, and it occurred to me it was shaped exactly like a fetus.

The bathroom door opened. A second later, Naomi appeared in a
pink checkered skirt and black t-shirt. Her square feet were bare. Water
from her hair dripped onto the floor. She sat on the end of my sofa bed—
jaw fixed, feet turned in—and brushed her hair down over her face. Sit-

ting there, behind her hair, she looked small, almost helpless. I wanted to sustain my anger at her, but my adversary had disappeared.

She looked up at me as if to say, *Okay, mister, go ahead. Hate me.* "I know you want me to leave," she said. "I'll go when I get the money."

I couldn't just hand her a check for a thousand dollars. How did I know she wouldn't spend it on drugs or give it to the first man who said a kind word to her? I wasn't a financial genius, but I had heard of protecting your investment. Besides, it would have been cruel to ask her to leave before her hair dried and before she had a good night's sleep. There was some logically correct move to make here. There had to be some common ground, but for the life of me I couldn't find it. "We both have adjustments to make," I said. "Before I agree to give you the money, we need to settle on some behavioral guidelines for the brief time you are here and discuss how exactly you'll use the money."

She started to get up. "That's it. I'm telling Howard."

"For example, my first guideline is that we discuss things like adults, that we don't threaten one another."

"You promised me a thousand. Now you're attaching all these conditions." Naomi tapped her knuckles with the back of my hairbrush, and one corner of her lip curled up as if this was giving her bad gas.

I suggested we start at the beginning. I asked to read Helen's letter again.

"It's on the dresser in the bedroom," she said.

Helen described Arthur Shade as a man who climbed mountains, flew planes and played tennis like a gazelle. As far as she knew, neither he nor she had any inheritable diseases. She said she was deeply in love with Arthur. She planned to leave Howard so she and Arthur could raise their baby together. Then things came unwound—the war, the draft, and, ultimately, Arthur's death.

"Have you found out anything more about Arthur Shade?" I asked.

"You heard Howard talk about his Japanese garden. Turns out Arthur Shade was the one who helped Helen build it." She lifted and poked at her hair, trying to tease some curl into it, but it fell straight. "Guess they made boom-boom in the old Zen garden."

Helen wrote she had never told Howard about Shade or the baby. Near the end of her letter, Helen described her favorite music. She said she liked Vivaldi and, in her wilder moments, the Grateful Dead. *Are you as beautiful as I imagine you to be?* she asked. *Do you dance or sing or play an instrument? Have you traveled much? So many times I've imagined the two of us sitting in my garden, sharing our secrets, laughing, talking for hours. Sometimes I can almost hear the sound of your voice. Your father had the most beautiful voice I've ever heard. I send you my love and deepest wishes for a full and happy life.*

I folded the letter and handed it to Naomi. "She obviously loved you."

"Loved who? Someone she never met? Someone she made up?"

"Try to see it from Helen's point of view."

"Okay, how's this? I'll dump a kid in the delivery room and write a note to her ten years later, telling her how much I love her."

"Maybe she wanted to meet you some day."

"If she wanted that, she'd have said so. I think she wrote that letter more for herself than me."

"Why didn't you get an abortion?"

"I don't know why. Money, maybe. And I hate doctors. Maybe I just wanted to shock all those Christian Reformed assholes in Pella."

"How about adoption. You could just give your baby up for adoption."

She nodded her head slowly as if this was the first time she'd thought about giving the baby away. "I don't know what I'm going to do," she said.

"Maybe your parents could help."

She shrugged. "That ain't gonna happen."

"Have you asked?"

"My mother ran away with another woman over a year ago to do the Thelma and Louise thing. My father hates me."

"You don't know that."

"He put me in that place."

"What place?"

"None of your business."

"I'm trying to help."

"I won't stab you to death while you're sleeping. You don't have to worry about that."

There was a long silence. I was on the verge of asking her to pack her things and leave when she said, "I hate my feet. Do you like my feet?"

I glanced down. They resembled two loaves of bread with toes. "Feet are feet," I said.

"Liar. Mine are uglier than most."

"Beauty is in the lie of the beholder," I said.

"Howard makes me sick, the way he goes all mushy about how much he loves Helen. He doesn't love *her*. He never knew her. He and Helen made each other up and spent their life playing house." She pulled a baggie from her pocket—some of Helen's ashes. She opened it, sniffed it. "I stole some of her."

"Why? You hate her."

"It's a totem. I'm going to buy one of those necklaces and carry her around my neck just to see what happens."

"I don't get it. You hate her, and you want to carry her around your neck?"

"I had this idea for getting even with Helen. I'd show up on her doorstep pregnant with a black baby and wreck the intense and prissy Grateful Dead life she'd invented for herself."

"Black?"

"Yeah, a guy named Raül. Carnival worker I met in Des Moines." She pulled one leg under her. "Then on the bus to Tucson, I started daydreaming about having my own room with white fluffy curtains. Helen and me sitting in that garden, pushing a baby carriage together, going shopping, having tea, all that crap. Now Helen is ashes, Shade is pushing up rice in Vietnam, and Howard's head is permanently stuck up his ass."

Naomi picked at a toenail while I drank a glass of water.

"My mother left my father and me when I was twelve," I said. This was one subject I hadn't talked about much.

"No one's who they pretend to be," Naomi said. "My father, the town liberal, turns out to hate blacks. Brendan, the big rock and roller, is now the great Alaskan fisherman in rubber boots, plaid shirts, and one of those knit caps. I was the only one who knew how scared he was that someone would find out he liked boys." She looked directly at me. "And you. You're a lonely old man, trying to be some clunky knight on a broken-down white horse, trying to make yourself feel good about your miserable life before you die."

"Are *you* who you seem to be?"

She sneered. "You don't know what to do with me, do you?"

"Nor you with me," I said.

"Give me the goddamn money."

"First, read this." I handed her the Spock book.

She refused to take it.

"I'm serious. Read this entire book. Discuss it with me along the way. Prove you've learned something about raising a baby. Then I'll give you the money."

She took the book, fanned the pages with her thumb, and dropped it on the floor. She picked at a loose string in the hem of her skirt. "Your mother walked out on you too, huh?"

"Moved to Philadelphia with a shoe salesman and died six years later."

"Of what?"

"Excessive everything, my father said. I never found out the real story."

"How'd your father take it? Mine hardly flinched."

"After a year he married his accountant. They moved to Florida and left me to run my father's business. All I had to do was send him two thousand a month. After a year, his new wife developed a thyroid problem. Eyes popped out like two ping pong balls."

"Yuck, I hate people with eyes like that."

"My father called and said he needed four thousand a month. Six months later the cleaners went belly up."

Naomi chewed at a hangnail. "Brendan and I were—tight, you know? It's been over two years."

I stood up, locked my hands over my head and looked out the kitchen window. On the sidewalk, a drunk stood on the curb. He looked right and left, then stepped off and fell on his hands and knees.

Naomi joined me at the window. We watched the drunk struggle to his feet. He brushed himself off and fell into the darkness.

The moon was just a sliver, the street empty and still. After a long silence, Naomi sighed and pulled the hair back from her face.

"You're having a baby," I said. "Read a little Spock tonight. Tomorrow we'll talk about your future."

"What future?"

"Well, for example, have you thought about what college you'll send your baby to?"

"Boy, have I. I mean I'm always thinking—Harvard, Yale, Iowa State?"

"I'm serious. It's not too early. You have to plan these things. Stay a few days. It won't hurt."

She rolled her tongue around her lips. "Wanna hear something funny?"

I braced myself. "What?"

"I wet my bed."

NO WETTING YOUR BED. "I see."

She turned on the TV and sat on the sofa. "I don't do it much anymore."

"We'll get a rubber mattress cover. I'll stay out of your way. It'll be like having your own apartment."

She stared at the television. "You can sleep with me if you want."

I glanced at her thin lips and long neck and, for the first time, saw her as the child she was. "I don't want that," I said. "On my long list of things I want, that wouldn't be in the top one hundred."

"You don't think I'm pretty?"

"That's not the point."

"What is, then?"

"I'm going to take a bath."

In the tub I lay back and placed a washrag over my face. I heard newspaper pages turning, the click of a cupboard door, water running. I could hardly bear listening. There was another human in my apartment, another person with a heartbeat, who talked about and thought about and felt things.

I was feeling things I wasn't sure I wanted to feel.

october-november

 ELEVEN

Two weeks passed and Naomi was still with me. She found a locket big enough for a pinch of Helen's ashes and flushed what was left down the toilet. After that, she did very little except wear the locket and slouch around the apartment combing her hair. She'd let her guard down a little, become more of a child, less a woman impersonator. This drew me to her in a way I didn't completely understand. I didn't particularly like her, but she was becoming part of my life, something to pay attention to, like a new mole or a bruise.

Every time she'd go out and not tell me where she was going, I'd imagine her not coming back, half-hoping she wouldn't. And when she'd forget to close the refrigerator or refuse to clean her dishes, I'd work myself into a frenzy and swear to myself that I'd ask her to pack her things and leave. But one look at her swollen stomach, and my anger would go away.

Truth was, I was developing an attachment to Naomi's baby, similar, I imagine, to the kind of attachment people feel for children in Africa or Mexico, the ones they send twenty-five dollars a month to so they'll grow up strong and learn to read. I wanted to see this baby make its appearance. I wanted to greet it, shake its hand, make sure it had one head and two legs. Perhaps a small part of me wanted to teach it something. I knew a few things and couldn't imagine myself going to my grave without sharing them with at least one other person.

But I didn't allow myself to get carried away. I knew there was a good possibility I'd wake up one morning, and she'd be gone.

Mayflower took Naomi's presence as a matter of course. The two women talked all the time—female things I wasn't interested in, but nevertheless would have appreciated being given an occasional nod of inclusion. At Mayflower's insistence she and I started taking walks together. We'd walk to the university and often stop at the Epic Café to have coffee and look at the weird people. One of her favorites was a black man dressed in a silvery outfit made completely of beer can tabs. She struck up a conversation with him and discovered he was visiting from another planet with the explicit purpose of learning how to play soprano saxophone.

At the university Mayflower surprised me again by introducing me to an American History professor she'd known years ago, a Dr. Cameron Wilson. At one point, Wilson had served as an intern to her father and was now a noted scholar on the Civil War. Wilson had written several scholarly papers on the role of monotheism in causing wars. He gave me copies to read. It was good hearing his politics.

"Tobias is an expert on the Civil War," Mayflower said. "You should have him as a guest lecturer."

"Not really," I said, my head suddenly buzzing.

"You must," Dr. Wilson said. "That would be a real treat."

And so it was that, with incredible grace and ease, Mayflower arranged for me to sample my life's ambition. In two weeks I would speak to Wilson's class on some aspect of the Civil War. The moment I knew what I was going to do and when I was going to do it, I felt presumptuous and stupid. I confessed this to Mayflower, and she told me another of her stories about a poor woman who dropped her two children off at a McDonald's every morning before going to work as a motel maid. She bought them happy meals and told them to play until she picked them up after work.

As usual, I didn't get her point. "What's that got to do with my situation?" I asked.

"Well, at least you're not cleaning motels," she said. And for some reason I felt better.

At night, Mayflower often read to me poems by Rilke and Neruda and Whitman. Although I would never have bought a book of poems on my own, I was beginning to see some redeeming quality in poetry. She talked a lot, too, about literature and art, insisting that the true indicator of one's death was not when the heart stopped beating, but the absence of art in one's life. We talked a lot about being alone. She argued that we see our lives more clearly when others are present. I, of course, advocated hermitages and solitary contemplation, but with decreasing conviction.

"Then what are you doing here with me?" she asked.

"Sharing the wisdom gained by long periods of solitude," I said.

Our time together felt real, vital, deeply connected. I liked the person I was when I was with her. I discovered I could make her laugh, that at times I could laugh at myself. To discover I had a sense of humor so late in life was a real boon. Yet, despite our good times together, there was the unspoken recognition that our time together was limited, brought home in those unpredictable moments when her eyes would glaze over. Those moments scared us both, drove a wedge between us. And although we saw a lot of one another, we began to keep our distance emotionally, to maintain an unnatural formality.

And when we tersely discussed her eventual move, we agreed she'd be better off where she would have someone to take care of her.

"Yes, of course," she said.

"It's obvious," I said.

"Obvious," she repeated.

She made me promise to visit her for as long as she could still recognize me. I also promised to bring jellybeans and read poetry to her. She seemed fearless. I was in awe of her strength.

As for Howard, he transferred what was left of Helen's ashes into a small Japanese vase and displayed it next to a miniature Zen fountain and a Bonsai tree.

He also fell in love.

One morning when Naomi was out, Howard showed up at my door looking as wrinkled as his jacket. "I feel awful," he said. "I've done a terrible thing."

I braced myself. I had learned that being even remotely friendly with Howard had a lot in common with picking poison ivy. I kept him at arm's length. "Are you sure you want to tell me this?" I asked.

"Have you ever meditated?"

"As kids we held our breath until we passed out. Same thing."

"I meditated last night with Katherine Peterson," he said. His speech was quicker than normal, his pupils huge. "You know, she's the owner of the Windsong Gallery."

"Ah," I said. "Let me guess. You bought one of her paintings on her credit plan."

"Yes, but that's not the point. Helen appeared to me in my meditation. I heard her voice as clearly as I'm hearing my own. I saw her standing there in front of me."

"What was she wearing?"

"What does that matter? A kind of flowing white gown."

"Ah, the standard flowing white gown. Why don't heavenly beings ever show up wearing overalls, miniskirts, or Bermuda shorts? Why do they wear clothes at all? And where do the clothes come from? Is there a heavenly Sears?"

"She said my grieving was keeping her from her journey."

"Everything these days is *journeys*. We hate our lives so much we delude ourselves into thinking that, if we are really good, we'll end up someplace better. We're always on our way, but we never get there. So we die and go to heaven only to learn that even in heaven there are ever more journeys. This is grossly unfair."

Howard clicked his thumbnail on his front teeth. "We used Katherine's bong."

"What's that, a body part?"

"Have you ever smoked hashish? I hadn't. Do you know anything about Buddhism? Do you have any food? I'm starving."

"Take a breath, sit."

"Can't sit." He sat and slapped out a rhythm on his knee with the flats of his hands. "She smokes hashish and sits naked in her back yard. There's a bell, a rice bowl, a little fountain, some rocks—lots of rocks, beautiful round, wet rocks. She says sometimes she breathes through her nipples. Can you imagine that?"

"Sure. I've known several nipple breathers."

Howard scratched his scalp. "I felt something like a laser light shooting from my penis up through my body and out the top of my head. I told Katherine about falling off the building, how I wanted to spend the rest of my life feeling like that. We talked about everything. We even talked about your attitude."

"My attitude?"

"Yes, you know, your pessimism and cynicism. She said you would have a better outlook if you ate brown rice seasoned with Japanese radishes." He paused. "You listening?"

"Your pupils are as large as eight balls, and you're calling me cynical? You've been doing way too much bonging."

"Hashish is wonderful. All my thoughts seem to have grace notes, tiny afterthoughts that tinkle like toy bells. This morning, I took a walk. Maybe for the first time I actually saw things—sidewalks, the mountains, a dog pissing on a bush. I mean I *saw* that particular dog pissing on that particular bush. God is truly in the details. Now I'm seeing you, and I feel like, for the first time, I *know* you."

He tried to hug me.

I stepped back. "Howard, I seriously think you should consider some kind of counseling."

"I don't need counseling. I need to keep feeling like I do now—free, alive, in love. I've started painting."

"You're having a breakdown."

"Katherine asked if I'd ever experienced a threesome. Have you ever slept with two women?"

"Beatrice was the closest I came."

"I mean the same love flowing between three humans. Katherine says there's something magical about the triangle. Pointed up, it's a phallus; down, it's a vagina. Up, it's fire; down, it's water. Think about the three of us getting together."

"Happy to, right after I get back from climbing Mt. Everest."

"Loosen up, Tobias. Katherine says to desire anything impedes spiritual progress. Therefore, you deny yourself nothing, satisfy every desire."

"I have no desire to share Katherine Peterson's bong or to participate in one of her triangles."

"Fantastic woman, I'm telling you—alive, intelligent, funny, sensual. Talented, too. I feel as if I've known her all my life. Her paintings are sparse but layered with meaning. Wait here. I want to show you something."

He went across the hall and came back with a dozen or so drawings, which he handed to me. "Wait." He left again and came back with Mayflower. He sat her at my table and spread out the sketches he'd made on his walk that morning.

There was an art deco house on University Avenue I recognized, a couple sitting on a wall holding hands, a saguaro cactus with some kind of bird on one of its arms, a woman working in her flower garden, a man sleeping inside a tractor tire. Some were airy and merely suggestive, others detailed. I was impressed and said so.

Mayflower circled the table, eyeing the drawings.

Howard sucked in his cheeks as if to prevent his head from exploding. "They're just quick impressionistic things, gesture drawings," he said. "Nothing serious. Be honest, now. Tell me exactly what you think."

Mayflower glanced back and forth from sketch to sketch. She made a faint sound in her throat.

"What?" Howard asked.

"Interesting," she said.

"The whole thing is interesting or just a part?"

"Here, where these two lines intersect, how they draw the eye down, anchor that woman to the earth."

Howard flicked something off the paper. "I like that, too."

"And this is nice."

"What?"

"This woman's eyes, dear. So alive, so inquisitive." When she came to the one of the man sleeping in the tractor tire, she looked at it for a long time and said, "Powerful."

"What do you mean, *powerful*?" Howard asked. "Do you really mean that particular word?"

"Oh, yes. It's so perfectly conceived, so emotionally strong—symbolic, perhaps of birth and death in a throwaway society. Everything is beautifully simplified, there's nothing insignificant or superfluous."

Howard raised his eyebrows to me and mouthed, *powerful.*

Naomi returned late one evening, having discovered she had a natural talent for games and gambling. She had met Bennie the Hindu on the third floor, and he taught her dominoes and various kinds of poker. In less than a week she had turned the ten dollars I loaned her into forty-six. Bennie said he didn't mind losing. Her company was worth it. "She makes me laugh," Bennie said. "Maybe I'll marry her."

I couldn't imagine Naomi doing or saying anything funny. I couldn't imagine Bennie losing money and laughing about it. And I especially couldn't imagine Bennie and Naomi married. Nevertheless, Naomi beamed when Bennie invited her to his weekly game in the back room of the Epic Café.

Thinking her love of gambling might be the one thing to keep her in Tucson, I advanced her another fifty dollars to get her into the game. That evening she played poker with five business men, while I, perhaps influenced by Howard's discussion of Katherine's nipples, read Dr. Spock's chapter on breast feeding.

I read about retracted nipples, swollen nipples, bruised and chafed nipples. I read more about nipples than I ever dreamed existed. When I heard Naomi at the door at a few minutes past one a.m., I closed the book and pretended to be asleep.

Naomi switched on the light. "Oops." She turned it off again. She thumped over to the sink, drank a glass of water, belched, let out a loud "Ahhh," then stood over me.

I opened one eye. "What?"

"You asleep?"

"Where have you been?"

"I won sixty-seven dollars. Everyone there said I was a good player. 'Tough,' they said. 'Strong.' They invited me back."

Even in the dim light, her eyes sparkled. As far as I knew this was the first time Naomi had really succeeded at something entirely on her own.

"I'm proud of you," I said and meant it. I was now certain she was going to stay in Tucson, not only because of her newfound talent, but because her relationship with Mayflower had grown even closer.

Naomi started taking Mayflower a cup of coffee every morning. She sat with Mayflower while she ate. I could hear them through the wall, chattering away and laughing.

I was pleased that Naomi and Mayflower had found one another until it dawned on me that Naomi's attraction for Mayflower wasn't entirely good. Naomi had been abandoned by just about everyone she had ever loved—Helen, her adopted mother, her adopted father, the father of her baby. Although the boy she called Brendan hadn't technically abandoned her emotionally, he had gone to Alaska and was no longer available to her. Now it was only a matter of weeks before Mayflower would be moving to Elderhaven. No doubt Naomi would see this as more proof of her unworthiness. Naomi had to be told before she became too involved. She needed time to adjust to the fact that Mayflower was more ill than Naomi thought, that she would be leaving us.

Mayflower must have come to the same realization. One morning Naomi left with a cup of coffee and a book and ten minutes later came storming back to the apartment. She went into the bathroom, slammed the door and locked it.

"What?" I called.

"Mayflower's leaving."

I was about to ask Mayflower to come and talk to her when Mayflower showed up at my apartment. "I told her about Alzheimer's and Elderhaven," she said. "She got very angry."

"She doesn't want you to leave her."

"No, it was more than that. When I told her, she turned rigid. She ripped her necklace from her neck and threw it at me. Her anger frightened me. She wouldn't talk. Her jaw was clenched so tight, I'm not sure she could talk. I tried to massage her back, but she pushed me away. You must get her to a doctor, let him give her a checkup, arrange for the delivery."

"She locked herself in the bathroom," I said.

Mayflower tried to talk to her, but Naomi told her to go away, she never wanted to see her again.

That afternoon, while Naomi napped, I came up with up a plan. Mayflower would call University Hospital, ask about costs, and arrange for a consultation. Meanwhile, I would take Naomi to Tucson Mall and buy her some maternity clothes. While there, we could look at baby clothes in Baby Gap. Surely, a few babies would show up. My idea was to give Naomi some exposure to real babies. Seeing real babies might be just the thing to jump-start her mothering hormones, snap her out of thinking only of herself.

Next morning over breakfast, as I poured Naomi a cup of coffee, I said, "So I was thinking we could go to Tucson Mall, look for some maternity clothes."

"Cut the crap." She brought the cup to her lips. I tried not to look at her inflamed fingers. They had almost no nails. She brushed drops of coffee from the front of her t-shirt, added another spoonful of sugar, then looked up. "Why are you staring at me?"

"I'm not staring."

"You are too."

"You want a scrambled egg?"

"How can you stand me?"

"Eat first. We'll talk later."

Naomi tilted her head forward and remained motionless, then she gagged, held her hands to her mouth, ran to the bathroom and vomited. Morning sickness and the way we managed it had become routine. My role was to wet a washrag, kneel beside her, wipe her forehead and tell her it was going to be all right.

She took the washrag from me to wipe her mouth, then spat in the toilet and shivered. She returned to the kitchen and went straight for the toast and jelly. "This has been going on forever," she said. "Isn't it supposed to stop?" She gave me a glance and for the first time I saw real fear in her eyes.

I helped her to the sofa and looked up *nausea* in the obstetrics handbook under "Complications of Pregnancy," and read aloud: "Morning sickness, when present, usually occurs during the first four months, but it can last throughout pregnancy. Some women report that eating a green olive first thing after awakening has been tried with excellent results." I found a bottle of olives in the refrigerator, removed the pimento from one, and handed it to Naomi. "Eat this."

She curled her lip.

"Eat the olive," I said. "What do you have to lose?"

She ate one, then another.

"All the answers you need are in one of these two books," I said. I held the handbook in front of her and turned the pages. "Look—flatulence, heartburn, shortness of breath, hemorrhoids. Come to think of it, giving birth and aging have a lot in common."

She may have cracked a smile.

I showed her sections on cramps, vaginal discharges, hemorrhage complications.

"Jesus," she said. "Take that away!"

"We have to get you to a doctor," I said. "You need a physical—blood pressure, check for albumin in the urine. There's something called toxemia. It's related to high blood pressure. Have you had any swelling?"

"Just my entire body," she said. "I haven't been able to make a fist for months. I have to pee every five minutes. My ribs hurt from puking so much." She went back to the bathroom.

"Don't worry," I called, "Swelling and frequent urination are common."

"Will you shut up?" The toilet flushed. A minute later she called, "Hey, Tobias, come look at this."

I rushed to the bedroom, thinking miscarriage, but she was sitting cross-legged on the bed holding a rag doll. "My mother's crappy going away present." She flipped her hair back and half-smiled. "You look funny in your boxers," she said. "Your scrawny legs."

"I'm sorry. I hadn't realized—" I made a move to put on my pants.

"You don't need to do that. You're cute that way. I'll bet the girls came on to you when you were young." She picked up my pillow and held it to her face. "Smells like you. Sort of dusty and vinegary. An old man smell."

Her mood had suddenly changed. She was Lolita. She bit her lip. "I think Mayflower just wants to get away from us. There's nothing wrong with her."

I didn't say anything.

She pushed her hair back with both hands, gave me a teasing glance and held the rag doll up to my face. "Say hi to Tobias," she said.

I moved back.

Naomi gave the doll an unnatural, awkward hug then tossed it to the end of the bed. "I don't know why I brought that stupid thing with me. You keep her, pretend she's your baby." She lifted her suitcase onto the bed. "You want to see what else I brought?"

I held the doll while she dug through her suitcase.

"Nothing fits anymore," she said. She pulled out a dirt-stained wedding dress. "It was my mother's. I took it to the hog farm with me. I was going to burn it when I left, but Brendan said I should keep it. Brendan was like that. I told him I was never getting married, that he could wear it." She folded the dress and put it away.

I chose my words carefully. "I think it's time you told me something about the hog farm."

"This guy, Quentin Raines, runs it outside Pella, Iowa. Group home, he calls it. His wackos do all the work."

"You were one of his—"

"I was the head wacko for a while, the queen of all his losers—alcoholics, broken-down druggies, and one guy who thought he was Jesus. No TV, no radio."

"And your diagnosis was—"

"Unmanageable, my parents called me."

"And how were you unmanageable?"

She ignored my question. "I stayed at Quentin's for about six months. Helped raise pigs and make little Dutch windmills. Every year, just before Tulip Time, the City of Pella paid us to clear birds from the park. I mean the Dutch really hate shit, any kind of shit, especially bird shit during Tulip Time. In the early evening, when the birds were settling in for the night, Quentin used a scattergun. Wham, wham. It was like raining birds. Thump, thump, their little bodies hit the ground and fluttered around. We picked up their carcasses and stuffed them in garbage bags. Half the town turned out to watch."

"Yes, but why exactly were you in the group home?"

"Birds are really stupid, you know? I mean if you are lucky enough not to get corked the first time, you don't circle back to the same tree. You go to a different tree in a different town. It's like some kind of death wish."

"I don't understand."

"So Quentin would fire again and another bunch would fall. I'd get the weirdest feeling seeing all those birds falling out of the trees. I mean the lawn is covered with dead birds, and I'm laughing and crying at the same time, thinking this is how it is, thinking I'm trapped in this birdless Dutch oven for the rest of my life."

"Why didn't you leave?"

"I mean the Dutch hate shit more than the Devil himself. The day before Tulip Time, a thousand locals show up with their buckets and brushes and scrub bird shit off the benches and sidewalks. The Dutch have some of the best sewage systems on the planet, and their pig farms are cleaner than hospitals." Naomi laughed and looked at me.

"Go on," I said.

"That's it. Next day fifty thousand tourists show up in Winnebagos to gape at tulips and watch cloggers. Quentin and us boners would change into Dutch costumes and artists' smocks and sell the little Dutch windmills to tourists. The churches, all except one, were open, and the choirs were singing, and there's no birds or bird shit within five miles."

"Look, if you don't want to tell me why you were there, just say so. But please stop playing games with me. What do you mean, 'all except one?'"

"You said you were proud of me for playing games."

I waited.

"I stole a few things," she said.

"Like?"

"Some gasoline."

"And why did you steal gasoline?"

"To burn down that one church."

"Which one?"

"The one run by the jerk-off minister who tried to rape me."

"Oh," I said. "I assume you succeeded in burning it down?"

"There was this big cross and the baptismal left standing."

"Was anyone in the church at the time?"

"No one died, if that's what you're asking."

"And now you're cured?"

"I won't set you on fire while you're sleeping, if that's what you're worried about. If I'd been thinking right, I'd have shot the son-of-a-bitch."

"What was the minister's name?"

"Van Steeland, Reverend Van Steeland. He wanted me to call him Ronny." She picked up the doll again. "What about you? You didn't like being married, did you?"

"It wasn't all I'd hoped it would be."

"Nothing is. Did you screw other women?"

"No."

"You'd make a terrible poker player. You did, didn't you? Who?"

"There was this waitress at the Bread and Butter. Elsie was her name. She had diabetes and had to quit work. Our affair was filled with shame and guilt, mainly mine. It didn't last long, a few months."

"Did you and Beatrice have good sex?"

"After the first six months, we hardly had sex at all. We lost our desire."

"Bummer. Getting laid has never been a problem for me."

"That's sad."

"What?"

"That you are willing to humiliate yourself by sleeping with anyone."

She patted her stomach. "Don't have to worry about that for a while. Nobody gets off on this, not even old geezers like you."

"You're pregnant. You look pregnant and pretty."

She pulled up her t-shirt. "Look at these tits. They're huge."

"Please, don't do that," I said. "Try to respect yourself."

She rolled her eyes and pulled her shirt down. "Why didn't you get a divorce?"

"Commitment, laziness, fear, take your pick—maybe even a kind of love. We had our rituals, our routines. It wasn't all bad. We got along."

Naomi rolled her eyes. "It's boring here. This place is dark and smells like Lysol. It's like being dead or something. Don't you get bored?"

"Lonely at times, often afraid, but not bored."

Naomi switched on the bedside radio, tuned it to the oldies station and tried to sing along.

I grimaced.

"I played cello in middle school," she said. "I have a sense of rhythm, but I'm tone deaf. So naturally I love to sing, right?" She tried again.

I grimaced again.

"See? To me it sounds beautiful, but everyone else gives me that same look."

"I can't sing, either," I said, "I dance a little. Mayflower and I—"

"I dance." She stood, moved her hands to the rhythm, then held my hand and twirled under my arm and back again. She placed her hands on her hips and rotated her pelvis. "Your turn," she said. "Show me your stuff."

I moved my hips as best I could, holding my boxers up with one hand.

Naomi joined me. "Hey, check us out," she said.

I shook my shoulders and pumped my free arm up and down. I turned around and did a flashy jig just as the music ended. We sat on the edge of the bed, laughing, out of breath.

Suddenly, Naomi jumped up and stood in front of me. She pulled her shirt up over her stomach. "It's moving." She grabbed my hand. "Touch it."

There were spidery stretch marks etched on her white stomach, tiny blue-green veins. Naomi pressed my hand to her side. We waited, but the baby didn't move again.

I looked up. A tear was working its way down Naomi's cheek. "Don't look at me," she said.

"It's going to be all right," I said. "You'll see."

Naomi gulped for a breath. "There was a rat lady at the carnival in Des Moines. She wore ripped knit stockings and a faded black satin dress split up the thigh, and men bet on which hole a rat would run into. It wasn't fair, not to the rat. Whichever hole it chose, it always ended up in the same place. I'm just like that stupid rat. Just like those stupid birds."

"Get dressed," I said. "I'm taking you to the mall. We'll get you some nice clothes."

 TWELVE

At the entrance to Tucson Mall three teenage boys stopped talking when we passed. They stared at Naomi. "Hey, Big Mama," one said. Another held his hand to his mouth as if to cover his laughter.

Naomi flipped them the finger.

"Don't encourage them," I said.

"How do I look from behind?" she whispered. "Do I waddle?"

"Not at all," I lied.

"Everyone's so tan. I feel so—white."

In Mother's Day Maternity, a tired-looking saleslady with a sagging eyelid and smoker's cough sat on a stool behind the lingerie counter reading a copy of *The Enquirer*. Naomi sorted through the smocks, pausing every so often to sneer at me. I was admiring the engineering of nursing bras, the magic of Velcro.

The saleslady approached Naomi. "Something I can help you with, honey?"

"Do you have anything in black?"

"You're pregnant, sweetie. You don't wear black when you're pregnant, you wear pastels, you wear primaries." She told Naomi she'd given up a career in real estate to raise two girls, and both got pregnant before they were sixteen. "How old are you?" she asked.

"Old enough," Naomi said.

"Make sure you graduate high school. No tattoos, no piercings. Otherwise, you'll be busting your butt at Whataburger the rest of your life." She held up a huge pair of orange stretch tights. "These look about your size."

"Let's get out of here," Naomi said.

"Not until you buy some clothes," I said.

Within three minutes Naomi had selected two smocks, both blue, two blouses, two bras, six pairs of maternity panties, and a pair of black tights.

"Now can we go?"

"A positive step," I said. "Now I want to have a quick look at baby things." On the way to Baby Gap, we stopped at a pet store and bought two goldfish, a small plastic castle, and two sprigs of green fern. In a flower shop, I bought a potted philodendron because the clerk said it was something any idiot could grow. I felt organized, focused, confident that we were finally on track.

Naomi lagged a few paces behind. I understood. I sat on a bench directly across from Baby Gap and waited. She paused to look at herself in a mirror, turned sideways, glowered at her stomach, then stood in line to buy a pretzel.

"Join me," I said, "rest a while, take a load off."

Naomi sat at the far end of the bench, dipped her pretzel in a small cup of melted cheese and took a large bite.

I hiccupped.

"Stop it," she said, wiping cheese from her mouth.

I stopped. Amazing.

Two teenage girls walked by dressed identically in short skirts and platform shoes. "Let's get out of here," Naomi said. "I hate this place."

A Mexican girl was pushing a baby carriage in our direction. "Just a minute," I said. "I need to rest."

The girl sat on a bench facing us. She rummaged through her purse, found a pacifier, licked it, and shoved it into her baby's mouth. The baby, a round-faced little girl, was all eyes and forehead with a white bow clipped to a sprig of hair directly on top of her head. She reached out to be held. Her mother bounced her on her lap, rocked side-to-side, made faces and talked baby talk.

"Look at those little shoes and her pudgy legs," I said.

"This is stale." Naomi tossed what was left of her pretzel into the trash.

The baby reached for her mother's nose and mouth. "Ouch," her mother said. "You pinch too hard."

"How old is she?" I asked.

"Three months."

"Must be fun, being a mother, bringing such a beautiful child into the world."

"Sure, if you like being run over by a truck. When's yours coming?" she asked Naomi.

Naomi shrugged.

"Six weeks, maybe less," I said.

"It's a drag, ain't it?"

Naomi looked away and bit an imaginary hangnail.

"Everyone gives you this bull about how beautiful you look. Man, I didn't look beautiful. I looked dumpy. My back hurt all the time. My legs got these big veins. My butt's never going to be the same. They used this claw thing to pull her out of me. I named her Alexis after her father, Alex. When he found out I was pregnant, he joined the Marines. Says he's going to marry us when he gets discharged. You want to hold her?"

Naomi shook her head and fixed her gaze on me. "Let's go," she said between her teeth.

"May I hold her?" I asked.

"She'll let anybody hold her. It's like holding a sack of potatoes."

Remembering Spock's advice, I made certain Alexis' head rested in the crook of my arm, and that I supported her back. The weight of a living thing in my arms, another consciousness sizing me up, trusting me, felt almost dangerous. I raised my eyebrows, puckered my lips and made smacking sounds.

The baby's face puffed up and turned red. Her mouth drew down on both sides. She screamed and arched her back as if trying to catapult from my arms. I tightened my hold. She screamed louder.

The mother produced a bottle. "No problem. She's hungry." She handed me the bottle.

The baby sucked away. Gradually, her arms stopped flailing, and she closed her eyes. Her body let go. Like water in a vase, she filled the space of my arms. This was the first baby I had ever held. It felt natural, as if I'd held babies forever. I turned to say something to Naomi, but she was fifty feet away, hurrying toward the exit.

"You should go after her," the girl said.

Why should I? Naomi appreciated nothing I did for her, not so much as a small nod of gratitude. I took another look at the sleeping Alexis and returned her to her mother.

"Go after her. She's pissed about something," the girl said. "Pregnant women get like this."

I hesitated, then picked up my bag of goldfish and the philodendron and followed Naomi to the car.

"Why did you run out like that?" I asked as we pulled out of the parking lot.

Silence.

We stopped at a red light. My stomach was in knots. I'd always been a good problem-solver. If I knew what the problem was, there was a chance

I could solve it, but in Naomi's case the problem was too ambiguous. I tried focusing on one small part. "All I ask is that you take responsibility for your baby."

Naomi glared straight ahead. "You know what I especially don't need? I don't need your holier-than-thou crap, your Mr. Fix-it advice. If you know so much, why are you picking up alley trash like me?" She folded her arms and jiggled her legs. "I have to go to the bathroom."

I stopped at a Circle K. While Naomi was in the bathroom, I bought a stale doughnut and a cup of coffee. I felt I owed the store something for the use of their facilities. Then I waited in the car.

When Naomi came out, she headed straight for the pay phone. I guess the call didn't go through, because she kicked at the wall and hung up. Watching her limp back to the car, head down, cursing, I felt for the first time that Naomi was seriously disturbed, that she could do damage to herself or others.

We sat side by side in the car, drowning in silence. The coffee burned my lips. The doughnut seemed to expand in my throat. Naomi tore off a strip of jerky and moved it around in her mouth until her cheeks bulged. "I hate Brendan," she said, almost inaudibly.

"So you want to talk about it?" I said.

"About what?"

"About how, whenever a person tries to help you, he ends up being your worst enemy?"

She slid down in the seat and rested both knees on the dashboard.

I noticed thick dime-shaped burn scars on her ankles. I didn't want to know where they came from. My mind raced down a hundred roads at once. I needed to get to a library. Would she hurt other people? What about the baby? Was she safe to be around? Had anything she told me been the truth?

"What?" she said.

"Nothing," I said.

She bit off another hunk of beef jerky. "You know that minister I told you about?" Her voice grew louder, more confident. "It never happened. I seduced him. Seducing someone that fat and that holy was easy. I liked seeing him swear he'd never see me again, then come begging like a worm. I like making people hate me. I like it that you hate me."

"I don't hate you."

"Take me back so I can pack my things."

"Maybe you should call your father. Maybe he'll take you back."

Silence.

"What about the hog farm? You could go back there."

"It costs money."

"Maybe that thousand I owe you—"

"That wouldn't begin to cover it. Besides, I don't want to be smelling hog shit the rest of my life." She wrapped her arms around her knees. "I just want to get the hell away. I want to go to Alaska, but that bastard Brendan never answers his phone."

I started up the car, and we drove in silence back to the apartment. I put the goldfish in a bowl, added rocks and the small plastic castle and set it on the coffee table in front of Naomi.

"I have to check on Mayflower," I said.

"I'll be gone when you get back," she said.

I couldn't look at her. "Fine," I said. "I've done all I know to do." I left.

Mayflower told me she'd called the hospital to make an appointment for Naomi, but they wanted information Mayflower didn't know. She had found out that the earliest available appointment was a week away. I thanked her, knowing all her work was for nothing. Part of me said I should tell her about Naomi leaving, about the scars. But it didn't matter. None of it mattered. Naomi was leaving.

I warmed a can of soup and poured a glass of milk, but something was bothering Mayflower. She ate only a few bites.

"Are you okay?" I asked.

"Follow me to the bedroom," she said. "I want to show you something."

I liked Mayflower's bedroom. It was a comfortable room, carelessly put together with lace pillowcases, white curtains, a dresser with a hair dryer, powder, brush, colored ribbons. It smelled of lilac and talcum. She opened her closet, switched on the light, knelt down at the far corner and pointed to a tank. "Helium," she said.

"For parties," I said. "Balloons. It makes you sound like Donald Duck when you inhale it."

"Yes," she said. "It is also an effective and painless way to end one's life. In five to fifteen minutes the brain shuts down, and with it the other organs."

I stared at the tank, pushing back a rush of fear. "How long have you had this?"

"Months."

"Then you've known—"

"I want to ask if you'll assist me. It isn't legal for you to hook things up, but will you be willing to look over my shoulder to make sure I assemble the parts properly and, afterwards, call the funeral home? There are specific things you need to do, words you need to say to the officials to avoid implicating yourself. I've written everything down."

I held up a hand. "It's too early to talk this way. You have months, maybe years."

She sat on the edge of the bed. "I'm not sure I even want to do it. But I want to have the option. It terrifies me to think I might become so muddle-headed I won't be able to. If you don't feel comfortable helping me, I'll look for someone else."

I sat next to her. "Let me put it this way," I said. "I have a question. We lived next door to each other for a year or so, and we hardly spoke. Now, in the past six weeks, we're talking. I mean really talking, having conversations, taking walks, eating meals together. You laugh at my jokes. I've laughed, really laughed maybe for the first time in my life. I'm often amazed by your insights and observations. We've kissed. I don't mean to presume, but do you think this means we're, well, more than friends?"

"Yes, dear, I think it does."

"This being the case, I ask you—no, I beg of you—please don't gas yourself."

She looked down at her hands. "I think that might be the nicest thing anyone has ever said to me."

I rubbed my palms together, trying to shake the numbness from my fingers. I sat up straight. "Once, in ancient Greece, a king put a stop to a suicide epidemic by decreeing that self-slain women should be carried naked through the marketplace to their burial."

She smiled. "Being carried naked to my grave doesn't sound that bad."

"Yes. Well." I slapped my knees with both hands. "Hey," I said. "Anytime you need something—a cook, someone to help you find your way back to your apartment—just bang on my wall and Tobias Seltzer will come running."

"Who's Tobias Seltzer, dear?"

I stiffened.

She placed a hand on my arm. "I'm sorry. Just my attempt at humor."

"No," I said. "This is an excellent question. Just who *is* Tobias Seltzer? I used to know. Now I'm not sure."

"I don't think it's necessary to know who you are, dear. We're all so many wonderful things. Rilke has a poem that ends, 'I have been circling for a thousand years, and I still don't know if I am a falcon, or a storm, or a great song.'"

"I think you're a great song," I said.

She closed her eyes and took in a breath. "Thank you, Tobias." She lay back. "I'm so tired."

I covered her with a cotton throw. Such an intimate thing to do, this covering a person you care deeply for, and for her part such a trusting thing, to fall asleep in the presence of another person. I started to leave, then returned to the side of the bed and willed her awake.

She took my hand and held it in both of hers. "What?" she said.

"I'll help you," I said. "I mean with the helium, if it comes to that."

"Thank you, dear."

"You know, I don't understand death. It makes me angry when I think of it. I mean, when I die, I want to die a meaningful death. I want a few people to miss me, really miss me. But you know what? That isn't going to happen. We die, days or weeks pass, and the world goes on—gravity still holds us down, the earth keeps spinning in the void, the sun comes up, the sky stays blue. If I die, you'll feel bad for a while, then you'll continue your sorting and packing."

"Worse, I may not even know who you are."

"If you die, I'll grieve, but in time my life will return to normal. That's the thing that gets me. Nothing changes when we die. If it did, the world would be soggy with tears. Even the dump goes on as usual, collecting more and more garbage. Somehow, I wish our deaths could at least cause dumps to shut down for a few minutes, or a small leaf to fall from a tree." I struggled to find the right words, then I said, "You're so much more than your death. I want to do something for you. I want to—"

"Thank you, dear."

On my way out, I made a mental note. It was time to see if I could locate Charles Thomas Robins.

When I returned to the apartment, Naomi was in the same position as when I left, still staring at the fish.

"Have you named them yet?" I asked.

"Shit-head Tobias and Crazy Naomi." She leaned closer. "That's Shit-head," she said, pointing, "the one with the white around his gills."

"I'm sorry," I said.

She stood, got the potted plant off the kitchen table and set it on the windowsill. "I want to stay here until I have the baby. I'll have the baby, give it up for adoption and get out of your life. You can make yourself feel like a hero by helping me. But you have to promise to give me that thousand."

"Why are you staying?"

"Because being here is better than on the streets."

"How do you know I want you to stay?"

She patted her stomach. "Because of this."

"Would you do me a small favor? Would you, just for once, say 'Please'?"

One corner of her lip turned up. "Please, let me stay."

"No more hate," I said. "You have to be nice once in a while."

"Fine," she said.

"Okay. We'll start all over again. But I can't stand this chaos. We need a plan."

She rolled her eyes and let out her breath. "So plan."

A half-hour later we had decided I would cook and handle the laundry. She would wash the dishes, clean the bathroom and take care of the plant and the goldfish.

"A team," I said.

"You ever been part of a team before?"

"Never," I said.

"Me neither."

That evening I fixed Hamburger Helper, a salad, and opened a can of creamed corn. Naomi ate everything, then picked up her plate and licked it. "We have to talk about your table manners," I said.

Following a tense discussion, she agreed not to lick her plate again, at least not in front of me.

Afterwards, I read from the handbook and listened to the sound of dishes clinking together in soapy water. The doll lay next to me on the sofa. When Naomi had finished the dishes, she sat on the other end and put her feet in my lap. We'd never been this intimate before. I picked up the doll intending to place her on Naomi's stomach, but felt a small slit under a flap at the back. I stuck my finger in and pulled out a roll of money.

"What the—" Naomi said. She counted the money. There was over five hundred dollars in fives, tens, and twenties. She tore the doll apart, looking for more. "I don't get it," she said.

"What's there to get? It's yours," I said.

"*That's* why she wanted me to have this doll. She wanted to give me this money."

Watching her count the money again, I became aware of a sudden shift in our relationship. She had money of her own now, close to six hundred dollars counting her poker winnings. She also had the independence that came with it.

That night I awoke to a sound in the bathroom. I found Naomi there, sitting on the edge of the tub, sobbing. She looked up at me, her eyes distant and unfocused. "I'm really messed up," she said.

I wasn't sure what I felt—hopelessness, mostly. Then I heard myself say, "I'm not going to kick you out, no matter how hard you try to make me hate you."

"You are out of your mind, too," she said.

That night after returning to bed, I thought about how much I didn't know, how primitive people must have feared the blackness beyond the edge of the campfire. I certainly did. I thought how secrets must have been shared there in the dark, plots born, enemies invented. Night thoughts were more liquid and dense than day thoughts, more magical and scary. Day thoughts could be sorted out into neat little piles, but night thoughts clumped together, blurred the lines between fear and hope, pleasure and pain, love and hate.

# THIRTEEN

I sprang awake, startled, disoriented. Outside, the sky was washed red and orange from the rising sun. Maybe I'd dreamed I heard someone cussing.

"Bastard! Stupid bitch!"

It was coming from the bedroom. I burst in, certain I'd see something terrible—Naomi lying in a pool of blood, an aborted fetus—but she was in a rage, tearing her sheets off the bed. She tossed them to the floor, stomped on them, kicked at them, missed, hit the wall and fell to the floor holding her toe.

"What's going on?"

"Nothing. Get out. Where's the money that was in that doll?"

"There, on your bed stand."

She slumped against the wall and counted the bills, sorting them by denomination. "I pissed my bed."

"Look," I said. "We'll clean up later. Some food will give you a better perspective. I'll buy breakfast at the Bread and Butter, then we'll wash the sheets."

"I don't want you to touch—" She held her hand to her mouth, got to her feet, stumbled to the toilet and vomited.

A half-hour later she appeared in the living room wearing one of her new blue smocks and the black tights.

"You look nice."

"I'm having biscuits and gravy."

"I've never had them."

"Let's get out of here," she said. "I'm starving."

In a corner booth of the Bread and Butter, a teenage boy and girl were fondling and kissing.

"Yuck," Naomi said.

Virgil was whistling "There Is Nothing Like a Dame." He pushed two orders of biscuits and gravy through the opening to the kitchen and glanced out at me.

"Hey, Virgil," I said.

"Hey, Tobias."

Miss Choy delivered our orders. She raised an eyebrow at me. "You not introduce me to your friend," she said.

"Naomi, Miss Choy. Miss Choy, Naomi Kuiper."

Naomi mumbled something without looking up from her plate.

"Tobias order same-same every day," Miss Choy said. "Always toast and marmalade. Marmalade and toast. Now he order biscuit and gravy, like you. Now Miss Choy know why he not come back to work for her." She raised her eyebrows in a terrible imitation of Groucho Marx and left.

I handed Naomi a napkin and asked her to wipe the gravy from her chin.

"I hate pissing my bed."

"There must be some treatment available, some new drug."

"Will you stop trying to fix everything? Some people you can't fix."

"You fixed my hiccups."

Naomi chewed with her mouth open and looked at me as if daring me to comment on her manners. I sat up straight and spread my napkin over my lap. The least I could do was set a good example.

Miss Choy returned with the coffeepot. "You know Mr. Seltzer for long time?"

Naomi swallowed. "A few weeks."

"It's temporary," I said. "She needs a place to stay. She's pregnant."

"Oh boy," Miss Choy said, shaking her head as she walked away.

I heard little smacking sounds coming from the boy and girl in the corner booth and shivered when I realized that before sunset they might have made another child for this world. I held a newspaper up to block my view, and the first thing I saw was a headline: "Getting Babies Off to a Good Start: Arizona Near Bottom." According to a Dr. Leslie Snyder from University Medical Center, Arizona ranked forty-ninth in babies born in good health. Last year, over half the mothers who had given birth in Arizona had no prenatal care. Leslie Snyder was the name of the doctor Mayflower had made the appointment with.

"I've found you a doctor," I said, afraid to bring up Mayflower's name.

Naomi licked her plate.

"Stop it."

"I don't need a doctor." She pointed to my biscuits. "You gonna eat those?"

I pushed my plate in her direction. "This isn't something you have a choice in."

Naomi looked up, past me, toward the door.

I turned. Caravelo stood just inside the entrance. He wore tight black pants, a black shirt with a turned-up collar, and patent leather boots. He stood with his feet apart, his handless arm extended over his head.

One look at Naomi's face, and I saw the possibilities. She was smitten. "You know him?" I asked.

"I've seen him. I've never talked to him."

Caravelo tossed a ball high into the air and caught it on the bridge of his nose. The ball drifted around his neck and chest and down the length of his arm. He arched backwards, and the ball ended up on his forehead. He flipped it high into the air and caught it in a bag attached to his hip.

I applauded with the others and waved him over. "This man," I whispered to Naomi, "releases the fluid possibilities of solid objects, inspires children to dream, causes young women to swoon. There's no one like him anywhere."

Naomi's face was crimson. "You know him?" she whispered.

Before I could explain that I didn't actually know him, Caravelo called out to me, "*Buon giorno, amico mio*. You are the one who give bite to the Greaser," he said. "You are Caravelo's hero." He sat next to Naomi. "And you, my *amica bella*, did you know of this man's heroics? One Ear has not been on street for six weeks."

Naomi turned red and stared down at her plate.

"Caravelo," I said, "my name is Tobias Seltzer. This is Naomi Kuiper, my friend from Iowa."

"I have played in Iowa," Caravelo said. "In Iowa there are many churches and many peegs."

"There are colleges and art museums, too," Naomi said, tapping her fork on her plate.

"But none without the smell of peegs. Whatever you do—make love, eat a meal, take communion—you are also smelling the peegs. A man cannot juggle in Iowa." He took something from his shirt pocket. "Here, take one of my new business cards." He gave one to each of us and pointed out his new address. He'd rented upstairs studio space on the corner of Eighth Street and Fourth Avenue. "Caravelo's audience has become too big for the street. The policemans scare away his customers."

Naomi sat up straight, dabbed at the corners of her mouth with her napkin and folded it.

Caravelo's card indicated he performed for weddings and parties, gave juggling lessons, dance lessons, trained small animals and was an animal psychologist.

"You're a talented man," I said.

"Life has burdened me with many talents. I cannot list them all on such a small card."

"What about this animal psychologist part?" I asked.

Caravelo explained that he'd spent ten years with Barnum and Bailey as an animal pacifier, that his job was to "relieve" the younger lions before they performed. "Very dangerous," he said. "The lions fall in love with Caravelo. They teach me never to allow myself to be loved by something that can eat me." He told us of treating a depressed elephant after she lost her baby, curing a monkey from eating its paws, helping the depression of a seeing-eye dog that had gone blind.

"Really?" Naomi managed.

"I make ball with bell in it. He learn to fetch." He laughed. "I give him something to fetch, and he blossom in his old age."

"That's great," Naomi said.

"Animals attack me," I said. "Birds dive-bomb me. Dogs who have never bitten anyone bite me."

Caravelo wagged a long finger. "This is not the animal's problem. The birds and animals are threatened. You are a sexual rival. You have to show them that you are not afraid. Never run."

"Oh," I said, not believing a word of it. I sipped my coffee. "Have you ever done toilet training?"

"Actually, I—"

Naomi broke in. "How much do you charge for dance lessons?"

Caravelo pulled back a few inches and looked Naomi up and down. "For you, a beautiful woman of such delicate condition? Will your husband join you?"

"I'm not married."

"Then I charge practically nothing, maybe five an hour. If you help Caravelo clean and paint his studio, he gives you free lessons."

Naomi was staring at Caravelo's stump.

"Ah, you want to know about my missing hand."

"I'm sorry, I—"

"Every woman, she wants to know about Caravelo's missing hand. I tell very few, but Caravelo cannot keep secrets from such a beautiful woman. I was still learning the art of pacification. Both the lion and Caravelo were young and inexperienced. The lion, he became impatient and chewed off my hand." He laughed. "But who cares? The world has many two-handed jugglers, but only one Caravelo." From his bag Caravelo produced a red ball, balanced it on a fork he held in his mouth, flipped it to the top of his head, moved out from under it and allowed it to roll slowly down his arm into his hand.

Naomi's expression turned to pure delight. She dug through her pockets and gave Caravelo ten dollars. "Here's for two dance lessons," she said. "Maybe I'll help clean and paint."

When I left them, Caravelo was demonstrating a tango step, and Naomi was laughing.

On the way back I stopped outside the Windsong Gallery and looked through the window. I saw Howard helping Katherine hang her paintings—triangles leaning against squares, small ovals stacked on larger ovals, three tilted rectangles. Howard was talking non-stop, laughing, touching Katherine as they passed, eyeing the paintings from various perspectives. He saw me and came outside.

"New show?" I asked.

"We're preparing for the holidays. Katherine has agreed to show a couple of my drawings." Katherine waved and threw Howard a kiss. "Isn't she something? I'm thinking of asking her to marry me." Howard motioned for her to come out.

She wore tight eggplant-colored pants and a lavender scoop-necked sweater. Glasses tinted purple perched like two plums on top of her head. "Tell Tobias about your art," Howard said. "Listen to this, Tobias."

She described the Buddhist influence on her paintings, how she'd become interested in exploring the relationship between higher consciousness, geometry, and eroticism. She repeated the bit Howard had told me about how geometric figures such as triangles turned down were symbols of water and the woman's pubic region. Turned up, they represented fire and the erect phallus.

"Sensuality is fundamental to the Christian communion service," I said. "The words *sacrament* and *orgy* are second cousins."

Katherine drew in air through her nose, thus inflating her chest, and continued talking about the underlying sexual symbolism of the holy trinity. Howard grew visibly taller. "Do you own much art?" Katherine asked me.

I told her my financial situation placed me in the category of clip art and excused myself.

As I continued my walk back to the Coronado, I envied Howard his new life, his passion. His moods were infectious. Because Howard was in love, an old man crossing the street next to me began to whistle, a stray dog near the alley wagged its tail almost frantically, a woman choosing vegetables at the Food Conspiracy seemed to be choosing them as if they were diamonds. I myself walked with a bounce in my step.

That afternoon, while Naomi washed her soiled sheets in the basement, I went to the library to try to locate Charles. Truth be known, I preferred not to find him, but I didn't want to break my word to Mayflower. The reference librarian recommended I start with late editions of "Who's Who." A Charles Thomas Robins from Pittsfield, Massachusetts was listed in the 1987 edition. Using a pay phone and a fist full of quarters, I called a half-dozen Robins who were listed in the Pittsfield directory and found one who had known Charles and his wife. Charles' wife had died several years back, the woman said. Charles himself was ill. He had held on for a while, then moved west to live with his son in San Diego. The Pittsfield Robins thought the son's name was Morris, but couldn't remember for sure. Ten calls later, posing as an old friend of Charles from Washington, I located the son, Norris Robins, a retired contractor living in La Jolla. Norris told me that, after having a stroke, his father had gone to live with his sister in Scottsdale where, after six months or so, he had a second stroke. He was now in a long-term care facility in Chandler, Arizona, a place called Sea Breeze.

An hour later I sat before Mayflower, ready to tell her the good news.

She held up a plastic bag of multicolored jellybeans. "I've just found these. They must be a decade old. Here, dear, have one. I like the popcorn flavor best." She was reclining on the sofa, wearing a Mediterranean blue skirt, a frilly white blouse, and white shoes with a strap over the top. I imagined the two of us taking a voyage to Mikonos, eating Greek olives and feta cheese and drinking Retsina.

"Let's go to Greece," I said. "Leave all this behind."

"When do we get back, dear? I should tell my social worker. She'll worry."

I shook my head. "We can't go," I said. "There's the problem of money. And someone has to look out for Naomi."

"To think of an adventure is almost as good as doing it, isn't it?"

"You have turned me into a dreamer, a blithering romantic."

"How are you, dear? Is Naomi all right?"

"The truth is, Naomi and my hemorrhoids have a lot in common."

She laughed and sorted the jellybeans with her finger.

I studied her sprawling grace, her large mouth, her radiant goodness. "You're an amazing person," I said.

She crossed her ankles and popped a red jellybean into her mouth. "Tell me more about you and Naomi, how you feel about her."

I sighed. "I thought of helping her as a kind of *mitzvah*, some small contribution to improve the human condition. But there's a big difference between the principle of helping others and actually helping them. I'm beginning to understand why the great saints never had roommates."

Mayflower ate another jellybean. "I have never been one to go out of my way to help others. Perhaps that's my failing, worrying too much about my own little existence. Before I go into that dark night, perhaps I'll help someone, just to see what it feels like."

"You've helped me just by being who you are."

"But notice, dear, I have managed to turn the conversation away from Naomi and on to me. Tell me more about her."

"She seems to have no positive feelings for anyone or anything and, if she does, she can't hold on to them. No interest in the future. None."

"How are you holding up?"

"She ties my stomach in knots. I've never led this kind of life before. I've never been so involved in other people's lives. It's so—demanding." I got up. "I have to go," I said.

"Not yet, dear. Sit down. Tell me more."

I sat down and let Mayflower rest her feet in my lap. "A few weeks back you told me I was good and kind," I said. "I don't feel so good and kind. One minute I'm welcoming Naomi with open arms, the next I'm wanting her to leave because she uses too much toilet paper. A good and kind person does not make another person homeless because she uses too much toilet paper. I want to help her, but I also want her to do what I say."

Mayflower moved her feet to the floor, sat up and leaned toward me. "You are helping her. As far as her doing what you say, maybe you have to lower your standards a bit. The only way I know how to get people to follow my orders is to order them to do what they're already doing."

I laughed. I wanted to tell her I'd found Charles, but I couldn't, not at that pleasant moment. I wanted to keep it pleasant. "Naomi just met Caravelo, the juggler. She's smitten. He's going to give her dancing lessons. Maybe he'll be a good influence on her. Maybe he's Prince Charming. Maybe they'll get married and live happily ever after."

"What an amazing man."

"He worked with circus lions, you know. He masturbated them before the show to make them tamer. That's how he lost his hand."

"The lion took offense?"

"No, it became impatient."

Mayflower laughed. "I had no idea that masturbating lions was something one could make a living doing. If they had a convention, I doubt many would show up." There was an awkward silence, then Mayflower said, "Caravelo teaches dance, does he? Watch this." She stood erect, did a perfect pirouette and struck a seductive pose, hand on hip, head thrown back. "What do you think?"

"I am truly impressed."

She held my hands, pulled me to my feet and hugged me. This was not a polite inconsequential hug, but an all-embracing and caring hug that told me one thing—despite my efforts to keep my distance, I couldn't, I simply couldn't. Guilt be damned, I couldn't tell her I'd found Charles.

Early that evening, just after Naomi left for her first dance lesson, Howard showed up wearing paint-spattered jeans and carrying a plate full of tacos. He'd made them from a secret recipe, which he gladly shared with me. I had to promise not to tell anyone that the secret ingredient was melted Velveeta cheese. I poured iced tea for us and tried a taco. I had to admit, it was good. We had finished two each when Howard said, "Your ice melts faster than mine." He was right. My ice cubes were practically gone. He still had five or six.

"Hyperthermia runs in the family," I said. "My father had it, too. He thought it had to do with his intense Jewishness."

We'd almost finished a third taco when Randall Pruitt, the self-made retard from down the hall, poked his head in. For months he'd been pestering me to read to him. I always put him off. Now, he'd found a beat-up romance novel on the street and wanted me to read it aloud. I told him it was better to start with something simpler, so I found my copy of *Goodnight Moon* and gave it to him. He insisted I read that to him, instead.

Howard thumbed through the romance novel while I read to Randall. "Good, you're learning to read, Randall," Howard said when I finished.

"I'm not reading it. Mr. Seltzer is reading it for me. After I shot myself in the head, I forgot how to read."

"Perhaps your accident was the beginning of something big," Howard said. Howard gave Randall a taco and a glass of my milk and told Randall about falling off the roof, how the experience had sharpened his intuition and how this had helped him locate Helen's ashes at the dump.

I reminded him that Naomi had found the ashes.

"Whatever," he said, brushing my comment away with a flick of a wrist. He moved closer to Randall. "Listen to the still, small voice, Randall. It will tell you what to do."

"Mr. Coleman, the manager, tells me what to do. I help fix things. He has a list."

"No, no, no, Randall. Accident or not, in this life all of us are responsible for making our own lists, shaping our own destiny. Have you ever meditated, looked at the world through your third eye?"

Randall cocked his head. "It wasn't no accident," Randall said. "I meant to kill myself." He slipped his hand under his t-shirt and felt his stomach.

Randall was right. The bullet had ricocheted off the ear piece of his sunglasses, entered his temple at an angle, and traveled the underside of the skull before exiting just above his jaw bone on the other side. He had, in effect, given himself a lobotomy. I had heard the shot and found him sitting on the floor with the gun in his hand. There was hardly any blood. When he looked up at me, he said, "Maybe you should call an ambulance, Mr. Seltzer."

Bennie the Hindu poked his head in. "Busy?"

"Welcome to Grand Central," I said.

Bennie was looking for Naomi to tell her that the poker players at the Epic Café had decided it was inappropriate to invite her to their games. They found it offensive.

"It's hard to offend Naomi," I said.

"That is not the point I'm making," Bennie said. "They were offended by her."

Howard, apparently still taken with himself, blundered ahead. "I hear you're a betting man," he said.

"Now and then. Do you wish to propose a bet?"

"As a matter of fact I do. I'll bet you that Tobias's ice cubes will melt faster than your ice cubes."

Bennie's eyes narrowed. "I have never bet on ice melting. Are you tricking me? How much do you wish to bet?"

"No tricks. A dollar," Howard said.

"You are giving odds?"

"No odds. You choose the glasses. You fill them with ice cubes."

Bennie, after a moment's reflection, placed five cubes in each of two glasses. At the kitchen table, we held them in our right hands. Bennie concentrated so hard his eyebrows looked like two caterpillars crawling toward one another. Howard and Randall moved closer. No contest. In twelve minutes my cubes had melted. Bennie's were less than a third gone.

Bennie conceded. "You have the hands of a healer."

"And I have the hands of a dollar," Howard said. "Pay up."

Bennie gave his dollar to Howard. "How did he do that?"

While Howard gave Bennie a detailed explanation of my hyperthermia and how it related to Jewishness, it occurred to me that I was a sixty-eight-year-old man, a man with limited time left in his life, and I had just spent twelve minutes watching ice melt. The most interesting thing about this realization was how much fun I'd had.

Next morning I awoke feeling productive and focused. I had grown tired of questioning the turn my life had taken. It was time to accept my destiny and deal with the details of my new life. First, I called University Hospital to confirm Naomi's appointment and inquire about costs.

"And your name, sir?"

"Seltzer, Tobias Seltzer."

"And your relation to Naomi?"

"I'm the father," I said. It was a necessary lie. They wouldn't talk to me otherwise.

"And your insurance carrier?"

"Medicare," I said.

"I'm sorry, sir, Medicare does not cover pregnancy." Bottom line—the hospital required an advance deposit of five thousand dollars: three thousand for the doctor's prenatal exams, delivery, and two follow-up visits, plus two thousand for the hospital and whatever an anesthesiologist charged, maybe another twelve hundred.

I had exactly $5300 in savings. I swallowed hard and said, "No problem."

In my new mode of accepting my destiny, I put some numbers together, figuring a worst-case scenario: a couple of extra days in the hospital, a cesarean, an infection or two. The bill could come to fifteen thousand or more. On top of that were clothes and food and rent money once Naomi moved out and found her own place. This five thousand did not include an educational trust. The kid had to have an educational trust.

Figuring conservatively, I'd need a minimum of fifteen thousand in addition to the five thousand I had in savings. Ideally, I'd like fifty thousand more, but that was impossible. This dose of reality made the next decision easy. I had to call Naomi's father.

I found his number through information. The voice that answered carried the resonant, confident timbre of a man accustomed to getting his way.

"Mr. Kuiper?"

"Yes."

"You don't know me. My name is Tobias Seltzer. I'm calling from Tucson, Arizona. I'm a friend of Naomi." I waited.

The voice got lower, became almost a whisper. "What do you want?"

"As you know, Naomi is pregnant and about to have her baby. I've been taking care of her, giving her food and a place to sleep. She has no money, no place to go. I'm calling to discuss the possibility of you contributing something—money for food, clothing, rent, hospital expenses, an educational trust for the child, perhaps."

"Mr. Seltzer, I'm James Kuiper, Stuart's father. Stuart was involved in a severe accident a month ago, shortly after Naomi ran away. He passed away three days ago."

"Oh," I said. "I'm terribly sorry." I hesitated, took a breath and, having nothing to lose, went for the jugular. "Look, Mr. Kuiper, I know it's probably not a good time, but is there any chance he left something to Naomi in his will?"

"Mr. Seltzer, Stu asked me to make sure that Naomi gets nothing. And I will honor his wishes. He offered her every advantage, every opportunity to excel, and she did nothing but make his life miserable."

"She's a child."

"She is anti-social, pig-headed, mentally disturbed, self-centered, and evil. Please don't call here again." The line went dead.

I paced the floor and looked out the window. A skateboarder hit a crack and lunged forward down the sidewalk.

Out of curiosity I called the Pella police and learned that Stuart Kuiper had run head-on into a Dutch elm at a high rate of speed.

That evening I ordered pizza—extra cheese with anchovies and green olives, Naomi's favorite. We watched *Wheel of Fortune* while we ate. I couldn't stop thinking about Kuiper, wondering whether to tell Naomi or not, wondering if his death was accidental or a suicide.

"What is your father like?" I asked.

Naomi took a wedge of pizza to the sofa, sat cross-legged and took a huge bite. "Tall, thin, good-looking in that blond-haired, blue-eyed Dutch way. Gets a manicure once a week, goes to church twice a week, prays before every meal. Neat and tidy. Tries to keep things in order. He'd go nuts if my mother put the glasses in the dishwasher wrong. He insisted she place canned goods on the shelf in alphabetical order."

"You miss him?"

"There's a part of me that does. He has this arrogance, this total belief that God and all the forces in the universe are on his side, that he is one of the chosen few."

"Makes me think of the new Howard."

"You know what? If you hang around him enough, you start believing he *is* chosen. It's sort of comforting."

"Do you love him?"

"Maybe, in a way." She laughed. "I mean, someone beats the crap out of you, calls you a whore and kicks you out, what's not to love?" She drank a whole glass of milk and didn't bother wiping the white mustache from her lip.

"You want more pizza?"

"Sure."

"Milk?"

I poured the milk and placed the carton back on the table, fully intending to tell her that her father was dead, but the words wouldn't come. I had no idea how she'd react, and I was unwilling to deal with the uncertainty. I'd flunked the first test of living my destiny.

The nights had turned cool. I borrowed a blanket from Naomi's bed. It smelled faintly of seaweed and salt air. Before drifting off, I imagined myself an oyster tucked deep inside my shell lying on the dark floor of the ocean, being rocked and lifted by the rhythmic movement of the water, wrapped tightly around a single granule of sand, straining to turn it into a pearl.

 FOURTEEN

Naomi took three dance lessons in three evenings. After that she went two or three times a week. She came home more relaxed, almost playful, willing to demonstrate the new steps she'd learned. The first dance Caravelo taught her was the waltz. She said it made her feel graceful. She'd hold her mother's wedding dress to her body and practice her steps in the living room. She even smiled occasionally. She told me a joke Caravelo had told her. She told me what Caravelo wore, passed on any tidbit she'd learned about his life. I'd never seen her happier.

Then he canceled a few lessons. Her mood grew dark. She started wetting her bed again. She worried that Caravelo would hate her if he found out. And the more she worried, the more she wet her bed.

I tried to remain nonchalant, but the stench of uric acid combined with my obsessing over money robbed me of energy, made me edgy, kept me awake at night. I tried to pretend everything was all right, gave her little mini-lectures about all problems being manageable, but I couldn't fool Naomi. She had an uncanny ability to know when I was lying. She blamed herself for wetting the bed, vowed to stay awake all night, then threw a fit when she fell asleep and wet her bed yet again.

I opened every window in the apartment. It was in the low forties outside. "It's nice out," I said.

"Screw you."

"I thought we might enjoy some fresh air."

"You can't stand the stench of my piss."

I denied it, of course, but she was right. I hadn't told her about her father yet. That would only make things worse. Nor had I told Mayflower about locating Charles. Aside from running the risk of losing her, I couldn't decide if this knowledge would be good for her. Mayflower had created this part of her life mainly in her head. What if it turned out not to be what she expected? Was discovering your life wasn't what you thought it was a common malady? And, of course, I hadn't told Howard about Naomi being Helen's daughter. Suddenly, I had become the repository of secrets that, if revealed, would cause others to suffer.

Friendship, I was learning, was like riding a train. At first, I didn't understand that if I boarded one car, I had in fact boarded the whole train. Had I known this two months ago, I might have elected to take a cab. Now the train was well down the line, and I had no idea where it was taking me.

What I did know was that I couldn't take Naomi's anger and self-hatred any more. Something had to change, if not for her sanity, then at least for my own. I had to do something to stop her bed-wetting.

I spent three hours at the university library reading scientific articles on the psychodynamics of enuresis. Bed wetters tended to be overactive, passive-aggressive, talkative, insecure, extroverted, and deceptive. I found an article stating, in effect, that adults suffering from enuresis often needed extensive therapy, sometimes years, and, even then, the prognosis wasn't positive. The authors suggested that adult bed wetters were still children emotionally and, in effect, were avoiding the responsibilities of adulthood.

Later that day, I found a few scattered behavioral studies that countered the psychoanalytic interpretation and reported success using a mildly aversive Pavlovian conditioning technique that claimed to be effective in two to eight weeks. Critics of the technique claimed it treated only the symptoms, not the deeper neurosis. I reflected on this and decided I'd prefer living with a psychotic who didn't wet her bed to one who did. I made a few calls and found the equipment I needed at a nearby medical supply store.

Naomi stood erect, arms folded, as I took the parts from the box and displayed them on the bed: rubber mattress cover, absorbent pads, a tape measure, large pieces of graph paper, a urine-sensitive electric grid, two large batteries, lead wires, and two bells.

It felt good to deal with explicit procedures and clear instructions. Per the instructions to the "parent," although skeptical, I stayed as confident and upbeat as possible. "Guaranteed to cure you," I said.

"You're going to electrocute me," Naomi said.

"Not at all. The idea's simple. Your problem is that you don't wake up when your bladder's full. This gismo teaches you to wake up. When you pee, the first drops of urine close an electric circuit, this bell goes off, and you wake up. Nobody likes hearing a loud bell in the middle of the night, so after a while your full bladder becomes your signal to wake up to avoid setting off the bell. Nifty, huh?"

"It'll never work. I'm too messed up."

"Look at it this way. You have nothing to lose."

I placed the absorbent pad and grid under the bottom sheet and hooked up the bells, one next to Naomi's ear in her room, the other near my head on the sofa. I explained that we were to get up when the bells went off, measure the diameter of the urine circle, chart this information on a bar graph and remake her bed. I didn't tell her I was supposed to praise her like crazy if the second circle of urine was smaller than the first.

"It's like sleeping in an electric chair," Naomi said.

The first night I went to bed confident. At two a.m., the bells went off.

In the dead of night this was not the sound of two bells, but a ten-alarm fire. I was on my feet before I was awake, disoriented, not knowing where I was or where the noise was coming from. Then I thought the place was on fire and headed for the door. I stopped, went back to the kitchen, filled a glass with water—I have no idea why—and heard Naomi cussing. I remembered suddenly what the bells were about, but I couldn't remember how to turn them off.

Randall Pruitt was the first to bang on my door. Howard and May-flower showed up, then Bennie the Hindu, and the women from the third floor. Mass confusion. Randall opened a window. Howard opened my cupboard doors. Mayflower stood in the middle of the room with her eyes shut. Finally, I yanked the wires loose. The ringing stopped.

I peeked into Naomi's room.

"Get this off me." She was standing on her bed, tangled in wires—wires wrapped around her waist, wires around her neck. Her bell dangled from her hip. I helped untangle her. I didn't laugh, acknowledge complaints, or show any form of sympathy. I returned briefly to the living room where my neighbors huddled together, staring at me, waiting for answers.

"What's going on, Mr. Seltzer?" Randall whispered.

"Scientific experiment," I said. "Everything's fine. Go back to bed."

Apparently, sleepy people require less information than those fully awake. They shuffled out and returned to their apartments.

Naomi sat on the toilet, resting her elbow on the roll of toilet paper while I reassembled the equipment, measured the urine spot and recorded its diameter on graph paper. "Twenty-eight inches," I said. "Now let's change your bed."

"My heart is pounding," Naomi said.

"Go to bed." I switched off the light, said goodnight and returned to the sofa. I wanted this to work for Naomi's sake—for the sake of a better world, for her dignity, for my own sanity. Had I been at all religious, I would have prayed.

The next alarm sounded at six a.m. Things went more smoothly, and the spot was only twenty inches. "Twenty inches," I said with exaggerated pleasure. "Eight inches smaller. This is truly amazing. Fantastic. Good work, Naomi."

Naomi stared at me—disheveled, sneering—and crawled back in bed.

Three days later Naomi stood before the bathroom mirror primping for her doctor's appointment. She'd been up since six, getting ready. She'd wet her bed all three nights since I'd installed the conditioning equipment, but the circles were getting smaller. I sat on her bed, reading aloud from the handbook. "The first trip to the doctor marks many a young woman's first acquaintance with hospitals and the world of nurses and doctors. She might experience strangeness, loneliness and homesickness." Although tempted, I chose not to show her the picture on the facing page, a protrusion labeled "Extreme bulging of perineum showing patulous and everted anus."

Naomi stood before the mirror in her smock, her feet turned out, a scowl on her face, her hair bristling from static electricity.

"I'm past dumpy," she said. "I have marks all over my stomach and hips."

I closed the handbook. "What you're experiencing is normal. The book describes all of this."

In the car Naomi sat stiff-armed, hands pressed into the seat, complaining. She had to go to the bathroom. She couldn't breathe. Her stomach itched. She thought she was going to be sick.

"I've never had a pelvic exam before," she said. "I don't think they're legal in Pella. Do I have to undress?"

"Tell me more about Caravelo," I said.

Gradually, her mood changed. She told me how they sat around after her last dance lesson and listened to Greek music. "We talk sometimes," she said. "We really talk. He listens to me. I think he's going to ask me to marry him."

I almost cheered, but answered with measured restraint. "He's a good man."

"He doesn't know anything about pelvic exams, either. I asked him."

"He's an artist."

"This whole concept is weirding me out."

"This is not a concept. You are, in fact, pregnant. There's a real human person living in your womb."

Naomi gnawed at the corner of a fingernail.

I tried to keep the mood upbeat. "The Hindus believe we're born over and over again. Each time around, who we are depends on what kind of life we led before. I've heard you can see that in babies' expressions when they're first born, before they forget who they were. Some have old soft souls. They look around with understanding and wisdom and accept the fact that they have another round to go. A few have new crispy souls. They may have been a hyena or an armadillo in their past life. They're confused. They don't understand what hands and feet are. Most are somewhere in between."

"You missed the turn."

I drove around the block and pulled into the hospital parking lot. "I've been looking into babies' eyes," I said. "Crispy-souled ones have vacant expressions. They arch their backs and push away. Soft-souled ones fold into you, cuddle and look you in the eye as if to say, 'How's it going, old man? Great life, isn't it?'"

"You're making this up."

"Of course," I said, remembering something Mayflower had told me. "Reality is chaotic and senseless. We select. We interpret. We imagine. This is how we make sense of our lives. This is how we survive." I pulled on the brake and turned off the key. The engine ran on for a minute, then chugged to a stop.

The hospital didn't have the ether-disinfectant-blood smell I remembered. Here, the floors were polished. Chrome and glass everywhere. The elevator, one as large as my living room, was filled with sick people mingling with the well. Several were coughing. I'd done fine to this point. Now, the backs of my knees were sweating. When the elevator started, it was only Naomi's glare that kept me from sinking to the floor.

Maternity was on the fifth floor. We turned left, walked down the hall, and peered into a locked waiting room occupied by an old man, a boy wearing a football helmet, and an attractive woman who was sucking her thumb and rocking back and forth. It was the psychiatry ward.

"I'll leave you here," I said, "pick you up in a few years."

"Don't mess with me," Naomi said.

We walked to the opposite end of the floor. A pregnant woman—a refrigerator with legs—came toward us. She beamed and said hello.

Naomi ignored her.

I forced a smile.

"About this doctor what's-his-name," Naomi said. "How old is he?"

"Snyder, Leslie Snyder, highly regarded. Don't worry." I produced a paper with questions I'd prepared—hospital mortality rates, the number of deliveries Snyder had done, his personal mortality rate, his cesarean and breech presentation rate, his preferred treatment for postpartum hemorrhage and lacerations of the perineum.

Our plan was this: if Snyder turned out to be okay, I would pull my right ear lobe. If Snyder was a jerk, I'd cross my left leg over my right, and we'd find a way to make a quick exit.

"By the way," I said. "No big deal, but they think I'm the father of the baby. I had to tell them that so they'd talk to me."

"Jesus Christ," Naomi said.

The receptionist, a round, short person with the kind of wide eyes I associated with new contact lenses, told us the doctor would be late: "A difficult delivery."

"What's the particular difficulty?" I asked.

The receptionist shrugged. "I have no idea."

"Are you familiar with the *Handbook of Obstetrics* by Zabriske and Eastman?" I asked.

"I'm just a temp," she said. "I'm taking information management at the community college."

"Keep up the good work," I said, and shook her hand.

The girl gave Naomi a stack of forms to fill out—method of payment, medical history, diet, the advisability of having a living will—and sent us to accounting.

I made out a check for five thousand, figuring I'd stop payment if Snyder didn't pan out.

Naomi wrote "adopted" under history of father and mother. I told her Helen had died from ovarian cancer, and she wrote "cancer" on the form. "What's enuresis," she asked.

"Bed-wetting."

"Shit," she said, and checked the box.

We waited in a room just large enough for three chairs and an examining table equipped with stirrups. One look at that thing, and I gave silent thanks I wasn't a woman. A woman in a laboratory jacket entered, a tall beauty with shiny black, shoulder-length hair. She wore no lipstick or eye makeup.

"Miss Kuiper? I'm Dr. Snyder."

"I expected a man," I said.

Naomi said something between her teeth.

Dr. Snyder glanced at Naomi's forms.

"How'd it go?" I asked.

"What?"

"The difficult delivery."

"And you are?"

"Seltzer, Tobias Seltzer."

Naomi spit out a piece of fingernail.

Dr. Snyder checked the file. "The father?"

"Not exactly," I said. "I got confused on the phone."

"The father's name is Raül," Naomi said. "He's a black dude I met in Des Moines. He worked for a carnival and had some really good dope. That's all I know about him or want to know."

"The complicated delivery," I reminded her. "How'd it go? Any hemorrhaging or lacerations?"

Dr. Snyder bit the side of her lower lip. "That's confidential," she said.

I tried again. "I noticed the gift shop only sells magazines. No books."

"I didn't know that," the doctor said, still looking at Naomi's health form.

"Do you read much? I mean, other than medical books?"

She put her pen down and folded her hands. "Yes."

"I don't mean to pry, but what was the last book you read?"

She paused for a moment as if deciding whether or not she wanted to call security or answer my question.

"Just curious," I said.

"*Zorba the Greek*," she said. "Kazantzakis. I re-read it last week."

I felt like I'd met someone who knew my second cousin. "You read Zorba?"

"Yes. Why?"

"It's one of my favorite books. Kazantzakis' exploration of the conflict between spiritual and worldly desires is—"

"I don't see that there is a difference," the doctor said.

"Still, if you—wouldn't you agree one has to sacrifice to attain the higher spiritual aspects of—"

"No."

"Maybe I should leave the two of you alone," Naomi said.

I caught Naomi's eye and tugged my right ear, pleased with myself to have discovered a better way to judge the worth of a doctor.

The waiting area was filled with pregnant women. It was an ovarian, milky world, a world alive with laughter and talk, an abundant world based on the certainty that life is indestructible, a world resting in a darker, almost palpable, softness. The women here weren't merely sitting, they had settled in. They talked to one another freely about things that, on the surface, hardly seemed worth talking about—what they had for breakfast, names they were considering for their children, various oils for stretch marks. Here, ambition had been replaced by collaboration, a kind of team spirit, as if all these women were pooling their talents to prepare a pot of soup.

Some had men with them: uncomfortable men, over-attentive men, sweating men. One man's eyes darted about as if he were planning his escape; another stared at a copy of *Off Road Biker*; a third just smiled.

I felt lacking, fractured, self-conscious, too old, too slow, out of my realm. I felt much like I'd felt at the dump. I sorted through a stack of magazines and selected one called *Home Beautiful*. On my way back to my seat, I spotted a rack of brochures about parenting and delivery classes. I took one of each, thinking I might show them to Naomi.

I flipped open my magazine and stared at a full-page ad for Pella Windows. I hadn't thought of Naomi's father for a while. I wondered what might have happened to Naomi if her mother hadn't run away. I wondered if her father ever regretted anything, even for a second. I couldn't put it off any longer. I had to tell Naomi about him. But I needed to find the right moment. If all went well with the doctor, I would tell her on the way home. It made sense to tell her on the way home—one life ends, another begins, that sort of thing.

Naomi appeared carrying a plastic bag with a picture of a baby on it. "Let's get out of here," she said.

"What did the doctor tell you?" I asked as we walked, trying to keep up with her.

"She gave me all this stuff on classes, recommended a diet, some vitamins, free diapers, formula, crap like that."

"Did she examine you?"

"She took my pulse and blood pressure, listened to my heart and looked up my works with this metal thing. I'm never doing that again. I'm supposed to watch my blood pressure. I'm thirty weeks pregnant. The baby is due the first part of December." She stood before a plate glass window and looked at her reflection. She turned sideways and mumbled, "First part of De-fucking-cember. Then I'll be free." In the elevator she said, "I'll take the vitamins, but I'm not taking classes."

In the car, Naomi rubbed her stomach in slow circular motions as if she were polishing a large marble. She folded her arms and stared down. "Stop it," she said. "It kicked me. It's been kicking a lot lately." She looked at her stomach again and pointed. "There. See it?"

A spot on her stomach the size of a small fist moved, stayed extended for a second, then receded.

"Yes."

"That's the biggest one yet."

I felt faint. I had to stop driving. I turned into the parking lot at the Village Inn.

"What are you doing?"

"They have good pie here."

"I'm not hungry."

"It's called quickening," I said. "Nothing to worry about. I read about it in the handbook. Biblical. People believed the first movement marked the exact second the baby came alive."

"It's creepy. Put your hand here."

My hand shook as I placed it against the side of her abdomen. I was relieved to feel nothing. "It's nothing," I said. "Perfectly normal. All babies do it." My palms were sweating. "Quickening usually starts at the end of the fifth month, a tremulous fluttering—"

"Will you shut up?"

Thirty seconds passed, a minute. Then, without warning, a small animal was tunneling under my hand. I pulled away, gripped the steering wheel and focused on my breathing. A claw clutched at my throat. Half of me had stepped through Alice's looking glass. The half left behind was about to pass out.

"Are you all right?" Naomi asked. "You're white."

"I'm fine," I said.

"What's going on?"

"Nothing."

"You're lying."

I fought to hold back tears. "Zorba," I said. "I love Zorba."

"What?"

"There's a passage in the book when the narrator is returning home from a Christmas party, walking along the water's edge. It's so beautiful—the stars above, the land and sea on either side—and suddenly he realizes that life had accomplished its final miracle. It had become a fairy tale. That's the way I feel now. I feel like I'm living in a fairy tale."

There was a long silence, then I heard myself say, "Will you marry me?"

"Yuck," Naomi said. "Are you out of your mind?"

Suddenly, I felt stupid and helpless.

That evening, still embarrassed by my misplaced emotionality, I threw myself into fixing meat loaf, baked potatoes, and salad. I forced myself to concentrate on preparing the meal, refusing to think about babies or my stupid proposal.

Naomi sat on the sofa, staring at her stomach.

"You are in for a treat," I said. "My meat loaf got me nominated for a Nobel Prize."

"We should invite Mayflower," she said.

I stopped dicing a tomato. "Really. I thought you were never going to speak to her again."

"I miss her," Naomi said.

And so the rift between Naomi and Mayflower dissolved as quickly as it came. I invited Mayflower to join us, and she was at the top of her game. She praised my meat loaf and looked over every item in Naomi's maternity bag. I told her about the fellow with the smile frozen on his face, and she told a funny story about a psychiatrist friend of hers who was losing clients because he had a kind of smirk permanently etched on his face. He had to have plastic surgery in order to save his business. I laughed. Even Naomi cracked a smile. I remembered how uncomfortable I'd felt practicing my smile in front of the mirror. Now I was laughing out loud.

After dinner, the three of us went to Mayflower's apartment. There were a few boxes packed and stacked in the corner. I was shocked when Naomi asked Mayflower if she needed any help packing. Mayflower accepted her offer and told Naomi to take anything she liked.

Naomi took an orange scarf. She held it to her face, then changed her mind and gave it back. I could read her mind. She wasn't ready to take something that would remind her of Mayflower forever.

I stacked boxes and listened to the women talk about glassware, the color of scarves, a teaspoon, salt and pepper shakers, dresses, hats. Women, I said to myself.

That night, at 3:20 a.m., a wonderful thing happened, maybe the best sound I had ever heard. It was the sound of my toilet flushing. Naomi had awakened and, on her own, gone to the bathroom. This was a major *mitzvot*.

 FIFTEEN

The day I was to give my guest lecture at the university I asked Mayflower to go with me. "Not to hold my hand," I told her. Then I confessed. "Yes, to hold my hand."

We took the trolley that runs from Fourth Avenue to the university and back. I was too nervous to walk. I wore my seersucker suit, Howard's red tie, and oxfords. I carried my briefcase loaded down with books I'd randomly pulled from my shelves. I was terrified. I had no spit. I needed to hiccup, but kept remembering Naomi's chilling command to *Stop*. I hummed. I fidgeted. I had an irrational urge to apologize to every stranger I met on the street.

Mayflower patted my knee.

"This is a mistake," I said. "I should never have agreed to—"

"But you look so collegiate, dear, so—qualified and wise." She told me of an actor she once knew who fainted an hour before every performance. Once, he didn't faint, and it was the worst performance of his career.

"Yeah, but he knew his lines," I said. "I don't know even the name of the play."

The rocking motion of the trolley was giving me vertigo. The clacking wheels sent spikes through my gut. I thought I saw the one-eared greaser walking east on University Avenue. I looked again. It *was* him, striding along, throwing his poison at the world. I touched my ear. An ear for an ear. I felt none of the bravado I had felt that night.

"Remember to blink, dear," Mayflower said as the trolley arrived at the main gate.

It was a few minutes before eight. Students everywhere. I would have preferred a pit of poisonous snakes. Students were arriving by bus, car, skateboard, roller blades, wheelchairs, motorcycles, motorized scooters, and bicycles. They wore cutoffs, miniskirts, overalls, and t-shirts embla-zoned with the logos of companies owned by the world's two largest defense contractors. They carried portfolios, books, cups of coffee, puppies, guitars, bicycle tires, cell phones, pieces of cold pizza, laptops, and backpacks. Against this backdrop of ten thousand maniacs, my peashooter of a lecture seemed small, stupid, and inconsequential.

"It's so confusing," I said.

Mayflower stopped. "Take a breath and imagine everything is happening according to a plan, dear, that it's all a wonderful game being played by exacting rules, that every move is being made to fulfill some larger purpose."

"I don't believe in larger purposes. I'm not even sure I believe in small ones."

"Me either. It's something I used to do to relax myself when I was scared."

I took a deep breath and looked around. I imagined purpose and intention in everything—in every student made feeble-minded and overactive by hormones, in every harried teacher, in those clouds above us, in that grasshopper on the sidewalk. "It does make a difference," I said. "Not as scary."

"Excellent," she said. "Welcome to the world of purpose and meaning. A nice place to visit but, of course, we'd never want to live here."

"Still—"

"What, dear?"

"They all look alike. I can hardly tell the boys from the girls."

"More efficient that way. Old people look the same to them."

She walked with her arm looped through mine, a little too intimate for a college professor, I thought. More like my mother was taking me to my first day of school. I had a nagging concern that, because of her Alzheimer's or her total lack of inhibition, Mayflower might do something to embarrass me.

I had prepared a lecture examining the contemporary lessons about human nature to be gleaned from the Civil War. Taking my position from James Hillman's *A Terrible Love of War*, I would argue that war—all war—is fundamentally senseless and terrible, but irresistibly seductive, sublime, and essentially religious. While we detest war, we also harbor an irrational and primal love of it and, by inference, a love-hate relationship with evil. Historically, war has seldom been a necessity. It has been instinctual, primitive, and, to a large extent, driven by erotic and self-destructive impulses. The answer, I would conclude, is that we need a new kind of person, a new kind of awareness, a way of channeling our violent impulses in less destructive ways. If the students happened to infer that I, myself, was an example of that new awareness, so be it. I wouldn't mention, of course, the sacred and erotic pleasure I derived from biting off a man's ear. I opened my briefcase and took out my handwritten notes—thirty pages, enough for ten lectures. My hands were clammy.

"Give me a preview," Mayflower said.

"I want to change their minds about war," I told Mayflower, "at least make them think there's more to it than politicians would have us believe."

"Perhaps you can change their hearts, too," Mayflower said. "You underestimate your ability to change other people's hearts."

At that moment I believed Naomi was right, that we all make each other up to meet our own needs. I was making myself up, hoping the students would see my own fake image of myself and believe in it. Mayflower had made me up because she had needed a heart person, a person who felt things deeply. I was not a heart person. I was an idea person. The sad fact was that ideas of charismatic leaders like Hitler and Robert E. Lee could change hearts in terribly destructive ways.

Two women in scant silky shorts had just finished their morning jog around the quad. One said, "Good morning, Professor."

"I'm sorry, I—"

Mayflower poked me with her elbow. "Say good morning, dear."

"Good morning, ladies."

We entered the Humanities Building where Cameron Wilson taught his class. It smelled like a college. I loved that smell, a combination of chalk and floor wax, pencil lead, perfumes and colognes lingering from yesterday, and the metallic scent of overworked copy machines. We walked to the main lecture hall and found a sign on the door: AMERICAN HISTORY 201. CANCELED TODAY. DR. WILSON IS ILL. READ CHAPTER ON GETTYSBURG.

"Oh, dear," Mayflower said.

"He changed his mind," I said.

"He forgot," Mayflower said. "I should have called him."

I was crushed. "It's not that important," I said. "Let's go."

"Wait," Mayflower said. "Do you know anything about Gettysburg?"

"A little," I said.

"Oh, good," she said. "Then here's what we'll do." She tore the note from the door and dropped it in a wastebasket. "All set," she said.

"I can't just hijack a class."

"Of course, you can. This is your moment, something you've dreamed of doing all your life."

"You'll come with me?"

She looked perplexed. "I'm sorry, dear. I have a previous engagement."

"You do?" I said, appalled.

"Don't turn yourself into a hapless victim, dear. Of course, I'm coming. I wouldn't miss it."

Mayflower sat in the back row. I stood before the empty seats, one hand on the lectern, looking out over an enormous blackness as two, maybe three hundred students filed in. Had my knees not been shaking so much, I would have walked out. I closed my eyes for a moment and used Mayflower's technique. I was here for a purpose. Everything had meaning. Everything that was happening was happening according to certain precise rules. When I opened my eyes the room was filled with students. I imagined them to be trained seals. Suddenly, they were quiet.

"My name is Tobias Seltzer," I said.

"Can't hear you," someone shouted from the back.

I cleared my throat. "I'm Tobias Seltzer. Dr. Wilson is ill today. I'll be lecturing on Gettysburg. He asked me to assign the chapter on Gettysburg in your text."

After a collective rolling of eyes, the students, as if on cue, took out their notebooks and scooted down in their seats.

A frail girl with way too much eyeliner raised her hand. "We gonna be tested on this?"

"Yes," I said.

"Which? The lecture or the book?"

"Both."

"Equally? I mean, fifty-fifty?"

"I can't tell you that."

"Ah, man," the girl said. She tugged at her miniskirt and clicked her ballpoint pen.

I smiled and mentally tossed her a fish.

I had no idea where to begin, then remembered that the Battle of Gettysburg started with the accidental meeting of the two armies—the Confederates beaten down and virtually shoeless—in a small town in Pennsylvania. "Shoes," I said. "The desperate need for shoes and thousands upon thousands die." I told them the story of how the first skirmish resulted from a rumor about thousands of pairs of shoes being stored in a building in the city. I talked about Lee's attack on the left, then his arrogant and suicidal decision to charge the center of the Federalists' line. I told them of Lincoln's insistence that Meade wipe the Confederate boys out at all costs, and how, finally, on the third day, fifteen thousand Confederate troops—still barefoot and facing certain death—marched blindly across an open field and died, mainly from shots in the face.

I described the unimaginable stench of rotting flesh in the days following the battle, the ungodly heat, the hisses and groans and pops of bloated bodies as they rotted, the screams as thousands of untrained medics performed amputations without anesthetics. I told how Lincoln's two-hundred-sixty-six-word address that spring—the spoken text being slightly shorter than the written one—had turned this human travesty into a patriotic symbol, a source of national pride. I ended by quoting, with the help of my notes, Lincoln's address in full and pointed out how Lincoln, surrounded by the graves of thousands upon thousands of dead young men, had avoided talking about the blundering stupidity of the battle. I couldn't resist pointing out similar, perhaps less eloquent but apparently successful, efforts by other presidents to sell their own wars.

I talked about the history of wars, how over the centuries there is a major one every eighteen years or so, just in time for heads of state to harvest the next crop of young men and women warriors. I told them how, originally, wars were harmless initiation rituals in which young men, having reached puberty, were sent off to ceremonially steal a cow from a neighboring tribe and how, upon their return, nubile young women would welcome the conquering warriors and reward them with sexual favors. I pointed out the similarity between these ritualistic wars and today's athletes and cheerleaders.

I reminded them of a scene from the movie *Patton*, when the General, surrounded by devastation and death, holds a dying officer in his arms, kisses him and says: "I love it. God help me, I do love it so. I love it more than life." I wondered aloud if there was something in the human psyche that loved war—that, in fact, needed it. I talked about how modern technology had dehumanized warfare, turned mass killing into something resembling a video game, how such a powerful and unmanageable arsenal of weapons controlled by self-righteous arrogance, greed, and blind ambition, combined with naïve patriotism and the belief that God was on one's side, could mark an end of civilization.

I concluded by going back to the Battle of Gettysburg, describing the crush of Union and Confederate families as they slogged through the mud and sorted through the carnage to find the mutilated bodies of their loved ones. Then I paused a beat and said: "Historically speaking, I think this is what we humans do too much of. We spend too much time digging through the wreckage of war, trying to find the ones we love."

The room was silent for a few seconds. I'd either stunned them or bored them into a stupor. I couldn't tell which. Most appeared to be awake—some not fully awake, but awake.

The girl who asked the question about testing raised her hand again.

"Yes," I said.

"Do you really believe that all cheerleaders are sluts?"

"Of course not," I said. "I was merely—"

A boy behind her said, "My roommate is a football player, and he's a Mormon."

"And what about terrorists?" a girl at the back of the class said. "I don't like war, but what are we supposed to do, let them kill us?"

I looked up at Mayflower. She smiled and gave a little wave.

"I don't have the answer to terrorists," I said, "but I know we can't let them turn us into the same monsters they are. I know it will take more than a John Wayne swagger to deal with them. We must find ways to find the root causes of why we can't stop killing one another. We must—" I paused, trying to think of how to phrase what I wanted to say. Just then, the bell rang. I tried to finish my thought as they left the room. "I know that when you show even the slightest concern for another human being, when you so much as acknowledge their humanness, you have grasped a golden string that will pull you into a morass of pain and, if you're lucky, happiness and peace." No one heard that except Mayflower.

We walked home, hardly speaking, Mayflower's arm again looped in mine. She said she had no idea I knew so much, or that I was so eloquent and passionate.

"I'll never do that again," I said. "I don't want to be a teacher, leastwise not to students."

"I know, dear. They're quite young, the opening of their funnels a bit small."

Sunlight played on the leaves of the olive trees. On the lawn of a fraternity house across the street, two boys with baseball gloves tossed a ball. We stopped to watch, admiring their agility, the speed of the ball, the popping sound when it hit their gloves.

Mayflower squeezed my arm and said, "I still can't believe it. You were marvelous, dear."

That evening when I told Naomi that her father was dead, she hardly reacted. She went to the refrigerator and drank orange juice from the container. "How'd you find out?"

"I called your house to ask for money."

"That was dumb."

"You needed help. Your father had money."

She remained motionless for a few seconds, then went into the bathroom and closed the door. She flushed the toilet.

After fifteen minutes, I tried to coax her out.

"Leave me alone," she said, her voice flat, emotionless.

I knocked on Mayflower's door, explained what had happened and asked for her help.

Mayflower talked to Naomi, and in a few minutes she came out of the bathroom, her face a blank. She refused to look at me.

"Maybe you should leave us alone, dear."

I waited in the lobby for Mayflower to call me.

I must have dozed off. A half-hour later it was dark, and Mayflower was still with Naomi. I'd screwed up. This was not just a dead father, as if that weren't bad enough. This was a radical shift in the delicate balance of Naomi's world. I should have been less direct, more sensitive. For all I knew, Naomi was already packing her bags.

I made my way to the game room and turned on the TV, but there was no picture. I needed something to take my mind off what was happening upstairs. I tried the exercise bike. The seat was too high. I lowered it, climbed on and began to pedal, tentatively at first, then with greater force. The television came on.

I stopped pedaling, and the screen went black. I started again, and the picture came back. Someone had wired the bicycle and TV together. There was no picture unless someone was peddling the bike. Ingenious, I thought, a great way to encourage old people to exercise. I pedaled, stopped, and pedaled again. The picture faded and reappeared. I pedaled faster, then even faster. Fascinating. I couldn't stop pedaling. There was a kind of exhilaration in oxygen deprivation, in my pounding temples.

I stood and pedaled. I pedaled faster, trying to sharpen the picture, make the sound more resonant. My legs grew numb. Drops of sweat spattered the floor. I didn't have the strength to go on, but I couldn't stop. I was afraid I was going to die. Maybe I wanted to die, to see the little light in the middle of the screen shrinking, the final poof, then darkness.

"What on earth are you doing, dear?"

I kept pedaling, eyes on the TV, pain stabbing my sides. "Look," I said, gasping.

"At what, dear?"

"The television. Watch." I stopped.

"It went off."

I pedaled. "Now look."

"It's on again."

"It's me. I'm doing it. Look. No, at me." I stopped. The TV went off. I started. The TV went on. "I'm controlling it."

"That's really quite remarkable. Think of what must be happening to all the other sets in the neighborhood. People everywhere must be wondering what's going on. Little do they know, it's Tobias riding his magic bicycle."

I dismounted and wiped my forehead. "It's not magic," I said. "Someone's wired them together."

Mayflower pursed her lips and looked from the bicycle to the TV and back again. "How Rube Goldbergian." She smiled a little too sweetly.

"You already knew, didn't you?"

"I'd heard something, but I hadn't seen it work. May I try it?"

"Be my guest."

Mayflower mounted the bike and began pedaling. Suddenly, she was a young lady on a Sunday ride. I thought of a black and white photo I'd seen—a bicycle on a country road, a loaf of bread and bottle of wine in the basket. The TV came on. Colors washed across her face. "There's the picture. What fun. When I was a child, I could never stay on a real bike." She pedaled at a medium pace, back straight, eyes forward. "And what a blessing this will be for Randall Pruitt. It will give him an endless task to do. He's so much happier when he's busy. You are doing such a good thing, reading to him like you do. You are such a good teacher. You should teach him to read."

I started to tell her I wasn't interested in teaching a retarded person to read. Then I realized she was concerned about me. She wanted to give me some sort of teaching victory. "I'll give it a shot," I said.

I watched her pedal, her knees rising and falling under her nightgown, her focus on the screen, her slight smile. How long could she go on like this without telling me about Naomi? Had she ridden off into an Alzheimer's fog? Had she forgotten?

"How is she?" I asked.

"Who, dear?"

"Naomi."

"We talked. She's a little despondent and confused, but she'll be fine."
She stopped pedaling and extended her hand. I helped her down. "Whew,"
she said. "She told me about her adopted mother. She lives in Des Moines
with another woman."

"I know."

"She also told me about Howard and Helen."

"She told you—everything?"

"Yes."

"Do you think we should tell Howard? Get it out in the open?"

"Absolutely not. He's doing quite well as it is. He's drawing and painting. He has a girlfriend. Why spoil it?"

"You sure Naomi is all right?"

"I left her sleeping and came down to find you. And there you were,
so cute, so determined, pedaling away like a man on a mission." She
paused. "I'm afraid I forgot my point, dear."

"Naomi, her father."

"Yes. She both loved and hated him. I believe he didn't care for her,
that he was ashamed of her. My father felt that way about me. She's disappointed but not heartbroken—not yet, anyway."

"Her father left her nothing."

"She wondered about that. I told her she might want to call the family
lawyer and leave her name and address."

"We need to do some planning. Where will she live? How will she
earn a living? What colleges—"

"Stop, dear. Not tonight." She looped her arm through mine. "Young
people are resilient. The miracle is so many actually survive. Get what
sleep you can. Tomorrow morning, crawl back on your white horse and
take us to Camelot."

Naomi did call her father's lawyer in Pella. I didn't try to stop her.
Even a few dollars would help. Their conversation was brief. The lawyer
said her father had made no provisions in his will for either her or her
children. In fact, he'd specifically requested that Naomi and any of her
offspring be excluded. All his money was to go to the First Reformed
Church.

Naomi hung up and got ready to go to a dance lesson with Caravelo.
She stood before the mirror, held a strand of hair over her head and let it
drop. She didn't speak.

"I'm sorry," I said.

"My hair won't go straight," she said. "The ends on both sides curl in the same direction. I look like I'm tilted sideways."

"Wet it," I said.

"In Iowa my hair had a curl in it." She pulled the sides of her upper lip up and moved closer to the mirror. "My gums are getting darker. Does being pregnant cause your gums to darken?"

"I'll look it up in the handbook."

"My face is puffy. There's these little veins under the skin. What does your book say about little veins?"

"Try some lotion. Maybe a little olive oil."

"How do I look?"

She looked like the Helen I'd seen in the picture before she left for Iowa—tired, melancholy, swollen, disoriented. "You look like Helen," I said.

She turned her head slightly sideways and stared at me from the corners of her eyes. "I hate the way I look."

"Hate? Isn't that a little strong? Don't you ever crave something normal?"

She turned to the mirror and showed her teeth. "I wish I had a better smile. I hate my smile. I'm never going to smile again."

That afternoon, after her dance lesson, Naomi sat for an hour dialing and redialing Brendan's number. Finally, a former roommate of Brendan's answered and told her that Brendan had moved and left no forwarding address.

After dinner, Mayflower and I watched TV. We heard a dull thud coming from the bathroom. I forced opened the bathroom door. Naomi was on her hands and knees, butting her bloody head against the wall. She looked up at us. Her eyes were dead.

I dropped to my knees and restrained her. "Stop it. No more."

Mayflower joined us. We held Naomi between us. After a long time, Naomi's body began to soften. She rested her head on Mayflower's shoulder. Mayflower held her and smoothed her hair.

Later, Mayflower sat on the edge of Naomi's bed, her hand to her cheek. "You must never do that again, dear," she said. "You're going to be fine. Close your eyes now. We'll stay with you until you fall asleep."

Next morning, Halloween day, Naomi acted as if nothing had happened. She and Mayflower read a fashion magazine together and pointed out things they particularly liked and disliked. They lingered over an article on makeovers.

"I want a makeover," Naomi said.

"You can't afford it," I said.

Naomi insisted, said she could spend her money any way she wanted to. After lunch Mayflower and I walked her to a hair and nail place three blocks north on Fourth Avenue.

Naomi had brought the magazine. "I want to look like this," she said to a woman in black leather pants and painted face.

The woman cut Naomi's split ends, glued false fingernails to her stubs, used foundations, rouges, mascara, eyeliners, and two colors of lipstick. I tried reading an article from a magazine for women called "How to Make Your Wedding Night Memorable."

"Maybe this will improve her spirits," Mayflower whispered.

"I think she's doing it for Caravelo," I said.

"It's not without precedent for women to paint themselves for men."

"Paint covers character," I said. "This woman in leather pants thinks character is something we are on Halloween. She uses words like *sassy* and *perky.*"

The beautician insisted Naomi try a pair of sassy earrings. She stood back and took a long drag on her cigarette. "Edgy," she said.

I said nothing.

Mayflower held a hand to her cheek and smiled. "Different."

Naomi asked me what I thought.

"I went to a funeral once," I said. "My father's third cousin, Hiram Bloch, had fallen onto his head off a six-story building and the mortician had to give him a plaster of Paris head, the whole cranium. I'm sorry to say you look like my cousin Hiram at his funeral."

"It doesn't matter what we think, dear. Do *you* like it?"

Naomi looked in the mirror, turned this way and that, then said, "I think I look like a country singer."

When we got home, Naomi said, "I give up." She scrubbed her face with soap and hot water, then went into her bedroom and sulked.

I went with Mayflower to her apartment and waited there while she dressed for bed. I tucked her in and gently massaged the bones on the back of her hand with my thumb. It was one of those moments when nothing else mattered except her hand and my thumb.

"What are you thinking, dear?"

I stood, then sat down again. I squeezed her hand, cleared my throat and said, "I was reading this magazine at the beautician's and had an idea. If we, you and I, were to marry, I would become your legal guardian."

Mayflower squinted. "What exactly—"

"They'd have to get my permission to take you away."

Mayflower smiled and shook her head. "That's above and beyond, dear."

"No, it isn't. Think about it. Even if we get a few extra days, it would be worth it."

Her eyes welled. "Is this a proposal?"

"No. An arrangement. A way of beating the—" I stopped. "Yes, it's a proposal."

She looked at me for a long time. "Then I say yes to every minute we can squeeze in."

"Really?"

"How odd," she said.

"I know," I said.

 SIXTEEN

I was going to tell Naomi about my marriage plans over breakfast, but she had gone out by the time I woke up. She returned, excited and happy, as full of energy as I'd ever seen her. She sat on the sofa with her mother's wedding dress draped over her lap. I decided not to tell her. I didn't want to risk spoiling her mood.

"My adopted mother married when she was my age," Naomi said. She stood and held the wedding dress to her. "Looks like crap, huh?"

"I don't think those wrinkles will ever come out," I said. "I know the stains won't."

"Caravelo wants to talk to you. He's coming up in a few minutes."

"He is a fine man."

She folded the dress and put it away. "He likes me. He didn't for a while. Now he likes me again," she said.

"He told you this?"

"Not exactly, but I know. He's happy."

"Maybe you shouldn't count your chickens."

Naomi dropped to one knee. She held my hand and did a poor imitation of Caravelo. "Oh, my beautiful *señorina,* my perfect flower, my—help me."

"Swollen grape?"

"—my swollen grape, tell me you will marry me." She waited. "Answer me."

"I'll marry you," I said.

She rushed to the window, looked out. "He's coming." She smiled; her eyes danced.

I stayed in the bedroom while they talked in the living room. In a few minutes Naomi stuck her head in. "He wants to talk to you." She winked and gave a little wave of her hand. "I'll go to the roof for some fresh air."

Caravelo and I sat at the kitchen table. One look at his face and I knew something was wrong. He looked almost old. "My friend," he said. "I need to speak with you."

"So speak."

"Naomi has made a friend with me." He held up his hand and made a fist. "She is very bitter person, very angry, but I like her. We talk. We dance. I listen to her stories. I try to cheer her up, tell her joke."

"But—"

"She clings to me, refuses to let Caravelo out of her sight. Even when I am giving lessons, she is pawing at me like a cat. When I don't pay attention to her, she flirts, tries to seduce me. When I do talk, she mistakes it for love, insists she is in love with me. She is very confused. Caravelo wants to help, but—"

"You also want to be left alone."

"She tells me I feel things I do not feel. Now she believes I have intentions to stay with her after she places her baby for adoption. This is a sad thing. I don't want to make Naomi more sad, but I…I wonder sometimes if she will try to hurt herself—or others."

"You mean you?"

"Yes, but—"

"Don't tell her just yet," I said. "Wait until she has her baby. A matter of a few weeks."

Caravelo looked away. His expression changed. He bit his lower lip, then said, "I cannot wait, my friend. Caravelo is in love."

"Ah," I said. "Someone I know?"

"Katherine Peterson. Just this evening I ask her to be my wife. I am on fire; a volcano is erupting in me. She insists we not have sex until we marry."

"I thought she and Howard Gardener were—"

"They are only friends. She lets Howard help her. He needs to stay busy. You must tell Naomi. She likes you, trusts you."

"Are you afraid to tell her?"

"It's possible she will have—how do you say?—a crackup."

He was right. Better she cracked up in front of me than Caravelo. "Go home. Prepare for your wedding. I'll tell her," I said.

A few minutes after Caravelo left, Naomi returned, deflated, blood drained from her face. She sat on the sofa, hands folded tightly, staring at them. "I listened at the door. I heard. That lying son-of-a-bitch."

I had to move slowly, one step at a time. I sat on the end of the sofa and turned to face her. "Okay, here are the facts," I said, not sure where I was going. "We are friends. Is this correct?"

Naomi did not look up. "You're boring."

"Still, I rub your feet. I buy food and cook for you. I think of your baby. You want a good home for it, don't you? You want—"

She glared at the wall. "I don't care about a good home. I had a good home. It didn't do anything for me. I just want this—thing—out of me." She shuddered. "And I want me out of this place." She unfolded her hands, wrapped her fingers around her thumbs, rested them on her knees. She rocked back and forth for a full minute, then leaned back on the sofa, smiling sweetly, and said, "Remember that time on the way home from the hospital when you asked me to marry you?"

"That wasn't—"

"Okay, I'll marry you."

I swallowed back the panic. How could I say no? I couldn't reject her at a time like this. There must be a way out. I had to keep calm. Think. "There are many options," I said. "We can consider them one at a time. No need to—"

She held her hands above her head and studied her fingers as she moved them, snake-like, through the air. "You can do whatever you want with the baby—keep it, arrange for the adoption, whatever." She moved her hands down and held her stomach as if she were about to toss me a beach ball. "All you get is this. You understand? This is all yours. You wanted it, you got it."

I filled a glass with water and took a sip. "Look, even if we don't marry, I can help with the baby. Mayflower can help, too. I've read Dr. Spock. I know how to give baths, change diapers and sterilize bottles. I know about colic and what to do in case of emergencies. I'm an encyclopedia of information about taking care of a baby. All this information, all this help from Mayflower and me, is yours. We don't have to be married to—"

Naomi began to rock almost violently. "You saying you don't want to marry me?"

"No, I want to, except—"

"I want it legal. Clean. Final. Over with." She stood and walked to the bedroom.

I started toward her.

"Go away. You smell." She closed the bedroom door.

I lay down on the sofa, hardly blinking, my mind racing. Tomorrow morning I would have to tell Naomi about my pending marriage to Mayflower, convince her how much better it would be for her to be free to associate with people her own age.

During the night I heard Naomi calling as if from a great distance. I opened my eyes and saw her standing over me. "Will you sleep in my bed?" This was not the voice of a seductress or crazed woman, but the voice of a frightened little girl. She held my hand and led me to the bedroom. We lay together motionless, her on her side, me spooned to her back, wide awake. After a while her breathing slowed. I placed my arm on her hip, rested my hand on the side of her abdomen and wrapped myself around her as tightly as I could. In a few minutes the baby kicked and, for one brief moment, I felt as though it was I, not Naomi, who was pregnant.

I was out of bed at the crack of dawn, shaky, sleep-deprived, panicked. I'd spent the night holding Naomi, afraid to move, thinking, calculating, developing a plan. My whole right side had gone to sleep. But I had an idea. I called Mayflower and asked her to come to my apartment.

Naomi had just pulled herself out of bed and was taking a bath. I'd been drinking coffee for an hour when Mayflower showed up wearing a lemon yellow dress and white pumps. She sat at the kitchen table drinking hot tea. "What is it, dear?"

"I've been thinking about Thanksgiving," I said. I was stalling, waiting for Naomi to make her appearance.

"Let's not wait until then, dear. Let's do something today."

"Odd you should mention that. I have an idea."

"What?"

"Not until Naomi finishes her bath." I held up a brown egg and a white egg. "Do you have a preference?"

"I don't know if I approve of my future husband living with a young woman," Mayflower whispered.

"How about more tea? Let me fix you an egg."

"Shit," came from behind the bathroom door.

"She's trying to shave her legs," I said. "Having trouble reaching them."

I walked to the window and looked out. The sun reflected off a plate glass window across the street. Beneath the window lay a pigeon that had crashed into the glass. "What do you suppose a pigeon is thinking about the instant before it crashes into a glass window?" I asked.

Mayflower sipped her tea. "I doubt if he thinks at all, dear. All he sees is the reflection of an endless expanse of sky. I'd guess he feels free, happy."

"Then, bam, and that's it?"

"Isn't that the way you'd prefer to go?"

I thought about this. "No," I said. "I'd like some time to work things out. Get my place in order. Wash my underwear. Say my good-byes. Make a video of my life. Think about God. Make a list of things I'd like to do before I die. Clean my oven."

From the bathroom came the sucking sound of the water as it drained from the tub, curse words as Naomi struggled to extract herself from the tub, the toilet flushing, the rattle of the handle. A few minutes later she appeared, hair stuck to her face, tights bulging at the midsection. She was eight months pregnant now, but looked ten. Her size evoked the kind of awe I felt once when visiting the Grand Canyon.

She pulled her tights down, scratched her stomach and yawned a monstrous yawn. "I dreamed I was getting married," she said, tossing me a glance. She opened the refrigerator. "We're out of orange juice?"

"I bought some more," I said. "Move something."

She peered into the refrigerator, bovine butt and breasts, a sagging t-shirt. "So, Tobias, you told Mayflower the news yet?"

I rested my hand on the corner of the table, then crossed my arms, trying to counter my rigidity. "You want one or two eggs?"

"Wait until you hear this, Mayflower."

"We also have news for you, dear."

"Not like ours," Naomi said. She popped a green olive into her mouth. "Ours is big—*National Enquirer* type news. Tobias and I are—"

"Hold on," I said. I pulled out a chair. "Sit here, Naomi, next to Mayflower."

"I'm hungry," Naomi said. She tossed an olive above her head, tried to catch it in her mouth and missed. She kicked it under the refrigerator.

I held up a finger. "I have something important to tell you both, but before we talk I'll make eggs and toast for everyone. Coffee for Naomi and me. Mayflower, do you want more hot water?"

"Thank you, dear."

"Excellent. The three of us do quite well together, don't we? We eat, we have a few laughs, we look out for one another." I cracked three eggs. One yolk broke and spread across the bottom of the skillet.

"That one's yours," Naomi said.

I removed a piece of shell from the broken yolk and wiped my hands. "It seems," I said, "we have an unusual situation here. Let me explain. I have done something which at first may strike you as inconsistent, but in the long run may be for the best." I filled Mayflower's cup with hot water and buttered her toast. "In fact, at first I didn't understand it myself. I thought I might be going crazy, but I sometimes have an instinct for doing the right thing despite myself."

"Tell us, for Christ's sake."

I faced them, spatula in hand. "I have proposed marriage to both of you, and both of you have accepted."

Mayflower stirred her tea, took a sip and looked over the brim of her cup. "Hot," she said.

Naomi narrowed her eyes. "I thought I was the one who was messed up."

Mayflower touched Naomi's hand. "No, dear. Tobias tries hard to make things better. I think his blundering is one of his most endearing qualities."

"Before you leap to conclusions about better or worse, let me finish." I placed Naomi's and Mayflower's plates in front of them. "Here's my idea—"

"Go to hell." Naomi stabbed her yolk with a fork.

Mayflower straightened and folded her hands. "Let's hear what he has to say, dear."

I sat down, tapped my fingers on the table and stood up again. "Please look at me. I can't talk when you don't look at me."

Mayflower looked up, then Naomi. Their eyes followed me as I lowered myself to one knee. My head just cleared the top of the table. "Naomi and Mayflower, I am hereby proposing marriage to both of you and suggest that we, the three of us, do it today."

Naomi scooped up half the egg and placed it in her mouth. "In Iowa you can go to jail—"

I rose up just enough to peer over the table. "Hear me out, think about it. It makes sense. My reasons for wanting to marry each of you are still valid. Mayflower, you said yourself that sometimes the old rules no longer apply."

"We'll get arrested," Naomi said.

"No, just me. You're both in the clear legally because you're victims, so to speak. Theoretically, at least, neither of you will know that I'm married to both of you. You will still be legally married. Even if they arrest me—which is very unlikely—I'm still the legal father of your child, Naomi, and I'm your guardian, Mayflower. They won't be able to take you away without my permission, and chances are no one is going to know, anyway. The cops have better things to do than chase down aging polygamists. We'll go on living here. Nothing changes. Mayflower, you'll stay here at the Coronado for as long as I'm alive. Naomi, I'll see to it that your baby has the best possible care. It will have a name, a home."

"You'd keep it?"

"Maybe. I haven't decided. As soon as it's born, you'll be free to go where you want, do what you want, and I'll have the legal authority to do what's best for the baby. We'll get married today. One marriage in Tucson, the other in Nogales, Sonora. I seriously doubt that Mexico and the U.S. exchange marriage records." I waited. "Tell me what you think."

"I think you're an asshole."

Mayflower unfolded her napkin and placed it over her lap. She sipped her tea, cocked her head, pursed her lips. "It sounds rather naughty, doesn't it?"

"It's the end game," I said, "played by our rules, dictated by our needs. Even if we get caught, I doubt anyone will prosecute."

"Will I stay in my own apartment?" Mayflower asked.

"There, here, wherever you want. We'll have our breakfasts, take our walks, read aloud."

"What about sex?" Mayflower asked.

"What about it?"

"I was thinking perhaps we could have a little."

"Yuck," Naomi said.

I tried to make a joke. "You would have sex with this?" I asked, indicating my body.

"The truth is, dear, I would have sex with Calvin Coolidge."

"Calvin Coolidge is dead," Naomi said.

"That's right, dear."

"What do you think, Naomi?"

She shrugged. "Maybe if I were super-stoned."

"Not about sex, about my proposal."

"I could help with the baby," Mayflower said.

"Strictly business?" Naomi asked.

"Absolutely."

"I can leave right after the baby comes, and you'll take care of everything? I'm not keeping the baby. You understand that?"

"I'll keep it or work with an adoption agency."

"I still get the thousand you owe me?"

"Correct," I said, having no idea how I'd come up with the money.

Naomi picked up crumbs with the flat of her finger.

"You'll be off the hook," I said, "have a fresh start, be free to go anywhere you want, even go back to Pella to see your pig farm friend, what's-his-name."

"Quentin Raines." Naomi looked at me, then Mayflower. She raised the corner of her upper lip.

"Will you join us in marriage, dear?"

Naomi shrugged. "Sure. Why not?"

 SEVENTEEN

It was one of those prime Tucson days, days that people in the Midwest read about in *Arizona Highways*. No clouds, pale blue sky, birds foraging, cats stretching in the sun, creosote and sage in the air. Early risers strolled Fourth Avenue as if they had just fallen in love. A bicyclist whistled tunelessly as he rode by. I was on my way to Mr. Bill's Thrift and Gift to buy a new outfit, certain I was doing the right thing. Lives in today's society were complex. We needed more than two options to define relationships. We needed trial marriages, annually renewable marriages, contract marriages, same sex marriages, and group marriages of same and different sexes. Older women needed more options. They vastly outnumbered older men. Why shouldn't several of them share a man or feel free to marry other women in groups? I was on the cutting edge of something big. I was a pioneer, a part of the avant-garde. When things settled down, I'd become an activist for revisioning our concept of marriage. Maybe I'd write a book.

While Mayflower and Naomi dressed, I went to the bank to withdraw my last three hundred from savings. I gave thirty to a street vendor for three rings made from bent spoons. There was a stirring in me, a sense of confidence and purpose.

At Mr. Bill's, I bought an English tweed jacket for five dollars and a pair of wool and polyester blend slacks for seven. I got a store-bought haircut. I hadn't had my hair cut professionally in twenty years.

Earlier that morning I'd called the marriage license bureau, worked through the telephone menu and listened to a recorded message. No blood test or waiting period, sixty-dollar license fee. We'd need to show birth certificates or driver's licenses.

"I look frumpy," Naomi said as she climbed the stairs, one step at a time, to the courthouse. "My ankles are swollen. My knees won't bend."

She was right. She looked almost square. Her denim dress didn't help much with its large pockets and wide, buckled straps.

"Tell me, dear," Mayflower said. "Do you think this young lady looks frumpy?"

I looked at Mayflower and remembered I had not yet told her about Charles. A splinter of shame worked its way into my gut. But this was a special day. Neither Naomi's depression nor my shame would dampen my spirits. "I think she's beautiful. And you, too, Mayflower." I smiled so big my lips stuck to my teeth.

Mayflower was wearing her red dress, white pumps, white pearls, and a wide-brimmed white hat. Her braid hung almost to her waist.

I stopped them at the top of the steps, intending to comment on their bravery, to reflect on my feelings about the outmoded marriage laws in the U.S., to boost them up by casting them in the role of pioneers. But one look at Naomi's frog-like grimace, and I said none of this. Instead, I asked, "Who first?"

"Me," Naomi said. "I want to get it over with."

No flowers, no prayers, just the rings and a strictly secular ceremony. Naomi said she'd puke if the Justice of the Peace mentioned God. This did not set well with the Justice of the Peace, a severe Texan with scuffed boots and bad breath. He dropped hints about his Southern Baptist up-bringing and made no attempt to hide his revulsion at Naomi's pregnancy and the difference in our ages. He spoke in flat, hurried tones, obviously cutting whole sections from his canned ceremony. "Tobias, do you take this woman to be your wife? Naomi, do you—" We quickly exchanged rings. "Fine, by the authority invested in me, I pronounce you—" he took a breath, "husband and wife." He didn't say, "You may kiss the bride," nor did he offer congratulations. I stood for a second, my arms at my sides, not knowing what to do. Should I kiss Naomi, leave, or punch the JP?

"Let's get out of here," Naomi said. "This jerk-off gives me the creeps."

On the courthouse steps Mayflower used a disposable camera to snap a picture of Naomi and me. "Oh, dear," she said, touching the corner of an eye. "I think I'm going to cry."

It took two hours to drive from Tucson to Nogales via I-19. Santa Cruz Valley had a familiar magic feel about it. I'd felt it before when I'd driven to Tubac. The land tilted to the east in a massive geological shift. Shadows from jagged mountains crept over the surface. I felt richly human, connected to the earth, grounded, confident.

Naomi sat in the back. She said she wanted to be alone. As we passed the Cow Palace in Amado, she rested her arm on the back of my seat.

"So," Mayflower said. "How do you two feel?"

Naomi fiddled with the hairs on my neck. "Hey, hubby," she said.

"Stop it," I said.

"How about you, Tobias?"

"Like when I got my first library card," I said. "I was six and short. All I could see were the giant legs of the woman behind the desk. She wore hose that came just below her knees, garters that cut into her flesh. She stood up, peered down over the desk at me and handed me my card. 'Eef you looze zis, young man, you vill pay zee beeg fine.' I almost ran out, but my card had my name on it, printed in large letters. I'd never been so frightened and happy at the same time."

"How do you feel?" Naomi asked Mayflower.

"I feel like howling," Mayflower said. Then she howled.

I gave it a try, but nothing came out but a squeak.

I parked on the U.S. side, and we walked across. Mayflower spoke broken Spanish, and within minutes she'd found the license bureau. We requested a civil ceremony, expecting we'd get the same hostile treatment we received in Tucson, but this one was long and sincere. A sleek clerk named Carmen Ortiz raised our spoon rings to the heavens and talked about the continuing circle of the ring as symbolic of our great and beautiful love, our boundless respect for one another and for our daughter.

Naomi let it pass.

When it was over, Mayflower hugged Carmen and said, "It was the best wedding I've ever had, dear."

Carmen's brother, a young man with a mustache and tight-fitting rayon shirt who acted as a witness, hugged Mayflower and Naomi and kissed their cheeks. "You are a very lucky man," he said pumping my hand.

Mayflower asked Carmen to take a picture of the three of us. Naomi took one of Mayflower and me, I took one of Naomi and Mayflower, and a receptionist took one of the three of us with Carmen, her brother, and his second cousin, who suddenly appeared from the back room.

We three walked arm in arm back across the border, back into a world that had changed. The light from the low sun rimmed the buildings and trees. The air tasted of Mexican food and honeysuckle. Strangers smiled and nodded their greetings.

"I feel as if I've just robbed a bank," Mayflower said.

"This is very weird," Naomi said.

We stopped at the Cow Palace for a bite to eat. Mayflower showed the bartender our marriage certificate, and he bought us margaritas and a glass of orange juice for Naomi. Naomi showed him her marriage certificate, and he bought another round, apparently not noticing or caring that my name was on both certificates.

Near Green Valley, Naomi had to go to the bathroom. I pulled into a rest stop and parked between two eighteen-wheeler trucks. The idling engines rattled and clanked. Mayflower turned to face Naomi and me, took our hands and kissed them. "I love you both," she said.

"Me, too," I managed, looking out the window.

Naomi sat motionless, hardly breathing. "Let me out," she said.

When Naomi was gone, Mayflower said. "Don't let me frighten you, dear. My love hasn't that much to do with you. I don't expect anything. It's mainly for me. It allows me to express something I've denied myself my whole life."

Naomi returned. "Those places are filthy," she said.

I didn't start the car. We sat for a while in silence, each with our own thoughts and feelings. I felt connected to some unnameable something outside myself—not with the usual Tobias, but with something greater, something that contained all of us.

That evening it rained, a light sprinkle at first, then a heavy downpour. Mayflower and I sat at my table, sharing a tuna sandwich and slices of Valencia oranges while drops pinged against the kitchen window. Water formed rivulets that divided and divided again as they ran down the windowpane, intersecting, stopping, darting off to the left or right, splitting, rejoining. We tried to imagine some order and purpose in the paths they were taking and laughed.

Mayflower bit into a slice of orange and stared at the window for a long time. "I *like* rain," she said.

"Me too," Naomi said. She was on the sofa with her plate balanced on her stomach. "Once when it rained in Pella, Brendan and I went to the gazebo and read love poems to each other. We held hands. We weren't even stoned. We just held hands."

"The last time Charles and I were together, it was pouring," Mayflower said. "We stood outside the Queen's Hotel in Stratford sharing his umbrella, then shook hands and said goodbye. I spent that afternoon in the bar drinking martinis and watching the rain drip from a giant elm outside the window. Two tickets to *Macbeth* were in my purse, but I didn't go. Instead, I hooked up with an actor who had the night off from playing Richard III."

"It was raining when my mother left," I said. "She was wearing wool. The smell of wet wool still chokes me up."

Naomi rolled from the sofa onto all fours and used the coffee table to stand up. She pressed her hands to the base of her spine and bent back. "Someday, I'll see the ocean. I'll own a car, have long fingernails and paint them purple. I'll use buckets of mascara and wear those high platform sandals. I want to be young. I don't think I've ever been young. I'm never going to get married or have another baby."

"You are married, dear."

"I mean, again."

I was on the verge of giving her some advice on birth control and better things to do with her money than buying a car and makeup. But I held my tongue.

Naomi wandered to the corner where I had stored the baby things I'd been accumulating. She held up a diaper between two fingers and dropped it, touched a rattle, stuck two fingers in a bootie and wiggled them around. She went into the bedroom and came back with her baggy long-sleeved sweater wrapped around her. She lay on the sofa and stared at the ceiling. "I like the rain," she said.

Mayflower sat at the end of the sofa and massaged Naomi's feet.

Naomi held the sweater to her nose. "Smells like our fireplace. Every Christmas my mother made rib roast. She'd coat it with mustard before roasting it. My father would fix eggnog, get a little drunk, drag out his clarinet and squeak his way through 'Silent Night.' I thought the words were 'Sleep in heavenly peas.' He thought he could play that damn clarinet." She grew quiet. I didn't notice she was crying until Mayflower comforted her.

"I can't believe he's dead," Naomi said.

Mayflower stroked Naomi's head for another fifteen minutes, then sat in the chair next to me and played with her necklace. I looked closer. The necklace was composed of small clay figures engaged in sexual acts. "A riddle," I said. "What is old, falling apart, and happy?"

"Me," Mayflower said.

"Me, too," I said.

Raindrops pelted the glass.

"Why don't you two go make out," Naomi said. "Just not in front of me. I have a weak stomach." She went into her bedroom and closed the door.

"Will you stay with me, dear?"

"Of course," I said. "I'll rest on the sofa until you doze off."

"I mean *with* me, in my bed, your naked body next to my naked body."

I swallowed back a hiccup. "Sure," I said.

In Mayflower's bedroom, I turned off the light. As I went about removing my clothes, every fear and self-doubt I'd ever had about sex surfaced. I was old. I wasn't sexy. I wasn't sure I could relax enough to perform. Even if I could, Mayflower was too needy. I could never satisfy her. My entire body was trembling. I was freezing as I slipped in beside Mayflower. We lay face-to-face, a lusty woman and a frightened alien, our bodies and mouths inches apart. I was shivering.

"Are you all right?" she whispered.

"I can't stop shaking."

She inched closer until our pelvises met and moved her knee slowly up between my knees. She touched my neck and chest with the tips of her fingers. Each point of contact was like a stone dropped in water that sent eddies of pleasure and fear rippling through my body. I thought I might faint. I wanted her to stop. "I like that," I said.

"That's what we have flesh for, dear, to keep us from breaking our bones when we love each other." Her hand inched down over my stomach and cradled my scrotum. She stroked my penis and kissed my stomach, and slowly took my penis into her mouth.

I lay still, willing my penis hard, silently threatening it, demanding that it respond, but it retreated even more. "I'm sorry," I said, turning over on my side, my back to her. She snuggled against my backside and held me close. Her arm fell over me like a giant wing.

The next morning I awoke and the first thing I saw was a picture of Charles on Mayflower's nightstand. I looked at it for a long time, wondering if Charles was old and impotent, too.

Mayflower stirred. "Good morning, love."

"There's something I need to tell you," I said. "Charles lives three hours away, just south of Phoenix. He's had some kind of stroke—two strokes, actually, I assume fairly serious. If you want, I'll take you to see him." I waited, hoping she might say no.

Mayflower lay still for a long time, then said, "I remember the first Christmas after I met Charles. He spent Christmas day with his family. I was alone, so desperately in love and feeling terribly sorry for myself. I drank too much cheap wine and ended up calling the information operator. We talked for over an hour. The operator was depressed, too, poor dear, about having to work on Christmas. She told me about her mother's sage dressing, and I told her about my affair with Charles. Then we talked for the longest time about our childhoods, our fascination with fireflies and the sound of crickets. Do you like fireflies and crickets, Tobias?"

"A little outdoorsy for my taste," I said.

She rose on one elbow and faced me. "Of course, I want to see him, dear. Why wouldn't I? I must buy him a gift." She thought for a moment. "A music box would be perfect. They're so—comforting. He must need comforting. You're so unselfish, Tobias. Thank you."

"Of course," I said, aware that I had taken yet another irrevocable step in the destruction of my life, that this so-called unselfishness could be my undoing.

 EIGHTEEN

After an hour at the mall Mayflower found a suitable music box—one that played "Blue Danube"—and we were on our way to Chandler. Mayflower sat next to me, cradling the music box in her long fingers. The speed limit was seventy-five. I could barely hit fifty.

A truck almost blew us off the road.

Naomi woke long enough to say, "What the hell—"

"Go back to sleep, dear."

The sun was burning my left arm. An image of Charles and Mayflower making love came to mind. I pushed it aside and gripped the steering wheel with both hands as cars and trucks hurtled by. We drove for two hours, the wind blowing sand and weeds across the highway. Finally, I saw the Chandler exit.

"We're here," I said.

Naomi sat up, looked around and went back to sleep.

Mayflower checked her teeth and lipstick in the rearview mirror. "I wonder if I'll recognize him," she said, "or he, me."

Twenty minutes later I pointed to a square cinderblock building in the distance. "That's it," I said.

"Oh dear," Mayflower said.

We walked from the parking lot to the front door. She did not loop her arm through mine.

Piped-in rock and roll music played through cheap overhead speakers. In the middle of the lobby, lights on a large Christmas tree flickered occasionally. Naomi hunched her shoulders and folded her arms. "It's freezing in here," she said.

At the front desk a woman in her mid-thirties, wearing a red sweater, greeted us. Her name tag read SHEILA LAMONT, SHIFT SUPERVISOR. She was wearing too much perfume.

"We're here to see one of your residents," I said.

"Charles—" Mayflower said.

"Don't you ever turn up the air conditioning?" Naomi asked.

"We keep it on the cool side, hon. Good for the residents, keeps them active, more alert. If they get too warm, they sleep all the time."

"His name is Charles Thomas Robins," I said.

"Sure, old Charlie Robins. You're his first visitors since, let's see—" She took a card out of a file. "Last Christmas. He shares a room with Harv Miller. We try to keep our strokes together, cancers with cancers, and so on. They prefer it that way. Makes 'em feel normal. Great old guys, though. Follow me."

We followed Sheila down a green and tan corridor with handrails on both sides. The place smelled of Lysol, urine, and something familiar I couldn't identify. Then I saw the sign BEAUTY PARLOR and knew I was smelling chemicals used by beauticians. Outside the beauty parlor door, a dozen or so women waited in wheelchairs. Some talked, some slept. One was missing both legs.

"Our ladies live for hair day," Sheila said. "Good morning, ladies."

One or two looked up blankly. I looked away and caught up with Mayflower.

"Are you all right?" I asked.

Mayflower cleared her throat and straightened her back. "No."

"We feed them at eleven," Sheila said. "Food makes them drowsy. They usually sleep for a couple of hours." She tapped on 107 and opened the door.

One man lay on the bed, bone thin, transparent, yellow, hollow-eyed. "Hey, Harv," Sheila said.

Harv's mouth contorted, and he managed to say, "Hello, Sheila."

"Charlie, you have visitors," Sheila said to a man standing facing the window. He wore a navy blue blazer and wrinkled institutional pajamas. He turned. Matted patches of spidery white hair floated above his scalp. His left arm hung at his side; he dragged his left leg. His hands were cracked and swollen. In spite of it all, he still had a veneer of State Department reserve and dignity.

"Hello, Mayflower," he managed.

"Hello, my love." She approached Charles, stood in front of him, picked up his hand, held it for a moment, then kissed it. "Can you believe I recognize that jacket?"

He sat on his bed and looked up at her. "I thought I'd never—" He stopped and reached for a tissue.

Mayflower held the box for him. "Are you all right?"

Charles nodded. "Yes. So much time. I'm sorry, I—"

Mayflower turned to Sheila. "Is there any place we can be alone?"

"No problem. We'll wheel Harv out in the hall and leave you two to catch up. Want to go outside, Harv?"

Harv was in no condition to object to anything.

Naomi said she'd wait in the game room and motioned for me to follow her.

I stayed. I didn't want to leave Mayflower alone with Charles. I could sense from the way she looked at him that she still cared deeply for him. His broken body wasn't affecting her. I doubted she was even seeing it.

Mayflower opened the music box and placed it on his lap. "This is for you, dear." She turned to me. "And this is Tobias Seltzer. He found you."

Charles held out his good hand. "Pleased to meet you, sir."

I took a few steps forward, held Charles' hand and shook it. "Likewise."

Mayflower looked around the room as though she needed a place to hide for a few minutes. "Stay with him, Tobias, until I come back." She took her purse and went into the bathroom on the other side of the room.

I looked out the window, and Charles looked at the music box. He opened it, listened to its tinkling waltz for a minute and closed the lid.

"Nice place," I said.

Charles said nothing.

"I tracked you down through the Internet."

Charles' left eye was tearing.

I handed him the tissue box.

Charles closed his eyes and managed, "I never thought—I want to thank you. I should have married her."

I sat in a bedside chair. "She cares for you a great deal," I said. "Her memory of you has sustained her." I almost told him she was already married to me, that she was in the early stages of Alzheimer's, but I didn't. It seemed unnecessarily cruel, not to him, but to his memories.

The bathroom door opened and Mayflower reappeared—head erect, shoulders back, in control. She was wearing her red silk dress. "Play the music box, dear. I'll dance for you."

I excused myself and left them alone, Mayflower standing before Charles, dancing.

I waited in the lobby. The room was filled with gaudy prints of seascapes and fishing scenes, artificial flower arrangements, the fake Christmas tree. I wanted Mayflower to hurry. I didn't want to see Charles again. I wanted to go home.

Naomi joined me. She'd been watching TV in the game room. "I'm never getting old," she said.

An hour later Mayflower came down the hall. She'd changed back to the dress she'd worn in the car. Her heels echoed on the tile floor. For the first time I noticed she had begun to walk with a slight shuffle, arms held mainly at her sides. I made a mental note to keep a closer eye on her, to make sure she didn't wander away.

I rose. "Ready?"

She stopped a few feet away. "I have to stay, dear. For a while, at least. I'll take him to a motel. He'll pay my fare back, if you'll still have me."

The life went out of me. "Fine," I said. "I understand." I had lost her. I knew she'd not come back. I hated Charles.

Mayflower took my hand and squeezed. "I told him I loved you with all my heart."

"Will he—watch over you?"

"Mentally, he's very alert, dear. He'll keep me out of trouble."

She touched Naomi's cheek. "I hope you understand, dear."

"You told me once to do what I wanted to do," Naomi said. "You, too."

Naomi and I said an awkward goodbye to Mayflower and left. We drove for almost three hours in silence.

The next day, two days before Thanksgiving, I bought enough supplies to equip an orphanage. I stocked my cupboards with jars of baby food and formula, cleaned and disinfected everything, did laundry, ironed. I called Mayflower's social worker and told her I was now Mayflower's legal guardian, and she would not be moving to Elderhaven. She told me I was making life hard on myself. I told her I wasn't sure what that meant, that maybe that's exactly what the best lives turn out to be.

I washed the bathroom mirror where Naomi had left her fingerprints, cleaned the ring around the tub, dusted, bought reserve toilet paper, made notes from Spock, massaged Naomi's feet with lotion, read aloud to her, brushed her hair. Naomi had gained nearly seventy pounds and was past caring. She cried for no reason. She'd refuse to talk, then break into a rage and curse Mayflower, me, her baby, this stupid marriage, Brendan. She had begun dropping things. She dropped cups of coffee, spoons, and dishes. She tripped on the rug, knocked over the floor lamp. When she sat on the sofa, she needed help getting up. If God created women, he treated them badly.

I bought four used CD's for a dollar each and used Mayflower's player to play Bach, Mozart, and Beethoven over and over again.

"You like that crap?" Naomi asked.

"Music is good for the baby."

"It's driving me nuts."

I agreed I'd play it only during dinner and only Bach, the one she hated least. But in exchange for less music, she agreed to let me turn the volume up.

The afternoon of the day before Thanksgiving, I sat at the end of Naomi's bed watching her sleep. Sunlight filled the room with an orange glow. There was something extremely attractive about seeing such an angry person sleeping so peacefully. I had read about men in Japan who paid money to watch a woman sleep. They're called *Kawabata*. I wondered if I was a *Kawabata* and concluded I was. I remembered that first night in the basement with Mayflower, being worried about her thinking I was a peeping Tom. Now it turned out I was indeed a kind of peeping Tom.

Naomi sat up, frowned into the sunlight. "You're looking at me. I can feel it."

"Go back to sleep," I said.

She lay back down and closed her eyes.

Outside, a truck driver changed gears, and the strain of the engine became a smooth hum.

On Thanksgiving Day I made a roasted chicken with herb stuffing from a package and opened a can of cranberry sauce. I asked Randall and Howard to join us. Bennie said he didn't feel well. Before dinner I read to Randall from *Goodnight Moon* and taught him a couple of words. He was ecstatic and made me promise to teach him more.

Apparently, Howard had been destroyed when Katherine jilted him, but his art seemed to sustain him. During dinner, Howard kept looking at Naomi, framing her face with his hands, doing that thing artists do with their thumbs. He said he was going to draw some sketches of her as soon as he finished a series on Helen. I stayed busy and talked a lot, trying not to think of Mayflower.

Earlier that week workmen had strung colored lights and draped red and green streamers from lampposts. Luminarias along the tops of buildings glowed a golden yellow. Tiny white lights spiraled around trunks of potted mesquites and flickered like cinders in the higher branches.

"You think I could hold your baby?" Randall asked Naomi.

"Ask Tobias," Naomi said.

"Just once, Mr. Seltzer? Mr. Seltzer?"

"Huh? Yeah, sure," I said, barely able to speak. I missed Mayflower so much I could hardly breathe.

Howard said he needed to work. I escorted him to the door. "Are you all right?" I asked.

"What do you mean?"

"About Katherine marrying Caravelo, about losing—"

"It wasn't about love," Howard said. "She—and you for that matter—brought me out of myself, helped me get back to painting. I have no regrets. I was out of my realm."

Randall sat at the table pretending to read *Goodnight Moon*. He was a huge man with zigzag scars on his face. I would never know what horrors had caused him to put a gun to his head and pull the trigger.

After Randall went back to his apartment, I fixed Bennie a vegetarian plate and asked Naomi to take it to him.

At last, the apartment was empty. I cleaned up and read a chapter from the handbook.

When Naomi returned a couple of hours later, she told me that Bennie's son in Dallas was insisting Bennie come live with him. "He said he wouldn't have to go if he had a wife to take care of him," she said. "So he proposed to me, told me he loved me and everything."

"What did you say?"

"I told him I was already married," she said.

Mayflower had been gone three days. At night I wandered the halls, looked in her apartment, smelled her pillow. Once, I took the stairs to the lobby, where watery splotches of light from the television moved over the walls.

"Hey, Mr. Seltzer," Randall Pruitt said. He was riding the exercise bike and reading his book.

Howard was there, watching a James Cagney black and white movie about a prison break. Gun blasts sounded far away. Howard said he was taking a break, that he had been working, doing a lot of thinking. "I'm missing Helen again," he said.

"He needed someone to pedal," Randall said. "I can pedal whenever I want. It makes the television go on." He stopped. "See?"

"Pedal," Howard said.

Randall giggled and started again.

Howard placed his sketchpad on the floor and pulled his sweater over his shoulders. He'd already taken off his shoes. A big toe stuck out from one sock. "Look at Randall there," he said. "That's commitment. He'd pedal until he fell down dead."

On the TV, James Cagney burst open a door, looked around, ran up a flight of stairs, kicked open another door, shouted a few accusatory words at a woman, and shot her.

"Do you ever think about dying?" Howard asked.

"All the time," I said. "I think about what poems I want read at my memorial, what songs I want sung. I've even thought about making a memorial video for those who might want to know more about me."

"I went to this funeral for a professor at the university. At the end we sang 'Happy Trails to You.' I always liked seeing Dale and Roy ride off into the sunset to that tune. I wonder if she ever cheated on Roy—in real life, I mean."

"Not Dale," I said.

"Still, we're all human." He let out a long sigh. "Where's Mayflower? I haven't seen her for a while."

"Visiting a friend," I said.

James Cagney leapt from the roof of one building to another, held up a fist to his pursuers and shouted, "Suckers."

I returned to my apartment. Howard stayed to watch the rest of the movie. And that's the last time I saw him. The next morning I found a note from him under my door. Howard had made a decision. He was going to travel the world, live in poverty, associate with the salt of the earth, write, paint, look for wisdom. "I wonder," he wrote, "if you would mind cleaning my apartment. Take what you want and throw the rest away." He signed it, "Howard"—not "Your friend," or "It's been great," not even a "Sincerely."

The walls of Howard's apartment were filled with sketches of Helen. On the north wall was a set of drawings of Naomi. The drawings on the east wall were ambiguous. They could have easily been Helen or Naomi. It was as if Helen had gradually morphed into Naomi. It was clear he had guessed who Naomi was. If he hadn't figured it out consciously, he knew it in the same way we know things just before we're conscious we know them. I didn't want to miss him but I couldn't help myself.

Later that night, I said to Naomi, "Whatever he did, he did with gusto."

Naomi shook her head slowly. She grimaced and bent over.

"I'm sorry," I said.

"Jesus," she said. She held her stomach and rocked.

"Are you all right?"

Naomi looked at me from the tops of her eyes. "I think the baby's coming."

 NINETEEN

The first thing I said was, "Wait." I grabbed the handbook and held it up. "It says that in the beginning the pains are short, slight, separated by intervals of ten or fifteen minutes. What's your interval?"

Naomi folded over in pain. She made it to her bed and lay down. "No interval."

I felt like I'd been kicked in the stomach. Fire shot down my legs and into my feet. I couldn't catch my breath. "I have to lie down," I said. "Move over." I knew what was happening. I'd read about sympathetic labor in the handbook, but the pain was real, and I couldn't will it or think it away. "Give me time to breathe here," I said.

"Shit," Naomi said. She stood and water tinted with blood poured out onto the floor.

The room was spinning.

Naomi pounded the wall with her fists. "Do something, goddammit." She was standing barefoot in her own amniotic fluid, sweating, gasping for breath. She lunged and threw herself onto her bed, heels churning at my side. She screamed. Halfway through her scream, I joined her, then finished with a solo.

"My legs are cramping," she cried.

"Mine, too." I couldn't breathe. I kicked at the air and somehow ended up on my feet. I had to walk stiff-legged like a toy soldier, but I walked. I walked to the end of the hall and woke Randall to help me.

"What if it comes before we get to the hospital?" Naomi asked.

The muscles in my legs were letting go. The pain in my abdomen was easing. I felt detached, as if I were watching a movie. "Don't worry," I said. "I've got things under control." I grabbed a stack of clean towels and asked Randall to help Naomi. She was having trouble walking, so he carried her to the elevator.

Randall got Naomi into the back seat and sat beside her. I headed west on Speedway.

Naomi had another long contraction and screamed.

"You'll be fine," I said. Soon the hospital was in sight. "We'll be at the hospital in just a few minutes."

We were at Campbell and Speedway, two blocks away, when Naomi screamed, "It's coming."

"It's coming, Mr. Seltzer."

I glanced back and a second later felt a jarring thud from the front, a second impact from behind. I had hit the car in front of me. The car behind had plowed into me. The impact had thrown Naomi against the back of the front seat. Randall helped her up.

"It's coming, Mr. Seltzer. I can see it."

The drivers of the other two cars were heading my way. I told Randall to get out and let me in the back seat. He stood at the open door looking over my shoulder. I sat on my heels between Naomi's legs.

"Somebody hurt?" one of the drivers asked.

"Having a baby," Randall answered.

"Jesus, I'll call an ambulance."

Naomi clutched herself with both arms and tried to sit up.

"Relax," I said, pushing against her shoulder, easing her down. "Concentrate on your breathing. Slow—in, out, in, out—slow, that's it. Between intervals—"

"No interval," Naomi said.

Sweat filled my eyes and blurred my vision. My overhead light didn't work. I told Randall to ask if anyone had a flashlight. Naomi tossed her head violently side to side. It seemed as if Randall was gone for an hour, but it must have been only few seconds. Then he was there behind me, holding a flashlight over my shoulder.

I saw the top of the baby's head, wet and black and bloody, pressing out like a curious giant eye. Panic shot up from my toes and stuck in my chest. My brain froze. I was a small dot suspended in blackness. I waited for the next thought, then something inside me burst open. My rational brain deserted me, and the primal hull that remained knew exactly what to do. I heard my voice, but I was not the initiator of the words that came out of me. From deep within the folds of my brain, I was channeling Spock, the handbook, a conflagration of scenes from movies I'd seen. "Naomi, your baby is almost here, don't push. It will happen in its own time."

A woman who looked like Prince Valiant appeared. "Is there anything I can do?"

"Are you a nurse?"

"No, an accountant."

"You can call an ambulance—and the police."

"Already done," a man said, and handed me some blankets.

Another contraction came. Naomi clenched her jaw and let out a high-pitched sound that had no relation to anything human. The baby's head butted against my hand. "Easy does it," I said, hoping the ambulance would appear. I covered Naomi with the blankets. Her hair was wet. I'd never seen human skin that white. I could feel the blood dripping, one drop at a time, into my heart.

Deep-set eyes peered in through all the windows, faces with skin that changed colors as the traffic lights turned from yellow to red to green. Intense faces, worried faces, smiling faces. Naomi's eyes were open, but rolled to the top of her head, her lips drained of blood and slightly parted. Her chest heaved—her legs stiffened and shook. At first I thought it was another labor pain, then I recognized the symptoms—toxemia, potentially lethal. Where was the ambulance? I could see the emergency entrance, less than a block away. I decided to take a chance that the baby wouldn't arrive within the next few minutes.

"Randall," I yelled.

"I'm here, Mr. Seltzer." He was practically breathing in my ear.

"We can't wait for the ambulance. We have to carry Naomi and the baby to the hospital. Quick."

Randall lifted Naomi from the back seat as if she were a rag doll.

"Run, Randall," I said. "Run as fast as you can. Run toward that big red sign."

Randall ran ahead carrying Naomi. I followed, unable to feel my feet hit the sidewalk.

Emergency was a blurred scramble: an IV set up for Naomi, someone asking us to wait in the lobby.

In what seemed like an eternity, a woman who called herself Nurse Rose told me I had done a good job, that both my wife and the baby were fine, that Naomi had given birth to a boy.

Later, in the men's room, I reentered my body and started shaking. I was standing over the basin, washing blood from my hands, hands that had touched the baby's head. My stomach still ached from sympathetic labor. My entire body shook. Somewhere far away a woman laughed, and for a moment I thought it was Mayflower. I continued washing my hands—clear tepid water flowing over white porcelain, Naomi's blood mixing with the water, circling the basin and swirling down the drain. I let the water run a long time until my hands stopped shaking, then cupped them, filled them, brought them to my lips and drank.

Someone knocked, and the door opened. "Mr. Seltzer. Nurse Rose." She held out a gown and mask. "You've been in here for over an hour. Here, put these on." She was a woman in her fifties, short and wide, earthy, as if she'd been raised in a root cellar. I imagined her sprouting rootlets each night, having to pluck them each morning before coming to work. I decided to submit completely to her will. I was no longer capable of making a decision. I would do her bidding exactly, think only the thoughts she put into my head. I put on the gown and mask and followed her.

We passed through the lobby. Randall was napping in the far corner. I knew I would never forget his huge shoulders, his lumbering gait as he ran ahead with Naomi draped over his arms.

Randall woke and spotted me. "You want me to do something, Mr. Seltzer?"

I told him he'd done well, thanked him, suggested he go home and get some sleep.

"Can I hold the baby, Mr. Seltzer?"

"Soon," I said.

"Just down the hall, Mr. Seltzer," Nurse Rose said.

What a pleasant face she had, what chubby, ruby cheeks. She left me at the entrance of yet another long hallway and told me to wait in 509, Naomi's room. "I'll bring the baby to you," she said. She paused. "Mr. Seltzer?"

"Yes?"

"You know, of course, the baby is—black."

"Of course," I said. A cloud of regret and self-doubt descended. I wasn't sure I could shoulder all these responsibilities. I could leave now if I wanted, take a taxi to the bus station, go someplace where no one knew me or depended on me. Mayflower had acted selfishly. Why couldn't I?

"Are you all right, Mr. Seltzer?"

"Fine," I said. I glanced at my watch. It was six a.m. Another nurse walked toward me and, for some reason, I clicked my heels and bowed. I followed her to 509. I peeked in. Three beds separated by curtains, three sets of feet under the sheets, the dim glow from three night-lights. I checked the first cubicle. A woman was nursing. I apologized for the interruption. I skipped the second cubicle and tried the third. Naomi was watching cartoons on a muted television. She held her wadded-up sheet tight against her cheekbone.

"How are you feeling?" I asked.

Her face showed no expression. No movement, no eye contact, no reply.

I sat on the end of her bed and bowed my head, intending to take a short nap.

"Mr. Seltzer?" It was Nurse Rose. I knew she had brought the baby.

I kept my eyes closed. I didn't want to look at it, not yet. A look would seal a bargain I had made but wasn't yet ready to keep. Naomi had refused the baby. How could I care for it alone? It had to be put up for adoption. I couldn't become attached. I looked at Nurse Rose instead of the baby.

"My, oh my, would you look at those big eyes," she said.

I couldn't help myself. I leaned in, at first a disinterested bystander, then a scientist looking through a microscope, then an atheist just after his first glimpse of God.

The baby looked right at me as if to ask, *Haven't we met before?* This was a soft baby, a baby with an old soul, a baby that let itself be shaped by the lumps and curves of Nurse Rose's body. Cheeks like glazed doughnuts. Hair so black it seemed almost purple. A button nose. Perfect lips. Tiny, tiny fingers. It twisted its mouth around in a crooked smile. I felt a swell of pride—something akin to the feeling one has after successfully assembling a new barbecue, only a thousand times more. I made *ga-ga goo-goo* sounds.

Nurse Rose brushed the corner of the baby's mouth with her pinkie. His head turned in the direction of her touch. His lips puckered. One eye closed. His mouth pulled up on one side.

"He smiled," I said.

"He's hungry," Nurse Rose said.

"No, it was a definite smile." I made more sounds and looked at his face for a long time. The baby yawned, a great cavernous yawn. I yawned too. His tongue moved as if making preparations for his first taste of something wonderful. Then he gave me a dopey look that seemed to say, *Let's have one last drink and call it a night.*

"He needs a name," Nurse Rose said.

Her voice was the voice of Abraham calling me down from the mountain. With a task to perform, something specific that needed to be done, the fatigue drained from my body. I said, "Naomi, do you have any thoughts on this?"

No response.

If she would name the child, maybe she'd develop a connection with it and, with such a connection, who knows, she might decide to keep him. "There's Abraham, Adam, Aaron," I said. "What do you think, Naomi?" I waited. "How about Benjamin or Bernard?"

Nurse Rose said, "He's so strong. How about Samson? Samson Tobias Seltzer."

My ears rang. Nurse Rose's suggestion seemed vaguely immoral, even illegal. "You can do that?"

"Of course," Nurse Rose said.

"Samson is a large name," I said. "A giant of a name. Nobody expects much from a Tobias, but a Samson—" I waited for a reaction from Naomi, but none came. I moved my face six inches from the baby's face and whispered, "Hey, Samson."

The baby's mouth twisted. An arm shot out from under the blanket.

I glanced up at Nurse Rose.

"Would you like to hold him?" she asked.

I lost my nerve. "Not yet."

"Babies aren't as fragile as you think."

"I've read Spock," I said. I lifted the blanket from the baby's head and watched a pulse beat in the fontanel. I imagined thin layers of tissue there, the only thing that protected his brain from the world. These were important times before the bones fused, when the brain was so close to the world, a time for great truths and learning. I found two chubby arms that felt like cool velvet. The elbows worked nicely. The hands were right— four tiny fingers and a thumb on each. But what of his character? I tried to be objective, but there was no doubt about it—this baby was clearly older than his six or so hours indicated. He was comfortable in his skin, curious but not afraid, wise in his gaze, perhaps puzzled as to why he had not been awarded sainthood in his last life.

The baby squeezed my finger. "Strong," I said. I opened the blanket. Chubby eggplant-shaped thighs. Wrinkled feet. Big toes that stuck straight up. Tiny, tiny toenails. He began to flap around and swell up, about to cry. I tickled the bottom of one foot. The toes clamped down. The leg shot out straight. He didn't cry.

"Good reflexes," I said. I pointed to the baby's diapered crotch. "May I—?"

Nurse Rose opened the diaper.

I checked the anus—no protrusion—and the penis. "What about circumcision?"

"It's not too late," Nurse Rose said.

"What do you think? I mean medically speaking?"

"I'd prefer you make that decision, Mr. Seltzer."

I thought about the comfort factor, the cleanliness factor, the sensitivity factor, the cruelty factor, the religious factor, and went against the strain of Jewishness left in me. "His penis seems fine as it is," I said.

"Oh, yes, it's quite lovely," Nurse Rose said.

The baby began to cry. Nurse Rose moved to Naomi's bed. "Don't you want to hold him? He's hungry as a logger."

No response.

Nurse Rose placed the baby on Naomi's stomach, moved Naomi's arms around him and helped him find the nipple.

Just as he started sucking, Naomi clenched both fists in little spasms of revulsion. "It hurts," she said. "Take it off." She narrowed her eyes and set her jaw. "I want you to leave me alone. All of you."

That afternoon, Dr. Snyder checked the baby and spent a long time with Naomi—pulse, pupil dilation, blood pressure, reflexes, pelvis, abdomen. She tried without success to engage Naomi in conversation. I looked for telltale signs in the doctor's face, some sign of concern, some judgment she was making without telling me. She lifted Naomi's hand and let go. The hand fell to the mattress. In the hall she spoke of toxemia, D and C's, transfusions, intravenous feeding, sedation, stress, bed rest, disassociation, postpartum depression. She recommended a psychiatric evaluation.

I asked how much it would cost.

"A thousand to three thousand," she said.

I told her I needed to think about it. I had no insurance, no idea where I was going to get the money. I went back in to see Naomi. "I thought you were going to die," I said.

She muttered something.

I moved closer. "What?"

"Wish I had," she said. "That baby, too."

I caught Dr. Snyder before she'd left and approved the psychological evaluation.

The psychiatrist, Dr. Zimmer, a gaunt man with a sparse beard and soft voice, tried to examine Naomi. She refused to talk. "She's very depressed," he said. "Perhaps even suicidal, or worse."

"Worse?"

"Homicidal," he said. "I don't think she should be exposed to the baby at this time." He prescribed an antidepressant, but Naomi cursed and threatened him and refused the medication. The doctor, with my permission, ordered the drug administered intravenously. He also ordered restraints and around-the-clock observation.

During the next three days and nights, Naomi was totally withdrawn and unresponsive. She refused food and had to be fed intravenously.

On the fourth night I awoke from a deep sleep to the sound of humming. The room was dark except for a night-light. I looked around but couldn't see anyone. I closed my eyes and tried to get back to sleep, but the humming kept on. I recognized the tune—"Me and My Shadow." I checked the closet, under the bed, in the other beds. I found Mayflower in bed with Naomi, spooned tight to her back. She had loosened the restraints and lay with Naomi in her arms, humming.

"Mayflower?"

She looked up at me, eyes glazed. "Go back to sleep, Charles."

Overjoyed, but too tired to argue, I went back to sleep.

When I awoke, Mayflower was combing Naomi's hair. She looked exhausted, her face drawn, her hair disheveled.

Naomi was sitting up, but still unresponsive.

"You're back," I said.

"Yes, dear."

"Are you all right? Are you and Charles—?"

"We talked," she said. "It was like straightening drawers, putting things in order, tossing out some false memories, adding some new ones. We discovered we'd changed, that we don't and probably didn't have a lot in common. We did agree that we had created one another in the image of our ideal lover. We also agreed that that wasn't entirely a bad thing, that somehow it may actually have changed the ordinary person into an ideal lover. And now—all I can say is that seeing Charles at this point in my life was a true boon, a gift. We experienced ourselves again, but this time with greater imagination and humor, more forgiveness, and profound gratitude. I feel that same gratitude for you, dear. I can't tell you how grateful I am for the gift of seeing Charles one last time." She paused for a moment and added, "For the last time."

I wasn't ready to forgive her. "Did you tell him about me?"

"I told him everything. About you, about Naomi, about my condition, about our interesting three-way marriage."

"What did you say about me, specifically?"

"I told him you were a good and kind man, a man with an enormous heart. I told him you were an excellent dancer. I told him you were very smart, a great lecturer, and extremely funny at times. I told him you made me laugh. I told him I loved you with all my heart."

A few seconds passed. I cleared my throat. "Fine," I said. "Did you and Charles—make love?"

"Yes, in a manner of speaking. Oh, dear, I hope you don't want to hear about it."

Another few seconds of silence, then Naomi said, "Yuck."

At Mayflower's urging, Naomi ate her breakfast and, for the first time, took her medication orally. She would not allow Mayflower to leave the room. She insisted Mayflower sit close enough to hold her hand. That afternoon she answered Dr. Zimmer's questions and, after some prompting from Mayflower, agreed to name the baby.

"Samson Tobias Seltzer," Naomi said.

Everyone looked at me. "It wasn't my idea," I said. "Nurse Rose—"

"Please be quiet, dear. It's a fine name. We'll call him Sammy, at least until he's older."

That evening Naomi tried to hold Sammy, but panicked and said she was afraid she'd hurt him.

december-march

 TWENTY

In early December, eleven days after her admission to University Hospital, Drs. Zimmer and Snyder released Naomi and Sammy from the psychiatric ward into my care with instructions to make sure Naomi took her medication and to have someone with her at all times. The charges came to over twenty thousand dollars. I was now fifteen thousand dollars in debt and close to hysteria. On the positive side, I had a family I loved that relied on me. On the negative side, I had a family I loved that relied on me.

I bought a folding bed from the Salvation Army and set it up behind the sofa for Mayflower. I put Sammy's cradle where the coffee table had been. At night I was sandwiched in between Mayflower's lapses, Sammy's needs, and the distinct possibility that Naomi would at any time attempt to kill us all. I didn't sleep well.

Lack of sleep and my around-the-clock caretaking responsibilities wore me down. Had it not been for Sammy's smile and Randall's willingness to help, I would never have made it.

Sammy's smile was a true blessing. It took over his face slowly, as if it were coming from some great distance. But once it arrived it ruled over the apartment and the hearts that beat there. In the radiance of such a smile, I could do anything. I had experienced several kinds of love in my life, but the love I experienced for Sammy opened great cavernous spaces in me that overflowed each time he smiled. This limitless and unrestricted love was the closest thing to happiness I'd ever known.

I'm not sure I ever actually decided to keep Sammy. It was a given, a fact as obvious as the sun and the sky. I was going to raise him as my own, home school him, prepare him for Stanford or Yale. He would be my companion and friend.

Randall moved furniture, peeled potatoes, washed dishes, cleaned bathrooms and looked after Naomi, Mayflower and Sammy when I had to go out. He listened when I needed to talk. It didn't matter what I talked about—Zeno's Paradox, Naomi's paranoia, or stewed prunes—he listened as though he understood and grasped every word. On one occasion I told him my concerns over being in debt and wondered aloud what I was going to do.

"I could get a job at the Bread and Butter," he said.

"I need you here," I said. But his suggestion kindled an idea. That afternoon I went to visit Miss Choy with a proposition.

She had a new cook, an older man named Cecil Phelps. Virgil had moved to Flagstaff to enroll full time at Northern Arizona University.

"Virgil no like to cook," Miss Choy said. "Want to be big shot business man. Cecil like to cook. He cook for Martians."

Cecil was a big, soft-spoken, hippie type who made his own wine and cheese. To add to his allure, he believed with total conviction that he'd been abducted by aliens and forced to teach them how to make omelets. I made a joke and told him I, myself, had, in a way, been abducted by aliens named Howard and Mayflower and Naomi. He called me Brother Tobias and offered me an omelet. I liked Cecil. I could tell Miss Choy liked him, too.

"You come back," she said. "I give you big raise, you keep books, punch buttons on register, you and Cecil make Miss Choy rich."

"I'd like that," I said.

She drew back. "You make joke with Miss Choy?"

"I need the money," I said. "I have a family to support." I suggested I start by keeping the books and working the lunch shift. As my life became more settled, I'd add breakfast and dinner.

"We get damn rich. Maybe we franchise Miss Choy's soup."

So I started working three hours a day for eight dollars an hour—almost a hundred a week take home. I used all of it to make payments to the hospital.

Although I trusted and relied on Randall more and more, every time he held Sammy, I recalled Steinbeck's *Of Mice and Men*, how Lonnie accidentally squished his beloved pet mouse by petting it too hard.

Every evening Randall asked me to read *Goodnight Moon* to him. He'd hold his breath, anticipating the last lines, and when they came we'd read together: "Goodnight moon / Goodnight stars / Goodnight noises wherever you are." By now, he could read the book aloud on his own, but he still liked me to read it to him.

One day I asked him if he'd like to walk to the university and get a library card. "You could check out all the books you want," I said.

"You mean take them home with me?"

"Yes."

Randall blushed and shook his head in disbelief. "They wouldn't let me do that, Mr. Seltzer. I don't know how to read other books."

"I'll teach you," I said.

That afternoon while Bennie watched over my flock, I walked Randall to the library. He was terrified and on the verge of bolting until I showed him the children's section, and he found a copy of *Goodnight Moon*. After he'd looked at dozens of books, he sat cross-legged on the floor while I read aloud from *The Cat in The Hat*.

"You want to take this one home?" I asked.

He shook his head. "They won't let me. I can't read it yet."

"Sure they will. Take it to the woman at the desk."

Randall insisted I go with him. His hands trembled as he took possession of his library card and first book. Or rather, it took possession of him. As soon as we got back to the Coronado, he insisted I give him another reading lesson.

Daily for two weeks during Sammy's nap, I taught Randall rudimentary phonics and read books with and to him. *Goodnight Moon* remained his favorite. He returned to it time after time, whenever I'd go too fast or the lesson became too difficult.

I walked him to the library a few more times, but as Mayflower's condition began to show signs of deterioration, our walks became impossible. I showed Randall an easy route, drew him a simple map and told him this was our last walk together, that from now on he'd have to go on his own. The following day he set out on his first solo trip.

Naomi, Mayflower, and I waited anxiously at the kitchen window. This was the first time the three of us had been this close in a long time. Naomi still clung to Mayflower and was showing small signs of participating in the household. She washed dishes once. She started combing her hair.

"Oh dear, I think we've lost Randall," Mayflower said.

"He couldn't find his ass in a snowstorm," Naomi said.

I was just about to go look for him when he rounded the corner, carrying books and a bag of popcorn and coaxing a dog to follow him. It was the wild dog that had prowled the neighborhood for over a year. I couldn't pass it without it snarling at me.

"Look out," I called.

"Watch this, Mr. Seltzer. Catch, boy." He tossed a piece of popcorn to the dog. The dog stood on its hind legs and snatched the kernel out of the air. It looked up at Randall and wagged its tail, waiting for more.

"That dog's dangerous," I said.

Randall petted him. The dog turned his head to get an ear scratched. "I'm keeping him," Randall said, "and I'm naming him Moon."

At first, Sammy slept most of the time. When he was awake, he was a joy. What was all the fuss about? I wondered. Anyone could do this. Then he developed colic and began to scream constantly, especially at night. The only way I could get him to sleep was to hold him over my shoulder and walk the floor with him, bouncing as I walked.

Now everyone was sleep-deprived. Mayflower stared out the window, her fingers playing with the nap of her dressing gown, tying knots with invisible threads. Naomi slammed doors and cursed Sammy. I hadn't slept more than a couple of hours a night for a week.

One morning at four a.m., I stood in the middle of the living room with Sammy screaming in my ear and found myself squeezing him, hating him, wanting to hurt him. I considered throwing him against the wall. I could understand why some mothers kill their children. I panicked. I couldn't trust myself. I was too tired to think. I put Sammy in his crib, walked down the hall and knocked on Randall's door.

"Will you help me?"

Randall's eyes widened. "Sure, Mr. Seltzer. Can Moon come?"

Randall was in charge. I was too exhausted to worry. I went to the basement, lay on the bench and slept six hours. When I returned to the apartment, Naomi and Mayflower and Moon were sleeping. Randall was cradling Sammy and feeding him. Randall looked up at me and said, "I'll do this every night if you want."

At that moment, all I wanted was to be held myself by this giant of a man.

I was the first to take Sammy on an outing, a stroll down Fourth Avenue—north one block and back on the other side. I walked vigilantly, waiting for a racial slur, prepared to fight to defend Sammy. The evidence was clear—children of interracial couplings were more beautiful, more emotionally stable, and vastly more intelligent and talented than products of pure strains. I was prepared to give this information to anyone who might need it, but no one seemed to notice the color of his skin. A bag lady stopped me to comment on how cute and well-behaved he was. A man selling balloons made into animals gave Sammy a giraffe. Everyone liked him. Sammy, it turned out, had charisma.

I dropped by the Windsong Gallery to show Sammy to Katherine and Caravelo. Caravelo wasn't there, but Katherine oohed and aahed and talked baby talk. As I was leaving, she invited me to a dance exhibit she and Caravelo were giving at the grand opening of his studio the following night.

I told Mayflower about the dance exhibit, and she insisted I take her. Naomi begged Mayflower not to go and refused to go herself. She never wanted to see Caravelo again.

"It's time you began to take care of yourself," Mayflower told her. "I want to go to the dance."

Mayflower wore a lime green dress and black pumps. She seemed especially alert and happy. For my part, my mind was scattered. I was mentally constructing lists of things I had to do.

I hadn't realized the grand opening of Caravelo's studio was also a party celebrating Katherine and Caravelo's wedding. They made their way through the crowd, accepting congratulations, gazing into each other's eyes, speaking in whispers and touching at every opportunity.

Caravelo took his eyes off Katherine only occasionally to look at the ceiling as though he might be considering juggling the hundreds of colored balls and sparkling stars that dangled there.

Card tables in three corners of the room held eggnog and bottles of wine. Another longer table held pastas, cold cuts, dips, breads, cheeses. A ten-foot tall Christmas tree took up the fourth corner. The air was heavy with perfume and pine resin.

Mayflower and I had something to eat and a glass of wine. We were about ready to excuse ourselves and go home when the room suddenly went dark. People stirred and whispered. A spotlight came on and moved recklessly about the room. Needles of reflected light bounced off the balls and stars hanging from the Christmas tree.

Mayflower looped her arm through mine and whispered, "I love you."

"I love you, too," I said.

"*Olé*," Caravelo shouted and appeared in the center of the spotlight like a black opal—fitted pants, a tight, black silk shirt with bloused sleeves, boots polished to a mirror finish, and hair slicked back Valentino-style. The crowd hushed as he walked like a Lipizzaner stallion to an arched doorway, stopped, extended his hand and shouted, "Tango."

Music began, four strong beats to the bar, the last beat swooping up like a trapeze performer to connect with the first beat of the next measure. Mayflower held her hand to her mouth and cleared her throat. I pressed my arm tighter against her and nudged her with my shoulder, remembering the time we'd walked like the King and Queen of England.

"*Mi amori, te amo,*" Caravelo called. At that moment a misty violet light came on illuminating the door. An ankle and hand appeared from behind the wall, then a knee and calf and a bare arm, then Katherine in a black, severely tight, backless and almost frontless dress. Caravelo's extended arm seemed to control her every step as she moved across the floor in spiked heels, each step revealing an electric flash of exposed thigh. Murmurs. A gasp. A giggle or two.

Katherine and Caravelo hadn't touched yet. Katherine's expression was severe, her eyes intense, neon, seductive. I wanted Howard to see this. This would have delighted him.

The dancers stopped, pivoted and faced one another, closer, but still not touching. Caravelo snaked his handless arm around her waist, and they stood face-to-face, motionless except for a brief shudder of lust. Suddenly, they pivoted and moved side by side across the floor. Katherine spun away. Caravelo pulled her back. They came together like birds crashing in midair, tumbling through the sky, enfolding, recovering in an embrace. With a quick turn of his head and a stare that would melt flesh, Caravelo rendered all two-handed tango dancers obsolete and delivered a message to every other man: if you dare to dance the tango with a real woman, you must first have your hand chewed off by a lion.

Pelvises bonded together by their own heat. Katherine leaned back, lifted one leg waist-high, came slowly forward, straddled Caravelo's leg and slid down it. She stood, hands fanned over her breasts, pulled away, turned sharply back, locked her leg around his and buried her head in his neck. Blue light washed over them. Touching, yet not touching—hand to thigh, to waist, to breast—their lips brushed moth-like and stayed together as the music soared and ended with a crash.

Silence.

As people rushed to congratulate them, Mayflower snuggled closer to me and gently kissed my ear. "Let's go," she whispered.

That night as we lay in Mayflower's bed, the one in her apartment, she wove her fingers through mine and moved my hand to her pubis, down between the folds of her vagina, moist and open. After a minute or so, she said, "Here, dear," and guided my finger to the right place. She moved the tip of it around in small, slow circles. "There," she said. "Don't stop."

"Touching," I said, "is—"

"Shh. Don't stop. Don't stop. That's it. Oh, dear." She seemed to forget I was there. In a minute or so, she raised her head, pulled in her knees, and moaned. "Don't stop," she said. She lay back, placed a pillow under her butt, rolled her head and moaned again, even louder. I felt as though I was driving a runaway truck. I started to pull away. "No, no," she said. She cried out a third time and, with tears in her eyes, lay back and shuddered. "Thank you, dear."

I was wide-awake and a little frightened. "What happened?" I asked. I knew in a general sort of way, but I wanted to hear her talk about it.

She told me, giving me ample credit.

I braced myself on an elbow. "Really? How does it feel?"

She used metaphors like warm butter and sea foam, images like blue pearls and golden light.

"Oh," I said. "I did that?"

"You did."

"Do you think we could do it again?"

Mayflower moved closer and asked, "Would you like me to do the same for you?"

She moved down over my chest and stomach. I grew more powerful and confident. At some point, I was beneath Mayflower, inside her, engulfed in willowy shadows while she moved like a giant bird over me, lifting us higher and higher, forward and back, lifting. I raised my pelvis as high as I could, reaching deep into her. Rumbling throaty sounds came from her. She moved faster, taking great scoops of me into herself. My hands found her breasts, her nipples. She emitted a muffled roar, braced herself with stiff arms against my chest, pulled up and slammed down on me.

Afterwards, I lay still, watching the bedroom curtain being lifted by a soft wind. We lay together, the same wind stirring in us, suspended in time. We giggled occasionally. Our hands, like roots, found new paths and discovered their natural places.

For days, my body buzzed with sensuality. Every waking minute, even when I was washing dishes or changing Sammy's diaper, I wanted to make love with Mayflower. I couldn't read or watch TV because I couldn't stop thinking about sex. At night, after making love with her, I'd fall asleep and dream about having sex with her. We fondled each other under the table, had intercourse in my bathroom and in the elevator. We talked dirty to one another. I was amazed at my staying power and Mayflower's capacity to arouse and be aroused.

"Jesus Christ, this is embarrassing," Naomi said. But it didn't faze us. We knew time was running short. Every precious minute took on the value of a week, every week a month. I confessed to Mayflower I was having problems turning off my switch, that I was obsessed, a satyr. I said I didn't want her to think I thought of her only as a sex object.

"Why not, dear?" she said. "I want to show you something."

Within sixty seconds we were in bed again. She had decorated her pubic hair with a dozen or so small purple bows. Those bows drove me wild.

Then Mayflower had several bad days. She spent most of her time sitting in her rocking chair and picking bits of imaginary lint from her dress. At times, she didn't recognize me or Naomi, and she cursed me once when I tried to get her to eat.

One evening while Naomi was napping and I was in the bathroom, Mayflower wandered off and ended up at the Lutheran church ten blocks away. I had placed a card in her purse giving instructions to contact me in case of emergency. The secretary at the church told me that Mayflower had been dancing up and down the length of the traffic island in the middle of Speedway. By the time I got there, she had collected twelve dollars and change from motorists. "New Yorkers are so nice," she said. She thought I was a doorman named Wallhausen. I gave her my arm, walked her to the car and held the door open for her.

She scooted over next to me and gave me the money she'd collected. "Let's use it to buy a nice bottle of wine and some raw oysters."

We spent an hour or so at a dark oyster bar called Jimmy's. We drank Riesling and shared raw oysters. It cost more than twelve dollars, but I didn't care. I wasn't sure who Mayflower thought I was. I didn't care about that, either. At that moment, playing the role of Wallhausen only intensified my pleasure.

As the days passed, Mayflower spent more time sitting in her chair or pacing. When she was alert, she seemed to enjoy brushing Naomi's hair, telling her how beautiful she looked, touching her, massaging her.

At night I would place my hand on the back of the sofa, and Mayflower would place hers on top of mine. Sometimes we kissed lightly. We didn't make love. Her Alzheimer's had transformed our lust into intense, almost desperate, caring.

A few days before Christmas, Mayflower said, "Let's read Sammy a poem or two, dear." I read a poem by William Blake while Sammy drank from his bottle and gazed at Mayflower's bracelets. *Tiger, tiger burning bright*— When I stopped reading, Sammy threw a fit. I tried Whitman. Sammy kicked his legs and waved his arms. Robert Frost elicited calm reflection. Hawthorne put him to sleep.

We tried different pieces of music. Beethoven provoked knowing little grunts. The Beatles elicited wide-ranging head movements. Sammy made swimming motions to the sounds of Bach.

Christmas passed, and no one seemed to notice. On Christmas day I made lists of fiction and non-fiction books I wanted Sammy to read by the time he was twenty-one—two hundred in all.

One evening Mayflower sat on the sofa brushing Naomi's hair. Her hands had become coarse and bony, her skin dry, her eyes dark and lifeless. "Will you get me my red dress, dear?" she asked me. "I have to meet Charles for the opera."

"I'll get it," Naomi said.

Naomi helped Mayflower put on the dress. She found Mayflower's beaded purse. They sat together on the sofa holding hands. They sat for over an hour, waiting. When Mayflower grew agitated, Naomi helped her change into her nightgown and combed her hair.

On New Year's Day, Naomi changed her first diaper. The next day she cleaned Sammy, rubbed him with lotion, powdered him and pinned on a new diaper. By mid-January, Naomi was grooming herself and wearing a touch of lipstick. Once, when I came up from the basement after doing a load of laundry, Mayflower and Naomi were leaning over Sammy's crib. Naomi was shaking the rattle.

"I stopped him from crying," Naomi said.

"I've been thinking about Christmas, dear," Mayflower said. "When is it?"

"We missed it this year," I said, folding one of Sammy's shirts.

"I've never missed Christmas," Mayflower said. After lunch, she insisted Randall take her to the lobby. There, in the December issue of *Family Circle,* she found an article on how to make artificial poinsettia and made a list of materials she needed.

"Naomi, you must help me," she said. "We're going to give poinsettia to everyone we know and wish them a happy holiday. And if some are left over, we'll give them to people we don't know."

I bought three pairs of blunt scissors, and the three of us sat at the kitchen table cutting out hundreds of poinsettia.

"Stupid scissors," Naomi said. She was thinner now and regaining her figure.

That afternoon Sammy, Naomi, Mayflower, Randall, Moon, and I distributed the paper flowers to everyone in the Coronado, then to dozens of people on the street. Next day Naomi took Sammy for a walk, the first time she had gone out with him.

"I couldn't believe it," she said when she returned. "People keep stopping me to tell me how cute he is."

"Let's give him his first real bath," Mayflower said.

Randall got the Bathinette while I reviewed the relevant section in Spock and laid out everything we'd need. "Watch it with the soap," I said. "A soapy baby is a slippery baby."

Naomi ran the water while I read aloud from Spock about how to test the water with elbow or wrist.

Mayflower laid out a towel, washcloth, tearless shampoo, baby soap.

We looked at Naomi.

"Not me. You're the one who read the book."

Mayflower and Randall stood on my left, Naomi on my right. As I undressed Sammy, he strained to keep Naomi in view.

"Don't expect me to rescue you," Naomi said. I slowly lowered Sammy into the water. His eyes popped wide open; his legs churned. He waved his arms as if trying to fly. Finally, he settled in, became motionless, and smiled his excessively charismatic smile. Everyone fell silent. An auspicious moment.

"Oh, dear," Mayflower said.

Randall handed me the washcloth. I soaked the cloth and squeezed water over Sammy's head.

"Look how the water shines on his skin," Naomi said.

I laid him back, supporting him with one hand. Sammy splashed, made grunting sounds, smiled and peed straight up into my face.

Everyone laughed, even me. "So you think this is funny?" I said, wrapping Sammy in a towel and patting him dry. I held him close and smelled the clean scent of his neck. I looked at the faces of Naomi, Mayflower, and Randall and felt at home.

 TWENTY-ONE

One morning I awoke and Mayflower wasn't there.

Randall and I looked for her in the basement, on the roof, on the street. I called the church she'd wandered to before, every store on Fourth Avenue, the Bread and Butter. Finally I called 911.

An hour later, a policeman found her in the alley behind Mr. Bill's Thrift and Gift. Instead of approaching her, the policeman was sensitive enough to radio his partner and have the partner tell me he'd found her.

The policemen waited a respectable distance away while Randall and I walked toward her. She sat on the ground, one leg straight out, the other folded under. Her hair was tangled. Her wide-brimmed white hat lay across her lap. If it were possible under these conditions to sit in an alley in a dignified way, Mayflower had achieved it.

"Mayflower," I said.

She didn't look up.

I knelt beside her and took her hand. "You all right?"

She lifted her hat and shook her head. She had soiled herself.

My first impulse was to turn away, not from repulsion, but in respect. Instead, I put both arms around her shoulders and held her close.

"Thank you, dear."

While I held her, Randall ran back to the Coronado for towels. When he returned, I wrapped the towels around her. We helped her to the apartment.

She insisted on cleaning and bathing herself. Naomi selected clean underwear and a dress for her and waited on the sofa, the dress draped over her lap. She looked up at me, eyes filled, and said, "I can't stand seeing her like this."

"I know," I said.

"I want to go to the hog farm," Naomi said.

That afternoon I called three certified counselors about Quentin and his so-called therapeutic community. They agreed that Quentin was crude and rough-cut, but tough and intuitively good. One said Quentin's was the place you go when you've reached the end of the road. "He deals with the toughest cases," he said.

I had also talked with Quentin at length. He told me he honestly didn't know if he could help Naomi. "Odds are against her," he said. "Of course, they're against everyone who comes here. Some get better, though—one in four, maybe. The ones who don't usually die or kill themselves." We discussed finances. I told him I'd send monthly payments.

Three days later, while Sammy slept, Mayflower and I listened to Naomi's end of a conversation with Quentin Raines. She told him everything and asked his permission to come back. She needed help, she said. From across the room I could hear the inflections of Quentin's voice at the other end of the line, but I couldn't make out what he was saying. Then Naomi hung up.

"Tell us," I said.

"He said he'd let me in, but it was against his better judgment. He said I'd have to work my butt off, take my meds and show up for therapy. He said one slip, and I'm out." She paused. "He said he'd have someone meet us at the airport."

I noted the "us," but didn't ask the question that stuck in my throat.

Naomi looked at Mayflower. "I'm sorry."

"It's time for you to go," Mayflower said. "You're doing the right thing."

I walked to the window and opened it. The cold air stung my face. The nights were coming sooner and lasting longer. It was nine a.m., and the morning sky was still streaked with pink and orange. Naomi came and stood beside me at the window. A chilly wind blew the curtain. There were hardly any cars on the street. "Fourth Avenue is dead," she said.

I pulled my sweater around me and folded my arms. "Cold nights drive people into shelters or under bridges."

"I've made reservations. We leave tomorrow," she said.

I closed the window. "I understand. No point drawing it out."

"You knew I'd end up keeping Sammy, didn't you?"

I shook my head. "I didn't know anything. I'm amazed at how much I didn't know."

Mayflower picked up Sammy and held him. The three of us stood in silence for a long time, huddled together, looking out at an empty Fourth Avenue. Mayflower put an arm around Naomi.

"I don't want to be here when you—" Naomi said.

"You're doing the right thing," Mayflower said.

"It's best." I said. "I—" I couldn't finish. I needed more time with Naomi and Sammy. There were things she needed to hear, things about life and death, love and hate, good and evil, things about education and books and trust and freedom. There were ideas I needed to have her understand so she could pass them on to Sammy. She wasn't ready to be on her own. Nor was I.

"I came with an old suitcase and a shopping bag," Naomi said. "I'm leaving with a baby and a locket full of ashes. How weird is that?"

Mayflower left and came back a few minutes later with her red dress. "Do you think you might like this?" She held it against her body and smoothed it with one hand. She looked at Naomi. "I'd like knowing you have it."

Naomi took the dress, gave Mayflower a quick hug and disappeared into the bedroom.

"My books," I called. "I've underlined them and written notes in the margins. I want you to pass them on to Sammy. My notes shouldn't go to waste."

She said she couldn't take them on the plane, that she'd send for them, but I knew she wouldn't.

Naomi's flight left at 7:15 a.m. She had to be at the airport no later than six. While Mayflower watched Sammy, Randall and I helped her pack. She was leaving with more than ashes and a baby. She was leaving with three suitcases, a playpen, a Bathinette, Mayflower's red dress, two of Howard's photograph albums, four peanut butter and pickle sandwiches, a travel bag filled with disposable diapers, bottles, clothes, and formula, and my list of two hundred recommended books.

The wedding dress stayed behind.

Randall carried her bags to the curb in front of the Coronado and waited for the taxi. He sat next to the driver. Naomi, Mayflower, Sammy and I rode in the back seat. Naomi seemed distant, as if her mind was already in Iowa. Mayflower and I played with Sammy, trying to make him smile at us just one more time, but Sammy would have none of it. The closer we got to the airport, the more I doubted I'd be able to do this.

"Don't forget to take your meds," I said.

"I won't."

"You'll be fine, dear," Mayflower said.

"And send him to a good college," I said. "I've made a list. It's on the back of the books list. He has an ear for music and poetry."

"No problem," Naomi said.

"And call. Letters take too long."

"Okay."

I got out the pictures we had taken on our wedding day. "Show him these when he's older. Tell him about your trip to Tucson. Tell him who we were and how much we—" I couldn't finish.

"Right," she said.

The airport smelled of jet fuel, car exhaust, and chorizo. The sky seemed too high, too far away. A new parking lot was being constructed. Traffic was stacked up for a half-mile. After checking in, we walked Naomi as far as the inspection area. The plane was already boarding.

Mayflower hugged Naomi and kissed Sammy.

I said goodbye to Naomi, gave her an awkward hug, took one last look at Sammy and squeezed his tiny hand. Then Mayflower, Randall, and I watched Naomi and Sammy walk away.

When we got back to the apartment, we found things Naomi had left behind—her wool sweater, the copy of *Goodnight Moon* Randall had given her, and one of Howard's photo albums she intended to take.

 TWENTY-TWO

The following week, Mayflower and I hardly left the Coronado, and when we did I always held her hand. Her lapses were almost continuous now, with only small glimmers of light in her darkness. I could feel in the touch of her hand when her soul left her body, when she changed from a woman to a frightened, bewildered child. I'd come to dread the cold loosening of her grip, the shuffling sounds of her soles on the cement.

In the evenings I brushed her hair, rubbed her arms and legs with lotion, coaxed her to eat, tried to comfort her when she cried, and read poetry aloud to her even when she showed no sign of hearing it. I read the love poems of Neruda, her favorite Rilke poems, long passages from Whitman's *Leaves of Grass*.

There was a quiet, almost plant-like melancholy about our days. My apartment became a kind of capsule moving through space, separating itself from the rest of the world, the two of us renouncing gravity, sinking deeper into a soulful oneness, all the while knowing, but refusing to admit, that the end of our journey was near. She smiled when I attempted to mimic Sammy's smile. We looked again and again at our wedding pictures. We assured one another that Naomi and Sammy would be fine.

One evening, after Mayflower had had a particularly lucid afternoon, she asked if we could go out for oysters and Riesling. We went to the same restaurant I'd taken her to the day she'd danced on the traffic island in the middle of Speedway and collected twelve dollars.

"Do you remember thinking I was Wallhausen, the doorman?" I asked her as we finished our first bottle of wine. She didn't remember, but got a great laugh hearing the story of her having sex with Wallhausen. Suddenly, she grew serious and took my hand in hers. She didn't have to say anything. Her hand said it all. I tried to pull away, but Mayflower held tighter.

"Look at me," she said.

"No," I said.

She squeezed my hand tighter, as if she were holding on to keep from drifting away. "It's time," she said. "Most of the time I can barely hear my own voice."

I stared at her hand clasping mine. "I think we have a few more days," I said.

"Shh, dear." Mayflower rubbed the back of my hand with her thumb. "It's time. Will you help me?"

I searched for the right words, but all I could do was stare at our hands and say, "Yes."

"Then we must hurry," she said.

We took a taxi back to the Coronado, still holding hands, unable to speak.

She led me through the lobby, pausing briefly at the door to the basement. "Remember our dance, you in skivvies?" she asked.

"I'll never forget," I said.

"Good," she said.

In her apartment she sat in her easy chair, ate two pieces of dry toast and drank a cup of sweetened tea. "To reduce the chances of vomiting," she said.

She was clear-headed now, focused, methodical. At her kitchen table she opened ten capsules and emptied them into a small dish of applesauce. Her hands were trembling, but only slightly. She dropped one of the capsules on the floor.

I moved to pick it up.

"No," she said. "I'll get it."

She placed the applesauce and a water glass filled with vodka on her bedside table, moved the plastic helium tank to the side of the bed and ran a tube from the tank to an oxygen mask. She sealed the exit holes on the mask with pieces of Scotch tape and lined the inside edge of it with Vaseline.

Our wedding picture was on her bureau along with a picture of Charles in a business suit with a handkerchief in his jacket pocket.

"Tell me what I can do," I said. "I need to *do* something. I can't breathe."

"Make the bed. I have clean sheets in the bottom drawer, and there's a rubber pad there, too. And pillows. I'll need to be partially sitting up." These sentences were said flatly, almost passively, with clarity and precision. Then she was mumbling. "Oh, dear. Hurry. I want candles. There's a box full of candles in the bedroom closet. You may light them."

With each lighted candle the room grew more and more yellow, the color of a fine leather glove. A calm settled around us.

She held a hand to her head as if forcing herself to remember. "Put some candles in the bathroom, too, dear. I'd like to take a bath."

She left an orange form on the table, instructing no resuscitation, and a handwritten note stating that the quality of her life had been diminished by Alzheimer's to the point that she no longer desired to live, that she was voluntarily, without the assistance of anyone, taking the steps necessary to terminate her life. All her possessions should be turned over to her husband, Tobias Seltzer, to dispose of as he saw fit.

She placed a living will at her bedside, along with a power of attorney and a copy of the book, *The Final Exit.*

"Don't dial 911," she said. "Wait for an hour after I've stopped breathing, then call the burial society directly."

I stood still, listening to the words, unable to make sense of them.

She opened the top drawer of her dresser, found her journal and gave it to me. "Read as much as you want, dear, then dispose of it."

"Maybe I'll mail it to Naomi," I said.

She thought for a moment, as if trying to remember who Naomi was, then said, "Yes, dear. That would be nice."

She used her list to check and double-check. She tried the valve on the helium tank.

"I can't loosen the valve."

I loosened it for her, and she wiped away my fingerprints with a washrag.

I filled the bathtub, tested the temperature and added more hot water. I thought about the day she'd told me I was a good and kind person. I thought about the time she told me about howling at the moon. I wanted to say something to her that would let her know how much I appreciated the time we'd spent together, what she'd done for Naomi, how much I loved her. But nothing I could think of to say seemed enough.

"Is there anything you need?" I asked.

"Yes," she said. "I want you to undress and bathe me. I loved seeing Sammy have his bath. I want you to give me one, too. I suppose somewhere in the distant past someone actually bathed me, but I can't recall."

I fumbled with her buttons. My hands were shaking too much to open them.

Mayflower helped. She slipped out of her dress, folded it, and placed it in a box. She folded her underthings, put them in the same box and held out her hand. "Help me, dear."

I helped her into the water. "How's the temperature?"

She settled in and laid her head back. "Perfect," she said.

I knelt beside the tub, rolled up my sleeves, dipped my hands in the water and watched it flow through my fingers.

She touched my cheek and forehead. "We loved and made good love."

"Yes," I said.

She lay back, slid down in the tub and parted her legs. "I want to be touched," she said. "Touch me everywhere. Look at all of me. I want to be seen and touched. I want your eyes and hands to take me into you."

I worked my way up from her feet to her head, touching and seeing every hollow, every crevice.

She held my hand to her breast. We kissed. It was like that first night when we danced. Neither of us existed separately, just one body, one breath, the beat of one heart.

I helped with her nightgown and robe, and she led me to her bed. Her death was inside her now. I could see it in her subtle nobility, her quiet reserve. She sat on the edge of her bed and ate the applesauce containing the drug, placed the empty dish aside and cautioned me not to touch it. It took less than a minute for her to finish the vodka. She placed the glass on the bedside table and lay back on the pillows. "Come here," she said, patting the bed.

I lay next to her.

She turned to face me. "Thank you, dear. I feel such gratitude for loving and being loved by you." Our lips touched. Then she turned away and placed the mask over her face.

To divert my mind, I thought of babies—silly, goofy-eyed babies, wise babies, moronic babies, babies in long gowns, flying babies.

Mayflower reached down and opened the valve.

A hissing sound.

She moved her back against my curved body. I held her close until her body went slack. A few minutes later she stopped breathing.

It took a long time for the hissing to stop.

one year later

 EPILOGUE

It's March again, eighteen months after I danced with Mayflower in my skivvies, almost a year since she took her life. I'm sitting in her rocker looking out the window at a full moon. Randall is at the kitchen table reading aloud from Huck Finn. "You couldn't go right to eating," Randall says, struggling with Twain's dialect, "but you had to wait for the widow to tuck down her head and grumble a little over the victuals, though there warn't really anything the matter with them." Randall is now working as a busboy for Miss Choy. He spends most of his money on books and treats for Moon.

Moon has sold out, traded his streak of wildness for a roof over his head and a scratch behind his ears. He's gained weight, sleeps most of the time and, like me, has to make frequent stops to pee or catch his breath. He lets me pet him now and then but, as if prompted by some flicker of distant memory, he'll sometimes wrap his tail between his legs, cast a suspicious eye at me and growl.

I didn't have a memorial service for her. Anything anyone could have said or done couldn't have captured her humor, her love of life, her courage while living. I think of this book as my homage to her. The story she wanted me to have. I keep her ashes under my bed where Beatrice's used to be. Someday, I'll figure out what to do with them, but for the time being I like having them there.

A week after Mayflower's cremation, I called Charles. "She's gone," was all I could manage. There was a long silent cry we both participated in, then Charles said, "She wanted life so much more than most of us."

"I know," I said. Then we hung up.

I'm working six days a week at the Bread and Butter, bringing in enough to make regular payments on Naomi's hospital bill and send something each month to Quentin Raines. I put what's left in an educational trust for Sammy. If I live long enough, he'll have enough to pay for college.

Miss Choy is doing well financially and personally. She and Cecil got married in Las Vegas a couple of months ago. She calls him her Dr. Spook and tells me with a wink, "He good fellow, good cook, plenty good other ways."

Katherine and Caravelo have a child, a girl with black hair and beautiful green eyes. They are the new directors of the Fourth Avenue Arts Festival and seem to be prosperous and happy. Once a month or so, as if to remind himself of his roots, Caravelo hits the streets with his juggling act. Randall and I never miss it or Caravelo's and Katherine's dance exhibitions.

Naomi hasn't written or called since she and Sammy left Tucson, but I call Quentin Raines to keep up on how she and Sammy are doing. Naomi is working in the kitchen eight hours a day and, like everybody else, has to help with the hogs. "She's taken to the hogs," Quentin said, "become our best slopper. Likes getting dirty. Probably good for her."

She still complains about having to take her meds, says they make her feel gray inside, but she can't seem to function without them. For the most part, she shows up for work and group therapy sessions. Quentin said that showing up is about all we can hope for right now. She still doesn't have much of a motherly interest in Sammy, but Sammy's doing fine. He's fourteen months old now, and Quentin said he almost runs the place. At any given time, at least ten wackos are arguing over whose turn it is to hold him.

I asked Quentin what were Naomi's chances for recovery. "Zero," Quentin said, "but she'll get better. Already is, since that friend of hers checked himself in."

"What friend?" I asked.

"Can't tell you his name. Client confidentiality," Quentin said. "Local kid, ran off to Alaska for a while. Back now. Wants to get clean."

I haven't heard from Howard. I like to imagine him as a monk in an ashram, painting his paintings, living simply and contentedly.

Randall and I walk every day. I feel safe with him at my side. On our walk to the university library last week, we took a detour through the Humanities building. I was half-hoping there'd be a sign on the door: AMERICAN HISTORY 201 CANCELED TODAY. DR. WILSON ILL. READ CHAPTER ON GETTYSBURG. But Dr. Wilson was there. We kept walking toward the library.

One night several months ago, I sat in the kitchen sipping gin on the rocks, thinking of Mayflower, remembering the short time we'd shared. A toilet flushed, then another. Someone coughed. Far away, the same dog was howling. I went to the roof and waited for him to howl again. When he did, I joined him for a few seconds. It wasn't Mayflower's robust and gutsy howl, but it was definitely a howl, a howl for Mayflower. That's the closest I've come to a real prayer.

ABOUT THE AUTHOR

Dan Gilmore, in his time, has been a fry cook, a jazz musician, a draft dodger, a soldier, an actor, a minister in a Reno wedding chapel, a psychologist, a single parent of Jennifer and Danny, a college professor, a dean, and a consultant to business. A Howl for Mayflower is his first novel. As a poet and writer, he has received awards from *Sandscript,* the Raymond Carver Fiction Contest, and the Martindale Fiction Contest. Currently, he lives in Tucson and divides his time between playing jazz, writing, and loving his two grandchildren, Quin and Graeson, his partner, JoAn, and his cat, Kitty.

Printed in the United States
62745LVS00005B/385-393